Candidly Cline

Candidly Cline

Kathryn Ormsbee

HARPER

An Imprint of HarperCollins*Publishers*

Library of Congress Cataloging-in-Publication Data
Names: Ormsbee, Kathryn, author.
Title: Candidly Cline / Kathryn Ormsbee.
Description: First edition. | New York : HarperCollins, 2021. | Audience: Ages
8–12. | Audience: Grades 4–6. | Summary: Cline Alden's grandmother says
that music is in the family's blood, but Cline's mother is dead-set against her
daughter's dreams of becoming a country music singer; Cline is determined
to find the money to attend a Young Singer-Songwriter Workshop in
Lexington (not too far from her Paris, Kentucky home), so now she has a
lot on her mind—she is hiding things from her mother, she is losing her
beloved grandmother to Alzheimer's, and she has begun to acknowledge, to
herself at least, that she is more attracted to girls than boys.
Identifiers: LCCN 2021006364 | ISBN 978-0-06-305999-3 (hardcover)
Subjects: LCSH: Singers—Juvenile fiction. | Mothers and daughters—Juvenile
fiction. | Grandmothers—Juvenile fiction. | Lesbian teenagers—Juvenile
fiction. | Alzheimer's disease—Juvenile fiction. | Paris (Ky.)—Juvenile
fiction. | CYAC: Singers—Fiction. | Country music—Fiction. | Mothers
and daughters—Fiction. | Grandmothers—Fiction. | Lesbians—Fiction.
| Alzheimer's disease—Fiction. | Paris (Ky.)—Fiction. | LCGFT:
Bildungsromans.
Classification: LCC PZ7.O637 Can 2021 | DDC 813.6 [Fic]—dc23
LC record available at https://lccn.loc.gov/2021006364

Typography by Chris Kwon
21 22 23 24 25   GV   10 9 8 7 6 5 4 3 2 1

First Edition

To my wife, Alli.

You are the reason love songs finally made sense.

1

PEOPLE SAY PARIS, France, is the most romantic city on earth. I wouldn't know. The farthest I've traveled from home is Ohio, for a school trip to the Cincinnati Zoo. I like to *imagine* Paris, though. I picture cobblestoned streets wet with April rain, almond-stuffed croissants that flake apart when they touch your tongue, and fireworks crackling over the river Seine. Paris is the perfect place to say "I love you" or to kiss the person you've been crushing on for the very first time.

Well, that's not Paris, Kentucky. Not even close.

Here's what my town has in common with the city of love:

1) It's named Paris.

That's it.

There aren't any Eiffel Towers here. No towers at all, unless you count the Shinner Building, which *Ripley's Believe It or Not!* reports to be the tallest three-story structure on earth. That's *our* claim to fame.

Don't get me wrong. I'm not bad-mouthing my hometown. Our Paris possesses, as Gram would say, its own bundle of charms. We've got Main Street, for one thing, which looks real pretty in the springtime, when the planters are full of begonias and the midday sun shines down on the Kentucky Bank rotunda. There's a big car dealership, which brings in folks from as far out as Lexington. There's a McDonald's, a Dairy Queen, and a Walmart. But the biggest deal of all—bigger, even, than the Shinner Building—is the Goldenrod Diner, where you'll find the best homestyle meals in Bourbon County.

That's where I am on Labor Day. My mama works the night shift on Mondays—even holidays. That means she's not home to fix her usual casserole supper, so Luann, the owner, lets me and Gram order free takeout.

Gram's order is easy enough. She always gets the biscuits and gravy plate, with one side of sweet baby carrots and another of turnip greens. Me? I like to keep things interesting, so I order a new entrée every week. Once I've made my way through the whole menu, I start over. Tonight, I'm getting the fried catfish, with hush puppies and tartar sauce on the side.

When I place my order, Delia Jones, my favorite waitress, tries to freak me out by saying catfish are bottom-feeders and basically the rats of the sea. I say I don't mind, so long as they taste good. Delia replies that I would eat an *actual* rat if it was battered and fried, but she goes ahead and places the order. That's what I like about Delia:

she knows how to joke around, but she's all business when it counts.

My mama, Judy Alden, head waitress of the Goldenrod for going on twelve years, is all business *all* the time. I watch from my stool in the kitchen as she whips to and from the order counter, shouting stuff at Bill, the chef, that you'd need the waitress's dictionary to understand.

I know the lingo because I basically grew up at the Goldenrod. When Mama puts in "a stack of Vermont," that means an order of pancakes with syrup. When she hollers for a coffee "blond with sand," that means with cream and sugar. This is "short order," aka diner secret code. My favorite code, which isn't *so* secret, is "Arnold Palmer." That means half iced tea and half lemonade, and there's nothing better.

I'm not allowed to order actual drinks any other time we go out. Sodas cost money, which we Aldens don't have. But Monday nights at the Goldenrod? That's different. Everyone here knows that Cline Louise Alden requires an Arnold Palmer with her meal.

I'm slurping my blessed drink from a Styrofoam cup, waiting for the catfish to finish frying, when it happens: the song on the radio changes, and a new one blasts out of the speakers. It's "Born to Run" by Emmylou Harris, who happens to be my singing hero.

There's only one thing a body can do at a time like this. I put down my Arnold Palmer, get to my feet, and dance, belting every last word of the song. From the grill, Bill—a broad-shouldered, big-bellied white man—shouts, "Rock on, girl!" I give a salute and grab a chili-crusted ladle from the sink. This becomes my mic, and if I squint real hard into the fluorescents, I can imagine I'm not in Paris, but Nashville, singing my heart out at the Ryman Auditorium, home of the Grand Ole Opry.

Delia swings into the kitchen, dirty dishes lined down her arms. She shoos me from her path, shouting, "Fire hazard! You'll be the death of us all." I smile and wink like the graceful song-stress I am, 'cause I know Delia's having fun.

"CLINE."

I whip around. Mama's glaring me down from the order win-dow, hellfire in her eyes. I lower the ladle from my mouth. It's not a mic anymore.

"Mind yourself," Mama orders, with a voice that could saw through the toughest skirt steak in town.

Like I said, all business all the time.

I plop the ladle back in the sink. My cheeks are hot—which must be obvious, on account of my pale skin—but it's not like I'm going to cry. Mama's scolded me for goofing off in the kitchen plenty of times before. According to her, I "ought to know better." Well, if knowing better means keeping quiet when a good song's on the radio, I'm happy to stay an ignoramus.

"Catfish up!" Bill announces.

I report to the order counter, where Bill's sliding my supper into a takeout box. Gram's biscuits and gravy are already boxed, bagged, and ready to go. See? The Goldenrod is a well-oiled machine. It's not like my singing changed that.

I take the big plastic bag, tell Bill thanks, and head on out of the kitchen. I don't bother telling Mama goodbye. She knows the Monday night routine.

When I turn into the back hall, I smack straight into Delia. Lucky for me, she's not carrying plates this time around. All the same, she grunts, "Cline, for the love of God."

I wince, feeling like an official nuisance, but then Delia cracks a grin and says, "Hold up."

She digs into her apron pocket and pulls out a piece of orange paper, folded in fourths. Handing it to me, she says, "Look what I found the other day on campus. I thought to myself, 'This couldn't sound more like Cline if it tried.'"

Delia is the coolest person I know. She's got cotton-candy-pink hair and tattoos on her fair-skinned arms. Sure, she works at the Goldenrod, but she takes night classes at the University of Kentucky in Lexington. So hearing she thought of me specifically the other day makes me feel real important.

I unfold the paper to reveal a printed flyer:

YOUNG SINGER-SONGWRITER
WORKSHOP

The Singletary Center for the Arts
invites students in 8th through 12th
grade to apply to its month-long course
for aspiring singer-songwriters.

Taught by UK professor of music Dr. Mireille Johnson, the course will cover songwriting basics and include a guest lecture by Lexington native and Grammy nominee Marcia Hayes.

Dates: Mondays, 6–9 p.m.
September 28–October 19
Applications must be postmarked
on or before September 16

I scramble to make sense of the words. UK, as in the University of Kentucky. September sixteenth, as in nine days from now. Aspiring singer-songwriter, as in *me*.

A singer-songwriter workshop? I didn't know such a thing existed. I'm out-and-out gawking when Delia says, "I know it's in Lexington, but you could figure out transportation, right?"

"Y-yeah," I squeak out.

What's a forty-minute drive when you're handed—literally *handed*—something this big?

That's when I read the final line on the flyer, which lists the price of this magical workshop:

$300, plus $15 application fee

My heart stutters. Stops. Revs up a few times before it beats again.

Three hundred bucks.

There's no way I can afford that. The Alden ladies don't have that kind of cash lying around. The reason Mama works late on Mondays is because we sometimes can't even make our gas bill. (I know, I've heard her talk to the gas people on the phone when she thinks I'm asleep.)

Three. Hundred. Bucks.

I feel like a party balloon someone's blown up, only to jab with a sharp pin. All the excitement's whooshing out of me fast. Still, I don't want Delia to think I'm ungrateful. That's why I slap on a rubbery smile and say, "Thanks."

"Sure thing," Delia replies. "I'd wager you could perform with the best of them. Even Emmylou."

With that, she hurries off to the kitchen, because Bill is calling an order up for the second time, and at the Goldenrod, there might be a second call but *never* a third. I fold the flyer and tuck it into my sundress pocket. It looks odd peeking out of there, an eye-smacking neon orange.

For as long as I can remember, I've dreamed about making it big as a singer. But maybe all big dreams look neon in reality—a sign they don't belong and won't work out in real life.

I grip the takeout bag hard in my fist and head for the back door.

2

"GRAM, FIRE UP the *Porter Wagoner!*"

That's what I shout every Monday night when I get home. It's part of the tradition. I know I'll find Gram in the den, but what's on TV is always a surprise. Sometimes it's cable news, sometimes it's an action-adventure movie on TBS, and other times it's a rerun of *The Mary Tyler Moore Show*. Once, I found Gram watching the Weather Channel. For *fun*. But as Gram herself likes to say, there's no accounting for taste. And I figure Gram's lived seven decades on the planet, so she should be allowed to watch whatever the heck she wants.

Mama doesn't agree. She keeps trying to get Gram to do sudoku puzzles and word searches, rather than watch TV. She buys Gram a book of brain teasers from the Dollar Tree once a month, like maybe Gram will start liking them one day. But Gram says those books are a waste of time.

"How's filling a box with numbers helping anyone?" she asks my mother.

That's fair. Though I guess it'd also be fair for Mama to ask, "How's watching *The People's Court* helping anyone, either?"

Mama says Gram needs brain teasers because they'll help her mind stay sharp. When Dr. Windisch diagnosed Gram with Alzheimer's back in May, he said her memory was going to get worse and worse. But I haven't noticed anything different, except that Gram sometimes forgets where she's put her glasses. Plenty of people misplace their glasses, and *they* don't have Alzheimer's. Which makes me think Dr. Windisch diagnosed Gram wrong. I've got a feeling Mama's thinking that, too, because she made a special appointment for Gram up in Cleveland. A "second opinion" is what she called it. A *better* opinion, that's what I'm expecting.

"Hey there, sweetie pie. Got supper?"

Gram grins at me from her recliner. Like me and Mama, she's got fair, freckled skin and a head full of hair, but where Mama's and my hair is bright red, hers is white. Tonight, Gram's wearing her floral dressing gown and matching green slippers and watching a recording of *Dancing with the Stars*.

"Biscuits coming right up!" I tell her, making a beeline for the kitchen.

There, I move our food onto ceramic plates and fetch real utensils. An Alden lady's got to eat with class, after all. I even pour what's left of my Arnold Palmer into my favorite glass—the only one of Gram's Bristol blue goblets that hasn't cracked over the years.

When I get to the den, holding our dishes waitress-style (I learned from the best), Gram's pulled up the menu of our current *Porter Wagoner* DVD. Here's a fact for the books: *The Porter Wagoner Show* was around for twenty-one years, which is almost twice the time I've been alive. Gram's got the whole collection, and we're only on season nine.

Tonight's guest star is Merle Haggard, who sings "Okie from Muskogee." I like Merle fine, and "Okie" makes me laugh, but my favorite part of the show is when Dolly Parton comes out and plays a number. Every week, Gram and I make a game of guessing how high Dolly's hair is. I'm realistic—"one foot and three-quarters!"—but Gram goes over the top, like "twenty thousand leagues under the sea!"

Gram's got a fine appreciation for the arts. She grew up here in Paris, but once Mama had graduated high school and started living on her own, Gram and Papaw moved away to Asheville, North Carolina, where they opened their very own music shop. They sold records and secondhand instruments, and every Saturday night they hosted live concerts on the back porch. Then, seven years back, Papaw passed away. Mama was starting to work more at the Goldenrod then and needed Gram to help take care of me, so Gram closed the shop and moved back here. I know Gram must miss her old home, and it doesn't seem fair she had to give up her musical dream. All the same, she believes in mine. Gram thinks

I've got what it takes to be the next Emmylou.

"We Alden ladies have music in our marrow," she likes to say. "It's no coincidence your mama named you Cline."

Sometimes I wonder about that. Gram tells me that Mama named me after the singer Patsy Cline. She says that when Mama was younger, *she* used to watch *Porter Wagoner* with Gram. She even says that the day I was born, Mama held me in her arms and sang "Blue Moon of Kentucky" like a lullaby. Gram says Mama cried while she sang. Of course, I don't remember any of that.

I *do* remember the piano we used to have in the house: an upright Yamaha, made of glossy cherrywood. Gram and Papaw would visit from Asheville, and all four of us would belt tunes as Mama's fingers danced across the piano keys. Gram told me that Mama was a star pianist, growing up. She won gold cups at competitions and performed Rachmaninoff for her senior recital.

But then Mama started taking on more shifts at the Goldenrod, and I heard her playing less and less. When I was in second grade, I came home from school to find a bare strip of carpet in the living room, where the Yamaha had been. Mama had sold it. I haven't heard her play piano since.

These days, Mama wouldn't be caught dead watching *Porter Wagoner*. She's almost always at the Goldenrod, and when she's not, she's at home sorting through the mail or folding laundry or haggling with folks on the phone. Even at home, Judy Alden is all business.

I just don't get it. I don't see how Mama could love music—*really* love it, the way Gram and I do—and then up and leave it behind. I would never sell my guitar. You'd have to pluck it from my cold, dead hands. Even if you took away all the records and speakers in the world, I'd still find a way to make music.

That's something Mama doesn't seem to understand. Years back, when I first asked about guitar lessons, she told me, "Maybe later, Cline. We don't have the money now." When I asked for a Spotify subscription in sixth grade, she said, "You can listen just fine with the ads." When I begged to go to last year's Brandi Carlile concert in Louisville—as my birthday and Christmas presents *combined*—she still said, "Concerts are a waste of money." That's why I know Mama would never let me do a singer-songwriter workshop, even if it were here in Paris and cost thirty dollars, not three hundred.

I guess music was all fine and good to Mama when we sang around that piano, 'cause it was just for fun. But then, when I was seven or eight and first announced that I wanted to be a singer, Mama changed her tune, talking about how music doesn't pay the bills.

Well, Mama should tell that to the likes of Dolly Parton, Tammy Wynette, or Shania Twain. I'm no fool. I know music isn't easy, but if you make the cut, you can make it *big*. That's what I intend to do, workshop or no workshop.

Still, that workshop could be a big first step for me. Something I could do in the here and now.

I tell Gram good night once we've finished our supper and

the show, but it's still early, and I don't mean to sleep. Shut up in my bedroom, I take my guitar out of its case. It's not particularly pretty, but it's one of the few things Gram brought here from her life in Asheville. I lie out with my head at the foot of the bed, guitar on my stomach, and pull out my phone. Like my guitar, my phone is an old, secondhand thing. It doesn't hold a charge for more than a couple of hours, and the screen is cracked in a dozen splinters, like spiderwebs. All the same, it's special, because it's home to my music collection.

Tonight, I queue up the song "Angel from Montgomery," written by the legendary John Prine and sung by Bonnie Raitt. As I listen, I strum along. I know these chords by heart.

I can't explain the way this song makes me feel. No matter how many times I've played it before, I get goose bumps all over when I listen, on account of my dad. I know the song meant something to him, because when I was ten, I found the DVD of my parents' wedding, and "Angel from Montgomery" was the first song they danced to that night. *Their* song. I wonder if, because of that, a little bit of Dad lives inside the music. Not in a scary, horror movie way. More like magic.

I never got to meet my dad. He died in a car accident before I was born. I've seen plenty of photos of him, though. He was tall and wiry, with a sand-colored beard, and his white skin seemed to be in a state of perpetual sunburn. I've heard people—Mama included—talk about the way he was, and I know certain facts about him, like how he took Mama's last name when they got married, rather than the other way round, 'cause he thought "Judy and Jacob Alden" sounded a whole lot better than "Judy and Jacob Judge." But those stories and photos don't make me understand Dad near as much as "Angel from Montgomery." So I listen, and I play my guitar, and I try to imagine what he would say to me at a time like this.

Would he say, *Listen to your mother—music won't pay the bills?*

Or, *Three hundred dollars is nothing when it comes to your dreams?*

Or, *Wait it out—your time will come?*

I don't know.

When the song ends, I set aside my guitar and pull Delia's flyer from my pocket. I eye the wastebasket by my wicker dresser. I could throw away the paper and move on. Maybe I will, in a day or two. But it seems wrong to let go of the possibility so soon— one I didn't know existed till tonight.

So I hold on a little while longer.

3

"NO SODAS, UNDERSTAND?" says Mama. "And bedtime at ten o'clock."

It's early Saturday morning—so early the sun is still blinking its eyes over the horizon. Today is the day of Gram's appointment at Cleveland Clinic, which is a whole five-hour drive from Paris. That's why Mama's in a not great mood. She's been fretting for weeks now about Cleveland. She's anxious about the drive and the expense of a hotel and how much the visit is going to cost "out of pocket."

But what Mama seems most worried about right now, parked in front of my best friend Hollie's house, is my consumption of carbonated beverages. When Mama's like this, the only thing to do is nod along. The way she's talking, you'd think I'd never spent the night at the Kendalls' before.

"C'mon, Judy," Gram says from the passenger seat. "You lighten up—kids need their fun."

Mama scowls at Gram, but they don't argue. It's too early for that.

Seeing my chance to escape Mama's lecture, I open my door, lugging my backpack after me. I'm not even halfway up the Kendalls' porch steps when the front door swings open. Hollie's standing there, beaming, with her tanned white skin and wavy blond-brown hair. She doesn't look near as tired as I feel. But that's Hollie for you. She's the same way at school: somehow chatty and full of energy when the rest of us want to fall asleep on our homeroom desks.

"Bye, Gram! Bye, Ms. Alden!" Hollie calls out, as Mama pulls our beaten-up Camry out of the driveway.

I wave goodbye to Mama and Gram, quietly hoping there's no traffic on the way to Cleveland and that however much Mama's got to pay from her pocket, it won't stress her out more. I think the trip will be worth it. I've got a feeling, deep down, that the doctors there will discover that Gram was misdiagnosed, and there's not a lick of Alzheimer's in her brain.

My family zooms off to Cleveland, and Hollie turns to me with a great big smirk.

"Chocolate chip?" she asks, like she even needs to.

My mama might've said no sodas, but she never breathed a word about cookies for breakfast.

∽∞∾

"Noah, stay *out*, oh my *gosh*."

I giggle as Hollie pushes Noah, her nine-year-old brother, back up the basement stairs.

"It's not fair," Noah yells. "You get the basement all to your-selves!"

"That's because I have a *guest.* If you want the basement, get a guest of your own."

"But you're not even using the Xbox! You're just watching mov-ies, and you could do that upstairs."

"Wah, wah, wah." Hollie scrunches her face like a fussy baby.

Noah stomps up the stairs to the Kendalls' kitchen and slams the basement door.

"Jeez," Hollie says, plopping down on the couch beside me. "He's so annoying."

"I guess he's right, though," I admit. "We're not using the Xbox."

Hollie grabs the remote and rolls her eyes. "Puh-*lease.* He doesn't want the Xbox. Noah's just a spoilsport. If we were using the TV upstairs, he'd be mad about that, too."

"Sounds exhausting," I say.

"Tell me about it. Boys are the worst." Hollie pauses, squinting in thought, and adds, "Well, *some* of them are."

I know what Hollie's hinting at. It seems that lately she and our friends at school have a *lot* to say about guys—the ones they like and the ones who might like them. Personally, I think we girls have the best time on our own. Take today, for example: after breakfast, Hollie and I made perfumes using old garden spray bottles and Mrs. Kendall's essential oils. Then we baked English muffin pizzas, and after that we went straight to the trampoline, jumping until we got stitches in our sides. Then we lay out in the sun, watching clouds pass over the dogwood trees. Mrs. Kendall baked a lasagna for supper, and now Hollie and I have the basement all to ourselves, where we plan to watch *The Princess Bride.*

This Saturday has been, as Gram would put it, a balm to my soul.

Hollie must notice I'm not giving my opinion on boys being the worst *or* the best, but she doesn't prod. She just turns on the TV and grabs a handful of chocolate-covered pretzels from the bowl of party mix on the couch.

She shoves the pretzels in her mouth, turns to me, and says, "Chocolate coating makes it go down easier."

I fish a peanut out of the mix. "Anybody want a peanut?" I quote back, and then we're both giggling.

Hollie and I have watched *The Princess Bride* together fifty times, probably, but it never gets old. We can quote the movie backward and forward, and we turn it on whenever we're bored. It's our thing. Actually, Hollie and I have lots of "things" on account of us having been friends for forever. Mrs. Kendall still laughs about something our kindergarten teacher wrote on Hollie's report card: *Tends to exclude other children, aside from classmate Cline Alden.*

What can I say? Hollie and I *were* exclusive. By first grade, though, we learned that other girls could be cool, too, like our friends Ava, Darlene, and Kenzie. And when we got to middle school, Hollie made some other friends in her church's youth group. I haven't met any of them yet, but I get that New Hope Church and Dunbar Middle School are two different worlds.

New Hope is the biggest church in Paris. So many people go there that they have *three* worship services. Since Mama won't be back from Cleveland until Sunday night, that means I have to go to church with the Kendalls. I don't mind, really. I've gone with Hollie before. I kind of nod off during the sermon, but I like the music. The worship leaders there can *sing*.

The only thing I don't like about the service is when the pastor says, "Take a moment to greet your brothers and sisters in Christ," and everyone goes around shaking hands and saying stuff like, "Peace be with you." That's when random old ladies tell me how cute I look in my dress, and do I have a church home?

I always tell them that yes, I do, because it's easier than saying no. See, us Alden ladies are what you might call "godless women." That's what Mama calls us, anyway, when she's trying to laugh off an invitation to someone or other's church. And she gets plenty. Seems the most popular thing to do in Paris, after going to church, is inviting whoever doesn't.

Personally? I don't know how I feel about God and all that. I don't particularly like the idea of someone watching everything I do and wanting me to follow his rules. As to heaven—the thought of living forever and *ever*, and everything being perfect? That plain freaks me out.

Mama and Gram don't talk about heaven or God, period. But

Bill from the Goldenrod once told me that for him, church is planting a new azalea shrub in his yard. I think I understand that, 'cause I do feel something stirring in my chest when I play guitar or listen to a good song. Like I've touched something beautiful and bigger than me.

And though I don't know about eternity, I do wonder if people live on after they've gone, in a way—in stories and melodies. Like how I get goose bumps thinking of Dad while listening to an old John Prine song.

Music. Maybe that's Cline Alden's religion.

⌘

Church starts early morning Sunday, and the Kendalls and I arrive just in time for the first worship song. A young man leads the congregation in singing while playing guitar, and a woman beside him sings harmony. "I'll Fly Away" is my favorite song we sing today, because the band plays it gospel-style, which gets the whole congregation clapping. Every line is a celebration, including the part of the chorus where we sing "oh glory." After a while, I focus less on the words and more on the worship leaders, and I wonder if *they* ever got to attend a singer-songwriter workshop.

I bet they did.

I haven't forgotten Delia's flyer. It's been on my mind this week like melted butter on toast. See, I can sing Emmylou's greatest hits till the cows come home. I know how to play the guitar with finesse. But I've never gotten a real lesson from a professional. I've learned music on my own. How much better could I be if I learned it in a classroom?

I know attending that workshop's next to impossible, but watching these folks on a stage, singing their hearts out? I can't keep my own heart from aching with possibility.

When we're through singing, the choir files out and the pastor stands up at the pulpit, announcing—sure enough—my least favorite part of the service: meet-and-greet. Hollie whispers to me that she's going to talk to a friend. She runs off just as an old man in the pew ahead turns around and tells me, "So nice to see you here today."

I tell him it's nice to *be* here, but then I turn around real fast, so he won't ask if I have a church home, and see that a woman in a floppy orange hat has filed into our pew and is talking to Mrs. Kendall. She's Asian, with fair skin and wavy black hair. Her hands whip around as she speaks, making her bangle bracelets clatter and sending a breeze my way that smells of honeysuckle.

"Exhausted, Paula," she's saying. "Pardon me, but the staff wasn't thinking of us nursery workers, adding that service. They seem to forget we're volunteers. I barely get to worship myself these days. This is the first service I've attended in two months."

"Oh no," says Mrs. Kendall. She clicks her tongue and shakes her head, as though to say, *The injustice of it all.*

"More to my point," the woman in the orange hat says, "the ladies and I have come up with our own plan, since the staff is too busy doing God knows what. We want to hire a girl to help out on Wednesday nights. We're pooling our money, and we can do fifteen dollars for the two hours—sometimes less than two, you know, depending on how long-winded—" She motions toward the pulpit, bracelets jangling.

"You're thinking of Hollie?" asks Mrs. Kendall, looking over at me—where Hollie *was* until a few seconds ago.

"That's right," says the woman, who notices me and gives a jangling wave. "Hey, hon, how are you?"

Then she's back to Mrs. Kendall. "What do you say? She'd really be helping us out of a bind."

But Mrs. Kendall is shaking her head again. "Hollie loves that youth group, Edith. I couldn't ask her to give that up. And she's babysat some, but I know for a fact she's not comfortable around the littlest ones."

The other woman sighs. "Well, I appreciate you hearing me out."

"You know I'd help personally if I wasn't teaching the women's group."

"Oh, I know. You're a dear." The woman in the orange hat pats Mrs. Kendall's hand. As she edges out of the pew, the honeysuckle scent drifts my way again.

That's when I do something real bold. Maybe it's the perfume that fills me with gumption, or the thought of those worship leaders attending workshops of their own. Whatever the reason, I step into the aisle, following the woman in the orange hat.

"Pardon me!" I call. "Ma'am?"

The woman turns around, clamping her eyes on me. She looks surprised for a split second, but then a smile stretches across her face.

"Why, hello! You're Hollie's friend, right? I'm Edith Yune."

Mrs. Edith Yune extends her hand, and I shake it, saying, "I'm Cline Louise Alden."

This *is* meet-and-greet, after all.

Mrs. Yune tells me, "It's nice to make your acquaintance," and makes like she's going to walk away.

"Wait!" I yelp.

Mrs. Yune turns back to face me, full-on. She looks at me intently, and, truth be told, I'm not used to that. Even though I just turned thirteen, most adults I know still treat me like a kid.

"You need help in the nursery?" I ask.

Mrs. Yune nods. "That's right! Wednesday nights. The nursery's bustling, and we're shorthanded. *So* many new babies."

"Well, I'm great with babies," I say eagerly. "Toddlers, too. I took my Safe Sitter course a year ago, and I've had lots of babysitting experience since then. I can give you references."

I'm fudging a little. I haven't had lots of experience, exactly. More like three jobs with Mrs. Nelson, a waitress at the Goldenrod. She *would* give a good reference, though.

Mrs. Yune's eyes light up. "You're interested in the job?"

I nod. "Is it . . . okay that I'm not a church member?"

"Oh!" Mrs. Yune waves a hand. "That's no problem, hon. Now,

I don't know if you caught this, but the pay would be fifteen for two hours. Would that be all right by you?"

"Sounds fine," I say, nonchalant, like all this time, I haven't been calculating precisely how many nights I'd have to work to pay for a certain workshop. (*Twenty.*)

"Excellent!" Mrs. Yune claps her hands, bangles jangling. "You know what they say: when God closes a door, he opens a window."

I *think* Mrs. Yune just called me a window, but I don't take offense.

"Now," she tells me, "I'm sure any friend of the Kendalls is trustworthy, and from what you've told me, you're well qualified for the job. All the same, we always do a trial run for new workers. Would this coming Wednesday work for you?"

"Definitely," I say, not missing a beat.

Mrs. Yune nods amiably. "Wednesday services start at seven, but we open the nursery early, at six thirty. If you could show up at six, I'll be there to show you around. All right by you?"

"Sure thing, Mrs. Yune," I say, trying to act calm and professional.

The worship leaders are back onstage, and everyone's heading to their seats. Mrs. Yune takes note and gives me one last big smile.

"Looking forward to it, Cline!" she says.

She heads for her pew, and I return to my seat in a dreamy daze.

Hollie shows up beside me a few seconds later, as the music starts up onstage.

"I just found out there's going to be a lock-in next month," she whispers excitedly.

I'm about to ask what a lock-in is when the congregation starts singing, and Mrs. Kendall gives us a look like we'd best behave. So Hollie and I look straight ahead and sing along. As we do, my cheeks burn, and I wonder if Hollie can tell. I can barely believe what I've done. I got a *job*, right here on a Sunday morning. Now a full-fledged plan is hatching in my brain. I haven't done anything like this before—leaping before I go looking.

But maybe it's time I tried.

4

"ABSOLUTELY NOT."

"But, Mama, if—"

"Fifteen dollars a week? I know you can do better math than that. It would take you *five months* to make three hundred, and this workshop starts in a quarter of that time. Land sakes, the application fee is due in four days."

"But I could ask about paying in installments, you know? Maybe they—"

"Not a chance, Cline Louise."

I stand before Mama, the neon orange flyer in my hand. I'm not sure how I mustered enough guts to be here, but I blame gospel music.

"I'll Fly Away" has been on my mind all day. For me, the words of that song aren't about flying away to heaven. They're about flying toward my *dream*. Those three words—*I'll fly away*—were somersaulting in my brain when we left New Hope Church. They were flipping around when we ate lunch at Hacienda Mexican Grill. They kept flipping at the Kendalls' house, as Hollie and I jumped on the trampoline. They were flipping even when Mama pulled the Camry into the Kendalls' driveway and I waved Hollie goodbye.

On the ride home, Mama was quiet, which usually means she isn't in a good mood. I didn't even care. I asked Gram what she thought of Cleveland and their chili, and the only thing Mama said was, "Cline, the special chili's in Cincinnati." When I asked how the doctor's appointment went, Gram said, "Real nice." And when I asked if that meant Dr. Windisch was wrong about her Alzheimer's, Gram said, "Now, honey, there's nothing to worry about." Which I suspected already, but it put an outright smile on my face. I bet Gram *did* get good news, and the only reason for Mama's bad mood was how much the doctor's visit cost.

When we got home, I helped Gram out of the car. She said she was plum worn out from travel, so I tucked her in bed and left the television on MeTV, like she asked. Then I went to my bedroom and picked up the flyer from my dresser. I figured, right then and there, that if I was going to be brave enough to ask, it'd have to be right away.

And that's how I've found myself in the kitchen, Mama staring down at me with a face sourer than pickle juice. I knew she wouldn't be *ecstatic*, say, but personally, I think I've made a good case for myself. Before, when Mama said no to music lessons, it was because *she* couldn't afford it. Well, I'm getting old enough to make my own money now. If I get the job at New Hope, I could pay for the workshop. Makes perfect sense to me.

Not so much to Mama.

"How would you even get to Lexington?" she's asking now. "You know Mondays are my late-night shift."

"But Delia works Mondays, doesn't she? She could cover for you."

"No, she couldn't," Mama retorts. "Labor Day was an exception. She's started back night classes at UK and takes off early on Mondays now. And Laila has the other late-nights 'cause she's got her baby to mind in the day. It was enough for me to get Monday."

"Even as head waitress?" I squeak. All that courage of mine? It's wiped clean out.

"You're too young to understand certain things about my profession," Mama says, shaking her head. "I know you think it's a boring job, but it's what has kept this family afloat. Playing that guitar is fine as a hobby, but it's not going to keep *you* afloat when the time comes to support yourself. There's no point in wasting good money on a workshop that isn't teaching you practical skills. I'd be failing you as a mother if I didn't say so."

You're failing me now, I want to say. *You're stabbing my dream in the heart and watching it bleed.*

"I love music, though," I whisper. I'm telling myself not to cry.

"Loving it's fine," Mama tells me. "But those musicians of yours are one in a million. The odds aren't good, Cline, and they won't be kind to you."

Rebel tears are coming on, hot and wobbly beneath my lashes. I wipe them away, but there's no chance Mama doesn't see. I think that's why her face stops scrunching so hard, and she says, in a nicer way, "I want what's best for you. I know you don't see that now, but you will. It was . . ." She looks at the flyer, which I'm holding on to so hard it's started to crumple. "It was a nice idea, but it's not going to work out."

It feels like I'm trying to swallow an apple whole—like it's jammed in my throat, and any minute it's gonna bust out, causing a mess. I've got no choice but to run out of the kitchen and into my room.

I don't want to hear if Mama's hollering after me. I especially don't want to hear if she's *not*. See, that's the trouble: I don't think Mama cares much about how music makes me feel. She thinks she's being noble, saving me from the life of a penniless artist. There's no softening someone who's set their mind like that.

I just don't understand *why* Mama's mind is set. So many times, I've wanted to ask her how she could ever sell her piano and stop playing music. Maybe I don't want to know. Don't want to even imagine how or why the person who named me Cline could turn her back on music for good, call it nothing more than a waste of money.

With my bedroom door shut, I plug my earbuds into my phone and press Shuffle on a playlist called "Cline Kicks the World's Butt." These are the songs I play when I'm in a real funk or when I want to punch someone in the gut for some awful thing they said.

"Music is medicine," Gram told me once, while *Porter Wagoner* was on. "It can take your broken, bruised spirits and heal 'em right up."

Well, my spirits? They've been through the wringer.

The first song's album artwork pops up on my phone, showing a blond woman with the floofiest bangs and bouffant you ever did see. It's Tammy Wynette, and I breathe a sigh of relief seeing her face. When it comes to spirit mending, Tammy is top-notch medical care.

"Your Good Girl's Gonna Go Bad" is about Tammy threatening to go hog wild on her unfaithful man. I don't have a no-good man to exact revenge upon, but the spirit-mending part of the song is this: when life gets tough, a girl can only go so long following the rules.

I've asked Mama to believe in my dream a hundred times before, and she's always said no. I never did get those music lessons, and I've probably listened to days' worth of Spotify ads by now. I can only hope that Brandi Carlile is still touring by the time I'm old enough to go to one of her concerts on my own. Maybe then I'll finally get her autograph and a chance to tell her she's been an inspiration to me. (Though I might *not* tell her about the crush I had on her all through seventh grade.)

I haven't asked Mama for anything music related this year. I know her wallet's already stretched thin. But this time around, it's *my* money. I told her I'd get a job, that I'd do this on my own, and she *still* won't say yes. There's no winning with her.

Mama says I'm too young, but who says being young's a bad thing? There've been plenty of girls like me who didn't let their age stand between them and their dreams. I know their stories: Patsy Cline wrote a letter to the Grand Ole Opry at age fifteen, asking to audition, *and they let her.* Linda Ronstadt was singing in a folk trio at fourteen. Dolly Parton and Tanya Tucker got discovered when they were *my* age.

I know I can be a singer, and if Mama's not going to help me, no matter how hard I try? Well, then it's time I helped myself. No more waiting around, dreaming of flying away. No more playing by Mama's rules.

This good girl's gonna go bad.

5

THE WAY I figure it, I need to check three boxes if I want my workshop dream to come true.

I've practically checked the first one already: money. I have seventeen dollars and twenty-six cents saved up from babysitting for Mrs. Nelson—I counted from my mason jar bank last night—and that's enough to cover the workshop's application fee. The tuition is trickier but not impossible. With the nursery job at New Hope, I can make the three hundred dollars. Not all at once, but that's what sweet-talking's for.

See, Mama bought our living room couch on something called layaway. She paid a chunk of the cost at first and then followed up with more money till it was paid off. Who says I can't do the same with the Young Singer-Songwriter Workshop? If I make a good-enough case, those workshop folks are bound to see reason.

Second, there's transportation. I've been thinking hard about that since Mama shot down my dream. My solution? *Delia*. Mama said Delia drives to Lexington on Monday nights for classes. She'll already be on the University of Kentucky's campus, plus she's the one who told me about the workshop in the first place. Of course she'd want to help me out.

Last of all, there's permission. I didn't figure that one out till early this Monday morning. After Mama left for the Goldenrod, I hopped on the computer and printed off the application form from the workshop website. That's when I saw that it doesn't say *parent* under the signature line. It says *guardian*. Well, Gram's as much my guardian as Mama. I'm positive Gram will sign that form. I just have to work up the courage to ask.

So, I've got two more boxes to check and three days to make the postmark deadline on the sixteenth. My work's cut out for me.

Gram is still asleep when I head out the door to wait for my school bus. Our house isn't in a fancy neighborhood, like Hollie's. It's an old farmhouse, built over a century ago, and it sits on the end of an old-as-dirt lane. I have to walk to the end of the lane every morning, passing under rows of shady oaks, till I reach the stop sign at Cherry Lane, the street where an actual neighborhood of newer, ranch-style houses begins.

I stand at the stop sign, nibbling a Pop-Tart and squinting into the sunrise. It may be September, but it's still hot as heck in Kentucky. I wipe a trickle of sweat from my neck and tick up the volume in my earbuds. I'm listening to "Right or Wrong" by none other than Wanda Jackson, Queen of Rockabilly. Most people only know about the King, Elvis Presley—and, don't get me wrong, Elvis is great and all. Personally, though? I think Wanda has the better chops *and* moves. She played a pink guitar and shook her fringed dress, all while singing about being a hardheaded woman. She deserved a royal title, no doubt about that.

I don't care what Mama says about odds not being kind to musicians. One in a million's a slim chance, okay, but I've been thinking . . . how many of those million are musicians who give it their all? Really put in the elbow grease? Mama wouldn't know. She may have been a great pianist once, with lots of potential, but she gave that up. And she never tried to be a singer, like me.

Wanda Jackson did, though. And she succeeded.

My bus pulls up to the stop sign, brakes squealing, and I tuck my earbuds away. Wanda's still singing to me, though, as I step on board. She's saying, "Go after your dream, Cline, right or wrong."

Only, I know I'm right.

∽∾

Before my first day at Dunbar Middle, Delia pulled me aside and said, "Listen up: middle school can suck, but you *will* make it through."

I know she meant well, but Delia scared me stiff, talking like that. I expected tougher classes, stricter teachers, and mean girls talking behind my back. None of that's been the case. Sure, some kids here are mean, and some classes are harder than others, but that was true at Paris Elementary, too.

Overall, I like going to Dunbar Middle School. I do okay in classes, especially social studies, and I get to hang with the same friends I've had since first grade. There's Kenzie Butler, who is Black and petite and has natural corkscrew hair. She's a real talented artist, and she loves watercolor sets. So far, she's collected fifty-six from all over the world. She even has her own Etsy shop where she sells custom portraits. There's Ava Zhao, who is Chinese American and has long hair she usually wears in a high ponytail. She's on the DMS color guard, and she can handle flags and batons like a pro. Ava's parents divorced four years ago, and now she visits her dad every summer and brings us back *delicious* blackberry preserves from his farm in Illinois. There's Darlene Flaherty, who's white and round figured and moved here from West Virginia when she was little. She's the star player for the school's volleyball team and went to state finals last year.

And, of course, there's Hollie, who's just taken a bite of food at lunch today when Darlene proclaims that she doesn't trust school pizza.

"C'mon," says Darlene, pointing her fork around our cafeteria table. "Where else does pizza come in a *rectangle*? I'm telling you, school kitchens exist in a parallel universe."

Darlene has been obsessed with this "parallel universe" theory ever since school started. She loves sci-fi stuff like that. At her birthday party in February, we watched a whole season of the TV show *Star Trek: Discovery*.

"So, what?" says Hollie, looking confused. "The kitchen is in some weird space-time vortex?"

"You mean I'm eating *alien* pizza?" Ava says with a full mouth. She makes a fake gagging noise and spits out a half-chewed pepperoni on her plate.

"Ew," says Hollie, but the rest of us laugh.

Ava is the funniest person I know. Not knock-knock joke funny, though. She's got the sort of humor that sneaks up on you. She'll act real unassuming, and then she'll pull a face or say something sly, and that's when you realize you're already halfway into a punch line. Other times, she'll pretend to trip in front of you and catch herself last minute. Or, like today, spit out pepperonis. Maybe that sounds silly on the surface, but it's the *way* Ava does it, all serious, like she's not in on the joke.

Even now, as we laugh, she stares ahead in horror, gulping down the rest of her food like she's ingesting alien slime.

"I didn't say *alien*," Darlene retorts. "That's different from parallel universe theory."

"But parallel universes *could* have aliens in them," Kenzie points out. "Like a Venn diagram."

Kenzie raises her pointer finger to illustrate, drawing two circles in the air. "Aliens here. Parallel universes here." She taps midair, at the place where the two circles overlap. "You can have both."

I could listen to Kenzie talk science all day. The past few summers, she's gone to Camp Quest, which is big on science and critical thinking. She one-hundred percent does not believe in ghosts, horoscopes, or the undead. She *does* think aliens could exist, though, and that's where she and Darlene make their own Venn diagram, I guess. Once the two of them start talking about extraterrestrial life, buckle up. I've spent plenty of sleepovers listening to the two of them swap ideas for *hours*.

Ava pokes at her tray and says, "Thanks for the info, you two. I will now never eat alien rectangle pizza again."

She glances longingly at Kenzie's bagged lunch, which consists of a PB&J sandwich, carrot sticks, and chips.

Kenzie smirks, raising a carrot. "No aliens *or* parallel universes had a hand in this."

"Totally non-GMO," Ava agrees solemnly. "You know, *Greatly Mysterious Origin*."

We're all laughing again when Trevor Larson—a tall, white boy with dark eyes and darker hair—walks up to our table and stops right next to me.

Darlene's eyes get big, and Hollie says, "Hey, Trevor."

I just smile, because there's not much to say. Trevor's in my grade, but he and I don't really talk.

"How's it going, Cline?" he asks.

Except for now, apparently.

I look around the table, sure he's got the wrong girl.

"Um," I say. "We're all good."

Trevor's not looking at the other girls, though. He's staring straight at me. I clear my throat and set down my spoonful of peas.

"I was talking to some of the guys," he says, "and one of them said you're named after a movie star. Is that true?"

That makes me smile. So this is just a question about my name. I'm used to that. "Not a movie star, exactly," I say. "A singer. Patsy Cline. You heard of her?"

Trevor scrunches his face, thinking. "Was she from the eighties? The one who sings 'Girls Just Want to Have Fun'?"

I laugh. "*Waaay* off. That's Cyndi Lauper. Patsy Cline was country, not pop."

Trevor's shoulders droop. He looks embarrassed, and that's when I realize that maybe my laughing could've come off as mean. So I say real fast, "Cyndi Lauper's cool, though. *Lauper* would be a fun first name, too."

Trevor's mouth tips up. "Yeah, it would." After a pause, he adds, "Not as cool as Cline, though."

I blink.

"Uh. Well." Trevor looks around at the other girls. "It's good seeing y'all."

He smacks his hands on the table with one big whump and walks away.

I'm squinting after him, trying to figure out what in the sam hill just happened, when Darlene whispers, "Oh my *gosh*, Cline. Trevor Larson was *flirting* with you."

"*Whoa,*" I say, whipping around to the table.

I'm greeted by a horrifying sight. Ava is smirking and Kenzie's covering her mouth like she saw a pig fly.

"He wasn't flirting," I say.

"Then why'd he come over here just to tell you what a *cool name* you have?" Ava asks.

"Yeah," says Kenzie. "Especially with the Harvest Dance coming up next month."

Kenzie is talking about the school's fall dance, which is taking place on Halloween this year. It is, without a doubt, my least favorite topic of conversation.

"Wait and *see*," Darlene sing-songs, when I don't reply. "Next time, he'll be down on one knee."

I roll my eyes, but the girls keep looking at me.

"*What?*" I say, kind of angry now. "Trevor's nice to everyone."

"Suuure, Cline," Ava drawls. "Sure."

"He's got such long lashes, don't you think?" coos Darlene.

"He's tall for his age, too," Kenzie says.

I feel like sinking down in my seat and melting into the plastic.

"Hey." When Hollie speaks up, her voice is firm. The other girls look to her.

"Cline's uncomfortable," Hollie tells them, placing a hand on mine. "Can't you tell? If she says Trevor wasn't flirting . . . well, then let's leave it be."

The girls don't say anything after that, but I can tell they think I'm dead wrong.

See, I know Trevor was flirting. The trouble is, I don't *want* him to. Trevor's nice and all, but I don't want to dance with him, and I especially don't want to kiss him.

When the girls get this way—Darlene gushing about Jared Rushford's swoopy bangs or Ava mentioning Mark Garcia's "hundred-watt smile," I can only shrug along. Jared has bangs, sure, and Mark smiles, but those facts don't send my heart aflutter. They never have. See, I don't like boys that way.

I like *girls* that way.

I haven't always had words for the way I feel. At first, it was only a niggling in my brain. While Kenzie was swooning over the muscles of her favorite K-Pop stars, I was thinking about how Brandi Carlile looked like a million bucks at the Grammys. When Darlene would talk about how her favorite YouTuber, Jeremy Falcon, had eyes like a stormy sea, I thought that was plain ridiculous. But then, months later, I found a channel called Sweets for the Sweet, run by this college girl named Georgie, and I couldn't stop staring at her face, and that's when it hit me that *Georgie* had stormy sea eyes, and maybe I felt about them the way Darlene did about Jeremy's. Soon, what started as just a niggling became plain as day.

There's no one girl in particular at DMS I have a crush on, but I do notice myself admiring Lindley Clifton's freckled nose and the way Odessa Long's laugh carries across the cafeteria. Little crushes. Nothing real.

Truth be told? I'm not sure I'm ready for real. I've overheard some diners at the Goldenrod saying how it's a real tragedy that the "gay agenda" has taken over the media and how Bible-believing folks need to stand against it. Those same diners called a lady in Rowan County a hero years back for refusing to marry same-sex couples on account of her "principles."

Granted, I also heard Delia tell those diners that the only item on gay agenda was to be treated equally under the law. *And* I heard other customers say that the lady from Rowan County was backward as a rearview mirror. I haven't heard my friends breathe a bad word about girls who like girls, but then again, they don't say *anything* on the subject.

Then there's Mama and Gram. I know that, on account of them being godless women, they don't hold to the religious ideas those Goldenrod diners have. Still, I haven't told either of them about my liking girls. It seems like such a *big* thing to say, and I don't have the words for it yet.

More than anything, though? I don't want people thinking of me differently. I'm the same Cline I've always been, but I'm worried that this part of me will make me stand out like a sore thumb. Cline Louise Alden, the girl who *doesn't* crush on guys. When I stand out, I want it to be for my music. The things I do. Not for a part of who I am and can't change, any more than Hollie could change the color of her eyes.

That's why, for now, my liking girls is a secret I keep to myself— safe and sound, locked inside my heart. But then something like *this* happens. Trevor Larson asks me if I'm named after a movie star, and I have to deal with a whole bunch of questions from the girls. It leaves me feeling worn out.

Hollie gets it, at least. After what she says, the girls quiet down about Trevor and start discussing Ava's upcoming color guard performance at the next football game.

As they do, Hollie shoots me a look that says, *Don't worry about it.*

I smile at her gratefully. Hollie will always have my back.

6

IT'S DEAD HOUR at the Goldenrod. That's the slow stretch between lunch and supper, when the loudest sound in the diner is Bill scraping bits of burned meat off the grill. It's around five o'clock when the old folks start showing up for their early suppers, and by six, the Goldenrod's packed as a sardines tin. Four fifteen, though? The place is deader than a week-old corpse.

Hollie and I have had an arrangement since the fifth grade: I get off our bus at her stop, and we hang out at her house, chatting or watching TV for a couple of hours. Today, though, I only stick around for one episode of *Sugar Rush* before heading out.

See, Mama told me that Delia takes off early on Mondays now, and my best guess is that she leaves in the dead hour, when she can make a clean exit. That's why I leave Hollie's house at four o'clock. But as I make my way down Main, I see Delia's beat-up Chevy truck already pulling out of the Goldenrod parking lot.

Panic pops in my chest like a soda bubble.

"DELIA!" I shout, waving my hands over my head.

She spots me as her truck chugs onto Main and slows to a stop at the curb. I run, huffing and puffing, to meet her.

"Hey there, Cline," she calls through her open window. The radio's on—Loretta Lynn singing "These Boots Are Made for Walkin'" with the utmost sass.

I love this song. Once, Gram and I belted it loud as we could, parading around the den and waving scarves from her cedar chest collection.

I take Loretta as a good sign.

"Early for your supper, isn't it?" Delia asks.

"Actually," I say, once I've caught my breath, "I came out to see you."

Delia lifts her thick brows—one of them pierced through with a silver rod.

"*Me*, huh?" she says. "Well, I don't work Monday nights anymore, sad to say."

"I know." I nod eagerly. "That's the point."

"Of what?"

"You know that flyer you gave me? For the singer-songwriter workshop."

Delia lights up. "You gonna do it?"

"Well. Thing is, Mama works the late shift Monday nights. But she said you go to Lexington for classes, right?"

"I do." Delia looks conspiratorial. "You wanna bum a ride, huh?"

I grin. It's awfully convenient when someone says what you want to say for you.

"I'll pay gas money," I tell Delia, but she shoos me off.

"You'll do no such thing. I'd be driving to UK anyway. But listen, Cline, I dunno if I'm your best bet. The workshop ends at nine, right?"

"Yeah."

"Well, I don't get out of class till nine thirty most nights. You'd have to wait around some, and—"

"I don't mind that," I interrupt. "Promise. I'm good at entertaining myself. I won't bother you a smidge."

Delia laughs. "It's no bother, Cline. I'm happy you're doing the workshop."

"It's not a sure thing." I look down at the cracked sidewalk, feeling suddenly nervous over the prospect of talking to Gram about her permission. "I have another box to check first."

"Huh," Delia says, looking sort of confused. "Well, for what it's worth, I can't think of anyone who'd be a better fit for that workshop than you."

I brighten at Delia's words. "If everything works out," I tell her, "I'll need a ride starting two weeks from now, on September twenty-eighth."

"The twenty-eighth. Got it." Delia's gaze hardens. "Hey. Your mama know about this?"

I freeze right there, on the spot. I've been planning up a storm, but here's one thing I forgot: how to explain to Delia that this workshop has to stay a secret—especially from my mother.

My silence is as good as an answer to Delia.

"Yeah," she says. "Wasn't sure how game Judy would be."

Like that, my hopes plummet down, down, *down* till they hit the pit of my stomach. I hang my head. It's over now. Doesn't matter if I can pay for the workshop or get Gram's permission if I don't have a ride into town.

"Thanks, anyway," I mumble, backing away from the truck and feeling a fool. I can't meet Delia's eyes. It's too embarrassing, getting found out this way.

"Hey!" Delia calls. "When did I say I wouldn't drive you?"

I look up quick. "You will?"

By way of reply, Delia winks. Quick as lightning, my hopes are soaring again.

I hold my hands to my heart and say, "You're the *greatest*."

"Normally, I don't condone cagey behavior," Delia informs me. "But I've got a feeling that even though Judy's not on board, Cynthia is. That right?"

All I can do is nod. Gram *will* be on board. I'll make sure of that.

"Well," says Delia, "that's enough to keep my conscience clean. Consider your secret safe with me."

I keep nodding, feeling like a happy-go-lucky bobblehead.

"See you soon, rebel musician." Delia tugs down her shades

from her pink hair and shifts the truck into drive. She pulls away from the curb, and I wave, feeling liable to float up into the sky.

Two checks down. Only one more to go.

A half hour later, as I leave the Goldenrod with supper, I'm still light and giggly. I start walking home, but then walking doesn't feel fitting. Running does. So I sprint down the sidewalk, bagged Styrofoam boxes tap-tapping against my leg and ice cubes sloshing around in my Arnold Palmer.

Loretta Lynn's boots were made for walking, but my purple Keds were made for *flying*—flying away, oh glory, like the old hymn goes.

7

IT'S REALLY HAPPENING.

My plan is coming along.

Only, this last box is easier drawn than checked. I'm beginning to second-guess myself. I know Gram supports me, but what if she thinks the workshop is impractical, or she doesn't like the idea of keeping it from Mama? If I've gotten this far, only for Gram to say no, I don't think my heart could take it.

That's why I'm sitting with jittery feet and bouncing knees as Gram and I watch *The Porter Wagoner Show*. Tonight's guest is Jumpin' Bill Carlisle, who I'd think was only a goofy one-hit wonder if Gram didn't tell me that, actually, Bill's a country legend. He got his start right here in Kentucky and went on to the Grand Ole Opry, where he played up till two weeks before he died. That's something, I suppose.

As we watch Bill perform, I eat the next meal up on my Goldenrod menu rotation: a Hot Brown with a side of collard greens. I especially like when I get to this combo, on account of the fact that the Hot Brown—an open-faced sandwich smothered in cheese—was my dad's favorite meal. There's even a framed photograph on the mantel of Dad beaming over his plate at the Brown Hotel, in Louisville, where the very first Hot Brown was served. It's my favorite picture of him.

When Bill is through with his act, Dolly Parton takes the stage and sings two numbers: the hymn "How Great Thou Art" and a song called "Just the Way I Am." I nervously chew my greens, listening to Dolly sing that she'll do whatever she pleases, thank you, whether or not anyone understands her. I tell myself Dolly is singing straight to me. I've got to do what I please, too, no matter how scared I am; and as the show is ending, I decide on what to say to Gram. I'll start by talking about Dolly's music, and then I'll nudge in my question about the workshop. Once I've done that? Well, I'll cross all my fingers and toes.

"Dolly really got it, huh?" I say to Gram, turning off the TV. "It's like, when she sings, she's giving your heart the words you didn't know it was speaking."

"That's a fact, Judy," Gram says.

I go still when she calls me by Mama's name. It's not that Gram hasn't called me *Judy* before. I don't blame her, because I've seen old photos of Mama, and I look a lot like she did when she was my age. It's only natural that Gram would mix up our names, same as other older folks in town tend to do. Only, before, Gram's always caught her mistake. This time, the seconds tick by, but she doesn't correct herself. Instead, she squints at the DVD menu, a faraway look in her eyes, like she's pondering life's great mysteries.

It's not that I'm real worried about Gram's memory. She got that good second opinion in Cleveland, after all. And Gram may have called me Judy just now, but only a minute ago, she was spouting facts about Jumpin' Bill like a walking encyclopedia.

Still, I decide now isn't the right time to ask about the workshop, after all. If Gram is a little out of sorts, the best thing I can do is stick to our regular routine. I heave a sigh, my stomach still fluttering from leftover nerves, but I've made up my mind: the plan can wait another day. I muster a smile and ask Gram what I always do after our *Porter Wagoner* date: "What's next for you, Gram?"

Some nights, Gram feels like watching more TV, but other nights she's worn out and wants to hit the hay. Either way, I help her out, punching in the right channel number or turning down the sheets on her bed. Gram calls this the "royal treatment."

Tonight, though, Gram doesn't have an answer ready for me. She's still staring ahead at the television, looking thoughtful but not saying a word.

"Gram?" I say, real soft, after half a minute's gone by.

She looks to me, the pondering fog finally clearing from her eyes.

"Cline, sweetie," she says, and I get a deep-down comforting feeling, like I've been bundled in a hand-stitched quilt.

Gram *does* know my name. Of course she does.

"Sweetie pie," she tells me, "I've got something for you in my room."

I stare in surprise. "Something . . . for me?"

"Mhm. Now help me up."

Gram uses my arm for balance as she gets to her feet, and we head down the hallway together. When we get to her bedroom, she points to her closet.

"Up there, top shelf. The blue tin box. You'll have to stand on a chair, most likely."

Gram's right about that. I spy the box, but my fingers can't stretch high enough to nudge it off the shelf. I drag in a chair from the breakfast room, set it up, and bring down a tin marked *Caramel Chews*. I hand the tin over to Gram, who's taken a seat in her favorite armchair.

Something tells me that what's inside the tin *isn't* caramel. Sure enough, when Gram opens it, there's not a candy in sight. Instead, the box contains a big stack of photographs. At the top, there's a photo of Gram and Papaw on their wedding day. Gram's holding tight to Papaw's arm as they smile on the front steps of the Bourbon County courthouse.

You can't see a photo like that and not grin, ear to ear, so that's what I'm doing when Gram digs deep, under the photographs, and pulls out a folded white envelope.

"Here we are," she announces, handing the envelope to me.

I take it cautiously, opening the flap, and I gasp when I see a wad of twenty-dollar bills.

"That's my rainy-day fund." Gram taps the envelope. "I've kept it for years now, knowing there'd come a time to put it to use. Well, the time has arrived."

"What?" I ask Gram, downright confused.

Gram gives me a knowing look. "I heard you telling your mother about that workshop in Lexington. Now, sweetie, I love Judy with all my heart, but, truth be told, she's forgotten how important music can be. She doesn't feel it in her blood anymore, like you and me, and that's all right. Mind your own fence, and to each their own, I say. But it's not right for something as common as money to keep you from going to that workshop."

My eyes well up as Gram takes the envelope back from me, counting out the bills.

"That's a hundred even," she says. "I know it's not enough to cover everything, but I'd say it's a start."

I can hardly believe it. All the time I was working up the courage to talk to Gram, she was ten whole steps ahead of me. She already knows about my dream. She *believes* in it. My hopes bubble right back up and come spewing out my mouth. I tell Gram about my three-step plan, my interview at New Hope's nursery, and my arrangement with Delia. Gram nods along, eyes twinkling, up until I tell her I can't take the money.

"Why ever not?" she demands.

"It's yours," I insist. "And I told you, I'll make the money at church."

Gram tuts at me. "Fifteen dollars a week won't cut it. Not in time to put down a good deposit, like you intend. Now, as you say, it's *my* money, and I get to do with it what I please. If you don't take it, you'll break an old woman's heart."

"Gram," I say, "that isn't fair."

Gram just smiles. "Take the money, sweetie pie. You go to Lexington, and you learn how to write better songs than Guthrie and Parton put together."

My eyes fill with tears all over again. Because Gram knows my heart. She sees me just the way I am.

This time, when she hands me the envelope, I don't say no. I hold the money close to my chest, even as I run to my bedroom, snatching up the workshop application form I printed off this morning. I bring it back to Gram, feeling suddenly jumpy— jumpier even than Jumpin' Bill Carlisle.

"And we . . . won't tell Mama about this, right?" I ask.

I feel a little bad, doing this behind Mama's back—two Alden ladies keeping a secret from one.

But Gram tells me, "Sweetie, that's a *given*."

She winks like we're coconspirators, which helps ease my mind, and takes the plastic pen from me, scratching her signature on the dotted line.

And like that, my dream seems within my reach—a tuned-up guitar just waiting to be strummed.

8

TODAY IS A real big deal.

For one thing, I've got my trial run at the New Hope nursery.

For another, I'm sending my completed application to the Young Singer-Songwriter Workshop, along with the fifteen-dollar application fee—practically every cent I have.

And on top of that? I have to keep my nervousness bottled inside, all to myself.

See, I haven't told Hollie about the workshop. She doesn't like music, especially *my* kind of music, all that much. The few times I've played songs for her—Loretta and Dolly and, naturally, Emmylou—she just shrugged and said they weren't her style. I figure Kenzie, Ava, and Darlene feel about the same way. It's not like I play guitar or sing around them, either. That's something I do on my own time.

Back in elementary school, I thought about joining the choir, or maybe even the school band. But, truth is, I didn't want to sing in a choir; I wanted to sing in a folk band or all on my own. And I didn't want to learn, say, the oboe or flute when I could play guitar.

When I was in fourth grade, Ms. Khatri caught me looking at the sign-up sheet outside the band rehearsal room. When she asked if I was thinking of joining, I told her how Gram had given me a guitar I wanted to learn to play, but guitar wasn't listed as a band instrument. Ms. Khatri didn't blink an eye. She whipped out her phone and told me about two YouTube channels I could check out—with Mama's permission, of course—that gave free guitar tutorials. That night, I headed straight to the computer to look them up, telling Gram about my plan to learn music on my own. And that's what I did.

That's the last time school had anything to do with my music. See, School Cline doesn't talk about singing or guitar playing. My musical dream feels delicate. Like, if I share it with too many people, it might dissolve in my hands. Hollie's my best friend, but for now, I want to share this secret only with the folks who get what music means to me, and that's Delia and Gram.

So after school, I tell Hollie I've got to head home early again, but I don't say what for. I've told her about the nursery job at New Hope, but I said it was for pocket money. Hollie gave me a kind of funny look at that. Maybe because she doesn't have to work for money; her parents give her an allowance of ten dollars a week.

But in the end, she said she hoped I had fun.

I take the long way home from Hollie's house, down Ivy Street, straight to the post office. Everything's in order. I've got a signature. I've got the fifteen dollars. I've filled out every line of the application, including a short essay on why I want to attend, and I've written the address on a manila envelope in big, fat letters, so there's no mistaking where this dream of mine is headed: straight to the city of Lexington.

My heart's beating fast as a hummingbird's wings when I step into the post office. It doesn't slow down—not as I stand in line, or as I hand over my last two dollar bills at the counter, or as I watch a postal worker named Gerry pick up my application and whisk it away to a giant cart of mail. Fact is, my heart's beating faster than ever when I leave the building. I've done something monumental, and all behind Mama's back.

But there's one thing I gotta face Mama with frontward. I *have* to tell her about tonight's nursery job. On Mondays, she'll be working late, so she won't know if I sneak out to Lexington. Wednesdays are different, though. Mama's going to know I'm gone.

I could lie, saying I'm hanging out with a friend, but I'm already keeping one giant secret, and I'd like to be truthful about this much. Gram says that there's no better recipe for a good night's sleep than a clear conscience.

Well. At least this way, I'll sleep *okay*.

Mama's at the kitchen table when I get home. She's filling up

Gram's pillbox—a colored contraption marked with each day of the week and fitted with containers for morning, afternoon, and night. Plastic pill bottles are lined up on the table, and Mama's using the pill splitter, cutting circle-shaped pills in half.

Mama does this every week. Gram has to take a lot of pills—mostly for her heart and blood pressure—which can get confusing if you don't organize. And if there's one thing Judy Alden's good at, it's keeping order.

I frown at the pill bottles on the table, counting them up. There are two more than the usual eight Mama works with. I notice a discarded bag from Gilchrist Pharmacy, which means Mama just picked up these new pills this afternoon. I squint at the unpronounceable word on the bottle closest to me, then at the name of the prescribing doctor. It's not Dr. Windisch, so it must be one of those Cleveland doctors.

I swallow hard, wondering what these pills mean. Gram told me not to worry about the trip to Cleveland. I took that to mean she'd gotten *good* news. If that's the case, though, why would she need new medicine? I think it over. Maybe the Cleveland doctors are just making sure they've got their bases covered, so in case Gram's memory is a *little* wobbly, it won't get any wobblier. Gram will stay perfectly fine so long as she's got the proper help—from the medicine, the doctors, and *me*.

I want to ask Mama about the pills, to be sure my theory is right, but something tells me that she'll get sour. She'll start thinking about how much the medicine costs, and Mama's always short-tempered when it comes to spending money.

Today, at least, I've got good financial news. That's how I'm going to frame it, anyway.

"Mama," I tell her, plopping into a chair. "You know that nursery job I mentioned before? The one at New Hope Church?"

She raises a finger, signaling that she's in the middle of something. Only when she's through splitting a pill does she look up and say, "Come again?"

"The woman in charge, Mrs. Yune, said I could do a trial run tonight," I explain.

Mama gives me a *look*, one auburn brow arched high.

"I'm not thinking about that workshop anymore," I add, 'cause even this much truth telling requires some fibbing. "You were right about it being impractical. But our talk got me to thinking how it'd be nice to have spending money."

Mama looks me over so hard she may as well be checking for ticks. Then she says, "I think that's a fine idea, to get a steady job."

I feel a whoosh of relief as Mama adds, "I'll want to meet this Mrs. Yune tonight, when I drive you there. And I would've preferred if you hadn't sprung this on me last minute. You're lucky I didn't already have plans."

I feel like I'm practically floating. I got my yes from Mama, *and* she's offering to drive me to work. I'd been planning for the worst: walking the half hour to the church and back.

"Really?" I ask, not sure I believe my good luck.

"Really," Mama replies, and I think she *almost* smiles. "Now fix yourself a snack. I've got to finish with these pills."

～∞～

I feel downright embarrassed as Mama and I walk across New Hope Church's parking lot. She doesn't need to meet Mrs. Yune, but Mama is this way about everything I do. She insists on meeting all my teachers at the start of each school year, and she asks a dozen questions about field trips and extracurriculars, and she *still* lectures me about not drinking sodas at Hollie's.

"What kind of mother would I be if I didn't?" she always says.

I'd like to tell her, "You'd be *cool*." I mean, land sakes, I'm thirteen. Shouldn't I be learning to make decisions on my own? Only, Mama seems to be worried that Mrs. Yune is an ax murderer.

Those worries must flit away real fast when we walk into the church's nursery wing. The walls are bright lime green and painted with cartoon animals: monkeys swinging from vines, a lion sunning itself, and a hippopotamus taking a bath. There's a check-in desk straight ahead, where Mrs. Yune stands, talking on the phone.

"Betsy?" she says into the receiver, when she spots me and Mama. "I'll call you back."

Mrs. Yune hangs up, breaking into a big smile.

"Why hello, Ms. Cline!" she just about hollers, coming round from the desk to greet me.

She's not wearing her orange hat today, but Mrs. Yune looks

just as fashionable as before, in swishy pink pants and a sparkly gray top. Her lipstick matches her pants precisely, and her black hair's teased high.

"This must be your mother," Mrs. Yune says, shaking Mama's hand. "I'm Edith. We're so happy Cline's interested in the job. We've been shorthanded, and it's difficult to recruit girls within the church, since most of them prefer to attend youth group."

That puts Hollie on my mind. It's weird to think we'll be in the same building tonight but probably won't see each other.

"Cline's certainly enthusiastic about the job," Mama says, eyeing me. "She told you about her CPR training?"

"Oh, yes," Mrs. Yune replies. "Cline was *very* convincing."

Mama asks Mrs. Yune a few more questions, like where she lives (the new Great Oaks subdivision) and how she came to work in the nursery (through a family friend). After a few minutes, Mama seems to make up her mind that Mrs. Yune is not, in fact, a serial killer, and tells me she'll pick me up around eight thirty.

I puff a relieved sigh as she leaves the nursery.

"Now!" cries Mrs. Yune, nodding as another woman bustles into the room. "Marjorie, hon, if you'll mind the desk, I'm going to give Cline the official rundown."

⁓

Here's how the rundown begins: with Mrs. Yune asking my favorite subject in school, complimenting my purple Keds, and making me a handwritten name tag to wear on my T-shirt.

She goes over the nursery's strict check-in policy and what to do if a kid is sick or causing trouble. Then she shows me around the nursery, checking rosters and cleaning off tables with Clorox wipes as she goes. I learn that the Antelope room is for infants, Elephant for young toddlers, and Giraffe for pre-K.

"Got it," I say. "In ascending animal height."

Mrs. Yune gives me a look, and then she busts out laughing, saying, "I've never thought of it that way."

That's when I know, for sure, that Mrs. Edith Yune and I are going to get along.

"You'll be working with Morgan in the Elephant room," she tells me, as parents and their kids start to file in.

She introduces me to Morgan, who is Delia's age, but nothing like her. Where Delia says things like "damn" and "right on," Morgan says "Lord willing" and "that's not the way."

For example, when I welcome our first kid—a two-year-old named Asher—by yelling, "Put your hands together for *Asherrr*!" and making a sound like an air horn, Morgan places a hand on my shoulder and says, "I appreciate the enthusiasm, Cline, but that's not the way to greet kids. It could scare them."

I get hot in the face and mumble, "Okay, sure." After that, no more air horns from me.

Even so, I keep managing to do things wrong. Once everyone on our roster has arrived, I suggest we play duck, duck, goose, since that was a game I liked playing when I was a kid.

"There's an agenda," Morgan tells me, looking cross. "A way we do things. It's your first night, but you'll learn."

Then she announces that it's story time, and she calls all the kids over to the big carpet square, where she reads a picture book called *Jesus's Twelve Disciples*.

I think the book's a snooze, and I sure don't hold it against a pigtailed girl named Margot when she gets restless and starts whimpering midway through the story. I think I'm helping when I get out an animal cracker for her from the big tub over the sink, but Morgan stops her reading to shout, "Cline! *No*. Snack time's not till later."

There's nowhere else to put the rhinoceros cookie I'm holding, so I eat it.

Then it's finger-painting time, and wow, are toddlers and finger paints a recipe for disaster. Margot ends up putting a big glob of green paint in her mouth before I can stop her.

Even after we wipe everyone's hands clean and hang their art up to dry, the kids who grab at my arms are sticky, somehow, with snot or spit or Lord knows what. It gets worse at snack time, when Rodney tries shoving a Goldfish up his nose, and Zoe pries her sippy cup lid loose and pours apple juice out on the floor.

"Cline," says Morgan, "can you watch the kids for *one second* while I get more paper towels?"

"Yep," I tell her, feeling just about fed up with Morgan and the Elephant room.

Once she's ducked out, Asher toddles up to me and says, "Tummy's funny."

"Tummy's . . . funny?" I repeat.

Asher's a pale kid generally, but now he's turned white as . . . well, *ash*.

I gulp, remembering what Mrs. Yune said to do if a kid gets sick: notify her immediately. Since Morgan's gone, I figure I'll have to open the nursery door, shout toward the foyer for Mrs. Yune, and hope for the best.

That's precisely what I'm doing—reaching for the door—when Asher opens his mouth, and out comes a big yellow spew that lands directly on my purple Keds.

9

AS FAR AS trial runs go, I'd say mine's been a disaster.

No way the New Hope nursery is hiring me now.

I'm standing in my socks in the nursery bathroom, scrubbing Goldfish chunks off my shoes, when there's a knock at the door.

I say a cuss word real low—one I've heard Mama use but am sure she wouldn't want to hear from me. When I open the door, Mrs. Yune's standing there, and I'm too ashamed to look her in the eye. I stare at the big toe poking out of my right sock, and I mumble, "I'll get packing."

I'm expecting Mrs. Yune to say that's the right idea and will I please never show my face in this nursery again. I'm *not* expecting her to laugh. It startles me straight out of my skin.

"No one's sending you packing, Cline," she says. "Stomach flu isn't your doing."

I shake my head in protest. "But I kept messing up tonight. Practically everything I did was wrong."

Mrs. Yune glances to the nursery foyer, where parents are bustling in, picking up their kids. Then she leans in and whispers, "Morgan's got a prickly side. I wouldn't take it personally."

"Really?" I say, unconvinced.

"You survived a whole two hours, didn't you? And so did the kids. Even Asher, poor boy." Mrs. Yune shoots her eyes heavenward. "Lord, his mother was in a *flurry*. Turns out his sister's home sick with the bug, too. Now that's just careless, I say, bringing him here." She tsks and sighs. "Well, that's what Clorox is for. Speaking of which, have your mother bleach those shoes in the washer first thing when you get home."

Mrs. Yune points at my Keds—once made for flying, now dirtied up on the sink.

"Won't bleach turn them white?" I ask.

Mrs. Yune nods apologetically. "I should've warned you before tonight: don't wear anything to this nursery that you'd mind parting with."

"Noted," I say.

"And let me tell you another thing." Mrs. Yune's voice turns confidential again. "Most grown women don't last more than a few weeks here. I think we're lucky to have someone as stalwart as you. No running and crying over upchuck—that's a real test of valor."

I blink, halfway shocked that Mrs. Yune said "upchuck."

"Then . . . you want me back next week?" I ask.

"If *you* want to come back, after that."

Standing here in a smelly bathroom, I get to thinking about all the Wednesday nights ahead, trying and failing to keep paint out of kids' mouths. If I could have my druthers, I'd hightail it out of this nursery and never return. But I can't do that *and* attend the Young Singer-Songwriter Workshop. As Gram would say, you gotta pick your pudding.

So I pick mine.

I tell Mrs. Yune, "I want to come back."

She smiles, making a show of wiping one hand across her forehead in relief.

I didn't like tonight, but I do like Mrs. Yune. I feel that way even before she hands me a whole twenty-dollar bill and tells me to keep the tip. My spirits are bright as I leave the nursery, even though I'm barefoot, carrying my socks and shoes in a grocery bag.

I push out the church's side doors into a muggy evening. The sun's started to set, turning the sky the color of orange soda. I'm sitting myself down on the curb when I hear a voice I recognize.

"Scott! That's so *ridiculous*."

I look farther along the sidewalk and see some folks my age hanging out on the church lawn. One of them is *Hollie*. I grin at the surprise. When Hollie and I talked earlier about my job at the church, she said we probably wouldn't cross paths, seeing as how youth group would let out before I'd finished up in the nursery. But here she is, along with who I assume are her youth group friends. I jump up from the curb and call Hollie's name.

She looks over her shoulder, surprised at first, but then hurries up to me.

"Cline, hey!" she says, giving me a hug. When she pulls away, she wrinkles her nose. "Where are your shoes?"

I raise the grocery bag. "Explosion in the nursery. Don't ask."

"I . . . won't." She's still wrinkle nosed as she waves her friends over. "This is Livy and Emma. And Scott."

Like that, my stomach turns. I didn't plan on meeting any other new people tonight—*especially* Hollie's friends. I know from Hollie that all of her church friends go to the private Christian school here at New Hope. That's *all* I've known about them for a couple of years, though. Now, suddenly, we're swapping names.

I feel Hollie's eyes on me as the others join us, and I hold the grocery bag low at my side so as not to draw attention to my puked-on shoes. I want to make a good impression and show Hollie's church friends how cool her best friend from school is.

That's a lot of pressure, though, and in the end, I don't come up with a great introduction. I just say, "Nice to meet you. I'm Cline."

"Nice to meet you, too," says Emma, a girl with dark brown skin and kind eyes.

Livy, a skinny white girl with pixie-cut hair, waves but doesn't speak. I guess she's shy.

Scott, a white boy with a big mole under one eye, says, "What's up, Cline?"

I'm opening my mouth to say something else. Something *actually* cool. Before I can, though, a voice behind me shouts, "Cline!"

I've been so distracted with this new kind of meet-and-greet, I haven't noticed my mother pull up in the Camry.

Great. The moment's over. No more chances to show these folks who Cline Alden is. I wince, telling the others again how nice it was to meet them and giving Hollie a real quick goodbye hug.

"See you at school!" I shout, getting in the passenger seat.

As we pull away from the curb, I notice that Hollie and her friends are watching me go. Scott's grinning in my direction, and Emma's waving. I bite my lip and wave back.

All right. Maybe it wasn't a top-notch impression, but it wasn't bad, either, and that puts me in a good mood. So much so that when Mama asks about my shoes, I smile and say, "Nothing the wash can't fix."

10

GRAM LIKES TO say a watched kettle won't boil, but my eyes are glued to my kettle for the next week. I go to school, hang out with Hollie, do homework, and play guitar. I've got distractions, but none of them last all day long. At night, as I fall asleep, I worry about the application and if I should've spent more time answering the question, "What makes you a good fit for our program?" In the morning, as I eat breakfast, I try not to think about how cool it'd be to get a songwriting lesson from Marcia Hayes, who's not exactly a favorite of mine but *is* a Grammy nominee.

And then there are the afternoons.

Sarah, our postal worker, shows up around four thirty every day, so by the time I get home from Hollie's, the mail is waiting for me. On Saturday, I spend maybe *too* much time looking out my window, waiting till the USPS truck pulls up our street.

No mail for me, though. Not for five days straight.

On Tuesday, I'm near exhausted from the waiting, especially

seeing as I don't want to share my secret with anyone else. That's the worst part: Hollie and Kenzie, Ava and Darlene—they don't know the state I'm in.

Instead, I listen to them talk about their lives. Ava is helping to choreograph a new number for color guard based on the school band's aquatic theme, *Atlantis*. Kenzie has reached one hundred orders on her Etsy shop and is going to be displaying some of her work in a school exhibit this November. Darlene and her volleyball team will be facing off with their biggest rival team, the Hawks, next week. I listen eagerly as everyone talks—at least, until the Harvest Dance comes up. There's always some new development, like how John Mahaffey's asked Kenzie to go with him a full *month* in advance. Today, when Ava asks Hollie who she wants to go with, she smiles and doesn't say a word. When Ava asks *me*, I get red in the face and say something about how I'm a bad dancer, which isn't true. Gram taught me how to Texas two-step like a professional.

After school, Hollie and I hang out at her place, and it's on my way home that I realize I haven't thought of the workshop for an hour at least. When I turn onto my street, though, the sight of the mailbox reminds me. I start running in my now *very* white Keds. I don't slow down till I reach the mailbox, and even then, I yank the lid so hard the whole post shudders.

There's nothing there. Sarah must running be late.

I heave a sigh, shut the lid, and head inside, where I hear Gram in the den, watching *The Mary Tyler Moore Show*.

Gram's pillbox is sitting on the kitchen table. I drop my backpack, tapping Tuesday's lemon-yellow row of containers: Morning, Afternoon, and Night. Then I frown. Morning's pills are gone, but Afternoon's are still there.

"Gram!" I call, picking up the box and heading into the den.

She's sitting in the La-Z-Boy, chuckling at the TV. When she sees me, she says, "Cline, honey! This episode's just starting."

"Sure, Gram," I say. "But what about your pills? You're supposed to take these with lunch."

A stitch forms in Gram's brow. "*Huh.* Could've sworn I did." She glances at the den clock and says, "Better late than never. Mind bringing me my iced tea?"

I leave the pillbox with Gram and fetch her tea from its customary place on the top shelf of the fridge. Mama insists on making it without sweetener, but Gram and I are in cahoots. I drop in a hearty spoonful of sugar before I bring the tea into the den.

"Bottoms up!" Gram declares, taking her handful of pills and gulping them down.

I smile, even though worry nibbles at my brain. Mama's around to be sure Gram takes her pills in the morning and most nights, but I've never known Gram to forget her midday medicine. That's just plain forgetfulness, though, *not* Alzheimer's.

I'm settling down to watch *The Mary Tyler Moore Show* when I spot the envelopes on Gram's TV tray.

"Gram," I say, trying not to shout. "Is that today's mail?"

"Sure is, honey. Sarah's a dear. Brought it to the door, since we had a package."

Then, all of a sudden, Gram gets an excited look on her face. "Gracious! I plum forgot that, too. There's a letter in here I think you'll want to see."

Gram sorts through the mail, turning over the envelopes so slowly, I want to rip out my hair. At last, she finds the letter she's after and holds it up for me to see. It's a no-frills business envelope, with the University of Kentucky logo printed on the top left corner.

I feel like my lungs are tied in a knot.

"Gram," I wheeze. "I can't look. Would you?"

"If you insist," says Gram. "Bring me the opener."

I fetch the letter opener from the coffee table, passing it to Gram with a trembling hand. Her hands don't shake a smidge, though, as she slides the opener through the envelope's top. She puts on the reading glasses she keeps on a sequined chain around her neck, and then she pulls out a folded sheet of paper.

My heart sinks. No good news comes on a single paper. That envelope should be stuffed with information and maybe a Congratulations card, to boot.

But then Gram announces, "Sweetie, you got *in*!"

"What?" I shout.

Gram holds up the paper. "Right there. My eyesight's not that far gone. I can read it clear as day: *accepted*."

I take the letter, staring down at the words:

Dear Ms. Alden,

We're pleased to inform you that you've been accepted into the University of Kentucky's Young Singer-Songwriter Workshop.

There's more to it, about the workshop's dates and location, and how an additional informational packet will follow in the next couple of days, but here's the important part: I'm in.

"Know what I think?" Gram asks, as I sit gaping. "This calls for a dance party."

I lower the letter, zombie-like, as Gram's words sink in. My excitement builds and then busts out of me like steam from a kettle—a watched kettle that's finally boiled.

"Yes," I declare. "Dance party!"

I grab my backpack from the kitchen and pull out my phone, notching the volume all the way up before hitting shuffle on "Cline Kicks the World's Butt." The first song to play is "Pursuing Happiness" by Norma Jean.

I jump and shimmy into the den, shaking along to the upbeat plucking of a guitar. From her armchair, Gram claps along, and together we belt the last line of the chorus, proclaiming that we're pursuing happiness.

I prance over to Gram, offering my hands to help her stand. It takes a few moments, but soon she's on her feet, and we're dancing together, swinging our arms and wagging our fingers along to the lyrics as Norma Jean puts naysayers in their place.

The music's so loud and I'm giggling so hard, I don't hear Mama walk through the front door. It's only when the song fades and a new one begins that Mama says, "Now, what's all this dancing for?"

She doesn't look mad, exactly, but she sure doesn't look pleased.

Gram and I share a look, and I shrug my shoulders up to my ears. "Feeling music in our blood, is all."

"Uh . . . *huh.*" Mama gives us both a look that says we ought to know better. Then she motions to me, saying, "Help me get these groceries from the car."

I follow Mama out the door, but not before Gram settles in her armchair, sitting right atop the letter from UK—no evidence left in sight. Once Mama's left the room, Gram shoots me a great big wink.

"Cline!" Mama calls from outside, and I stop dallying around.

In a mood like mine, I could carry in groceries for the whole city of Paris.

11

THE REST OF the materials from the Young Singer-Songwriter Workshop arrive the next day. As I tug the packet out of the mailbox, I think how lucky I am that I get home before Mama. Keeping this thing a secret would be a lot darn harder if she didn't work so much. Then again, if Mama didn't take on so many shifts, she'd have time to watch an episode of *Porter Wagoner* or listen to me play guitar. Could be, she'd open her ears back up to the music and realize how important a workshop like this is. Then I wouldn't have to be keeping a secret at all.

Only, as Gram would say, that's not the pattern I'm quilting with.

I'm still thinking about Mama at school—how, if I lived a different life in one of Darlene's parallel universes, I'd have a mother I could share this big news with. It feels kind of lonely, keeping this secret mostly to myself.

Now that I've gotten into the workshop, I've been wondering . . .

should I tell my friends about it? That would be a big change. For so long, I've been Singer Cline on my own and School Cline—no music talk—at Dunbar Middle. Am I ready to be both with my friends? To be fully *me*?

As we sit together at lunch, my workshop news bubbles inside me. It must show on my face, because Ava stops in the middle of her story about a girl on color guard getting smacked in the nose by a rogue baton.

"You all right there, Cline?" she asks, peering at me.

I look around at my friends. This could be it. I could tell them right now. My head spins with different versions of what I could say: "So, I'm doing this workshop." Or, "There's something you don't know about me." Or, "Guess what? I write and sing my own songs!" But all of those versions sound goofy. I glance real quick at Hollie, like maybe she'll give me the answer, but she's distracted, tapping away at her phone. I think back to when I played her Emmylou's "Magnolia Wind" and she shrugged—just *shrugged*—when it was over.

No, I decide. I don't want to share. What if the girls don't think my workshop news is that big a deal? That'd make it feel less special somehow. I'd rather wait till I've got something *really* impressive to share: an onstage performance, or even a record deal. For now, though? There's School Cline and Singer Cline, and never the twain shall meet.

"My food just tastes funny," I fib, pointing at the half-eaten burger on my tray.

Ava raises an eyebrow. "Well, you know, it *is* from another dimension."

"A parallel universe," Darlene corrects.

Kenzie snorts. "It's just a bad prefrozen burger, you all."

We laugh about it—including Hollie, who's put away her phone. It's only afterward, as I head to class, that I get to feeling low. I wish I weren't so worried about how the others would react. I wish I even knew *how* to bring up my music. Truth is, I'm not used to talking about it with anyone other than Delia and Gram.

I wonder if Emmylou ever felt that way about her songs. If Norma Jean kept secrets inside about the singer she wanted to be. I sure hope so. That would mean I'm in good company, at least.

⌒∽⌒

"It was *so* close. You should've seen Scott's face! Like a chipmunk."

I'm hanging with Hollie and her youth group friends on New Hope's lawn after my second night of nursery duty. Things went a little better this time around in the Elephant room. For one thing, none of the kids barfed, and for another, Morgan was nicer, which makes me wonder if maybe Mrs. Yune had words with her. Even when Rodney threw a Fisher-Price phone across the room and Zoe tried to eat a glob of hot pink Play-Doh, I kept my cool. I reminded myself that I am only five days away from the Young Singer-Songwriter Workshop. *That* will make the Elephant room worth it.

Hollie's friends have put me in a better mood, too. I have barely fifteen minutes to hang out with them before Mama is due to show up, but I already know I like Livy, Emma, and Scott. They're funny and sure of themselves, and they're busting with stories from youth group. Tonight, Emma recounts how Scott and another guy played chubby bunny—this game where you stuff marshmallows in your mouth, one at a time, and try saying "chubby bunny" until you *can't.*

Scott lost the game, but only, as Emma tells it, by one marshmallow.

"Next time," Scott vows, shaking a fist at the sky.

Beside me, Hollie bites her lip, twirling a strand of blond hair. "Maybe we'll play it again at the lock-in."

"That'd be dope," says Emma.

Livy makes a face. "I dunno. I still think it's a choking hazard."

"Wait," I say. "What's the lock-in?"

That word rings a bell, and it takes me a split second to figure out why: Hollie mentioned a lock-in the last time we went to church together. I'd meant to ask her about it during the service, but then we got to singing and I forgot.

Emma and Livy share a look, and Emma says, "Oh my gosh. Have you never done a lock-in before?"

I feel embarrassed, 'cause it's clear everyone else here has. I look at Hollie, hoping she'll speak up, so I don't feel so weird. She doesn't, though.

"Lock-ins are great," Livy tells me. "They're basically giant sleepovers for the youth group, and we get the whole church building to ourselves. You should totally come to this one. It's in a few weeks. Sign-ups are still open."

"I mean, hey," says Scott, "you should come to youth group, in general. You'd like it."

I try not to smile too wide. It's nice to know Hollie's friends don't think I'm annoying. They wouldn't invite me to stuff if they did.

"Yeah," I tell them, "maybe when I stop working at the nursery, I will."

Emma smacks Scott's shoulder. "She works on Wednesdays, remember? *But*"—Emma turns to me—"the lock-in is on a Saturday night."

"*Oh*. Yeah! I could do Saturday," I say.

"Awesome," says Scott. "It'd be great to hang out more."

I've noticed something: as I've been getting more excited, Hollie's stayed quiet. She's looking at her hands, picking at the silver ring on her thumb.

"That's . . . cool with you, right?" I ask her.

She glances up. "Of course. That'd be great."

Her voice is funny, like maybe she doesn't mean what she's saying. I don't know why she wouldn't, though. We're best friends. Why would she *not* want me to come to the lock-in? That doesn't make a lick of sense, so I tell myself, *Cline, you're making stuff up.*

"We can take you inside real quick," Emma tells me. "Show you where the sign-up sheet is."

This time, I smile as wide as I want and say, "That'd be great."

We run into the church, and Emma points out a clipboard stuck to the wall, next to a set of double doors labeled *Youth Center*. After I've written my name and phone number down on the sheet, I peek into the room, through the window slat.

It's dark inside, but I can make out a bunch of folding chairs in front of a stage. An actual *stage*.

"Whoa," I say, turning to Hollie. "You never said how cool it was in there."

Hollie shrugs. The funniness that was in her voice is now on her face. I want to ask if everything's all right, or if she's upset about something. Then again, I wouldn't want to ask about it, only for Hollie to say there's nothing wrong. Then she'd feel weird, and I'd feel bad, and that'd just be *too much*.

Instead, I get to wondering what my first lock-in will be like. Before, whenever I thought of Hollie's religion, I figured it only had to do with getting into heaven and doing what the Bible tells you to do. None of that sat right with me, exactly. I especially don't like what I've heard from certain Christians on TV who quote the Bible to say how God's gonna send other people to hell. But Hollie's friends aren't like that. They're nice. Maybe that's *also* part of religion: hanging out with friends every week and having a good time. I can get on board with that. In fact, it gets me curious as to what the folks at New Hope—Hollie and Emma and Livy and Scott and Mrs. Yune—believe about God and all that other stuff. I guess I'll find out more at the lock-in.

When we head outside, Mama's at the curb, waiting for me.

"You're late," she says, when I get in the car. "Everything okay?"

"Sure is."

"Who were those people you were with?"

"Friends of Hollie's," I say first.

And once I've thought it over more, I tell her, "Friends of *mine*."

12

NORMALLY, I WANT weekends to last. That's when I can sleep in, play guitar for hours, and relax in the den with Gram, watching reruns and drinking sweet tea. This weekend, though? It can't go by fast enough. For once in my life, I'm waiting for a Monday: September twenty-eighth—*the* first day of the Young Singer-Songwriter Workshop.

It took some thinking through, but I finally came up with a foolproof plan for the next four Monday nights: I go to the Goldenrod, as usual, to pick up supper for me and Gram. Only I go early, just before the dead hour. I take the food home to Gram for her to eat later with *Porter Wagoner*, and I scarf down my supper in the kitchen. Then I head out the door and run a good five minutes to Magnolia Square, which is on Delia's route out of town. That gives us just enough time to make it to Lexington for the workshop. Like I said, *foolproof.*

All the same, when the big day comes, I'm a bundle of nerves sitting on a bench in Magnolia Square, guitar case by my side.

Once upon a time, according to Gram, the square was better kept. There was a tall magnolia tree and planted gardenias, and the gazebo was new and freshly painted. That was in the sixties, when Gram was a teenager. In fact, she went on her first date with my papaw right here. They came out to see a local band play, and Gram swears up and down that she's never heard better fiddling than that night, when the band played the "Tennessee Waltz." There was a chill in the air, and Papaw lent Gram his suit jacket, and that's how she knew he was a keeper.

Now Papaw's passed, and the paint's peeling off the gazebo in ugly curls, like hangnails. The magnolia tree's a stump—struck by lightning or chopped down, I can't say which. The only flowers growing are yellow dandelions. Sooner or later, I guess the city will knock down the gazebo and pave the grass to expand the parking lot next door. But every so often, I like to sit here, on the bench, and imagine Paris sixty years back, bands playing under a starlit night and young folks going on their first dates. There's still a little magic in the air, I think, and I can do with some magic on the first night of my workshop.

Gram thought so, too, when I told her about the plan.

"That square's awful special to me," she said, with a pleased smile. "Turns out it's still good for something, after all these years."

Then she kissed me on the forehead and sent me on my way,

and I promised I'd tell her all about how tonight goes. Provided, of course, that my plan actually *works*. See, I still have one big task ahead of me: finagling my way into the workshop without paying the full three hundred bucks.

"Getaway driver, at your service."

I look up with a start. I've been so lost in my thoughts, I haven't noticed that Delia's pulled up in her ancient, pumpkin-orange Chevy. My heart's thumping as I lug my guitar case onto the floorboard and settle in my seat.

"Cline," Delia tells me, "this is Brenda. Brenda, meet Cline."

I glance back at the truck bed, even though I already know no one's there.

I say, "Brenda, who?"

Delia grins as she shifts into drive and taps the steering wheel.

Oh. I see now: Brenda's the truck.

"She's pretty old," I observe, not meaning it as an insult. I, for one, like old cars. They've got character.

"Born in seventy-five," says Delia, with pride, "but I've equipped her with the necessary modern amenities." She nods to the phone in my lap. "Got tunes you wanna share?"

Do I ever.

Delia hands over a cord for me to plug my phone into her cassette player contraption. When I hit Play on "Cline Kicks the World's Butt," a guitar and fiddle duet pipes through her speakers.

"Aw, yeah," Delia says, turning up the volume. "The Chicks. Classic."

That's how we find ourselves cruising down Paris Pike, wind blowing our hair—my tangled-up curls and Delia's bright pink bob—while we belt "Wide Open Spaces."

It's a thirty-minute drive to Lexington and another ten minutes before we reach the university campus. College students are all over, lugging backpacks and riding bikes and jogging along crosswalks. The buildings here are tall and a jumble of styles: pretty brick houses Delia says are for sororities and fraternities, ugly concrete buildings, coffee shops, and even churches. Delia points out the William T. Young Library, a gigantic building with columns that look to me like chicken feet.

Then Delia's pulling up to the address printed on my "Welcome, Students!" sheet. The front of the building is peculiar-looking: a white-stone entrance fitted with dozens of metal sculptures of human figures. Over the doors, a sign reads *Fine Arts Building*.

"Guess this is the place," I say, my knees bouncing higher than ever.

"Hey," Delia says, catching my eye. "You knock 'em dead, Cline."

I nod, trying to feel as confident as Delia seems. I can't wuss out now, so I grab my guitar from the floorboard and hop out of Brenda.

There's a car behind us honking, seeing as how they can't get around Delia. She shouts, "Hold your horses!" and then leans my way to say, "I'll be back a little after nine thirty. Earlier, maybe, depending on how long my professor goes on."

The car behind Delia honks again, and this time she shoots them the bird. I smile as she rolls her eyes and drives off. Once she's out of sight, though, my concrete stomach thuds to my feet. I walk real slow through the front doors of the Fine Arts Building and keep trudging till I spot a long fold-out table next to a printed sign reading *Young Singer-Songwriter Workshop Sign In*.

I suck in a big breath, steeling myself. This is it. I've got to convince these folks to let me in at less than half the workshop's cost. I've heard enough of Mama haggling on the phone to know what to do. I've practiced my lines and got them down pat. Now it's just a matter of saying them.

"Can I help you?"

A fair-skinned woman with big blond hair is waving me her way. Beside her, another woman is checking in a guy who must be a high school senior, at least. He's tall as anything, and when I glance over, I see he's got tattoos running up his neck.

Whoa. I steady myself, focusing on the woman in front of me, who's wearing a name tag that reads *Jocelyn*.

"Good evening," I say. "Name's Cline Louise Alden."

"Very good," says Jocelyn, looking over a sheet. "There you are. Alden, Cline. All we need from you is that workshop fee, and we'll have you on your way."

Here we go.

I take out the folded envelope from my back pocket and hand it over. I don't say a thing, just wait patiently as Jocelyn counts through the bills.

Her lips pucker, twisting to one side. "Hmm," she says, after counting twice. "We've only got a hundred and thirty-five. You think maybe your mom or dad forgot the rest?"

Here it comes. A good old-fashioned haggling.

"I know it's only half," I say, "but I was hoping we could do a sort of layaway plan?"

Jocelyn blinks at me. She presses her lips together, like she's thinking of words to say.

"See, I give you half the money now," I explain, "to show I'm in earnest. And then, once it's saved up, I give you the rest. A slight delay in between, is all."

Jocelyn sighs through her nose.

"Hon," she says, "I wish it worked that way. It should've said in that information packet, though." She nods to the welcome letter I'm gripping tight. "The amount must be paid in full at the start of the workshop."

I've been expecting this. They've got to give you the company line first. It's after that you sweet-talk them into a deal.

"I hate to ask a favor," I say. "That's a whole hundred and thirty-five you've got, though. Proof that I'm good for it. I wouldn't give you all that money just to bolt. Anyhow, you've got my full name and address. You know where to find me. We Aldens are honest people, I swear."

Jocelyn answers, "I don't doubt that. But we don't do layaway plans here."

This time, I'm the one blinking like a stunned deer. Jocelyn hasn't budged an inch. That's not the way it's supposed to work.

"B-but," I say, and I wince when I hear the quiver in my voice. "I came all this way. I've saved up that much. Couldn't you make an exception this one time?"

Jocelyn glances at the other lady, like she wants to ask her a question, but *she's* wrapped up talking to another student—a girl with light brown skin in a macramé dress.

Jocelyn looks at me again. "I don't think we can do that. I'm sorry, hon."

This was my bargaining plan:

Be confident.

Be calm.

Win them over.

This was *not* my plan: Break down and cry in front of a stranger.

Only, that's what I do. The tears are hot in my eyes, and they slip down my cheeks before I can stop them.

"I have a whole *plan*, though." My voice is one giant embarrassing wobble now, and I'm clutching the welcome letter so hard it's crumpling in my hand. "I got a job so I could make the rest of the money. And this workshop's my *dream*. It's—it's—"

I can't get out the words. As I wipe away my tears, I can feel the girl in the macramé dress watching me.

She's probably thinking, *What a loser.*

Jocelyn parts her lips, and her eyes water up, same as mine.

"Okay," she says, holding up her hands. "It's all right. Please don't cry."

I don't see the point in folks telling you not to cry, like you can help it. Like tears are notes in a song—things you can choose to let out of you. Jocelyn telling me to quit doesn't help. I'm already telling *myself* to stop. It's downright humiliating.

Jocelyn studies the envelope of money I gave her. I think she's about to hand it back when she leans in and says, low as can be, "How about we make an exception this *one* time."

The world around me slows, growing sludgy as molasses. I stare at Jocelyn.

"R-r-really?" I ask.

"Really," says Jocelyn, but she's quick to add, "It *will* be due at the end of the workshop. The final class, on October nineteenth. Is that possible?"

I'm no whiz at math, but I can solve this equation in my head: four weeks from now, I'll only be sixty dollars richer. That's not even half of what I still owe. But there's no way I'm telling Jocelyn that. This moment is fragile as glass, and I won't say a thing to break it.

I simply nod.

"All right," Jocelyn says. "I'll make a note of it here. And what I want is for you to send that payment to our mailing address on or by October nineteenth."

I keep bobbing my head up and down. Jocelyn looks uncertain, like maybe she's made a mistake. It's strange, but I don't think it was my bargaining plan that changed her mind. It was the only thing I *didn't* plan: my tears.

That thought puts a bad feeling in my gut, but I nudge it aside as Jocelyn hands me a name tag lanyard.

Cline, says the tag, and underneath that, *Young Singer-Songwriter.*

It's the first time I've seen my name and *singer-songwriter* written together in the same place—that is, anyplace outside my diary.

I'm sure hoping it won't be the last.

∽∞∾

The workshop classroom is more of a small auditorium—rows of desks set up on big, descending steps. At the bottom of them, there's a dry-erase board, a teacher's desk, and a podium. A woman sits at the desk, looking over a folder of papers. Her skin is dark brown and her long, braided hair is wound into a full bun atop her head. She wears a flowy silver dress. On the board, she's written her name in block letters: DR. MIREILLE JOHNSON.

I look around for a seat and notice an empty one a few rows from the front. There's a girl sitting there who looks closer to Delia's age than mine. Her hair comes down to her waist, and she's wearing bright orange lipstick. I'm sort of nervous to look her way, but when I do, she smiles at me.

"Hey," I say. "I'm Cline."

"Veronica," the girl replies. "You're . . . here for the workshop?"

Veronica sounds skeptical, like she thinks I wandered into this room by mistake.

"Y-yeah," I say, faltering. I point to my name tag, to prove I'm in the right place, but then realize that probably makes me look like a real dork.

I nod to the empty chair beside Veronica.

"This seat taken?" I ask.

The girl's smile turns to a wince. "Sorry. I'm saving it for my friend."

There's a sudden, sharp sting in my throat.

Nope, I tell myself, *you're not crying again.*

I try to act unbothered as I say, "Oh, that's cool."

I don't trust myself not to cry, though, so I keep right on walking until I reach a whole empty row at the back of the class. From here, I can see that there are lots of kids in the room—around thirty. It seems like most of them are in high school, and I'm the youngest of the lot.

That's all right, though. That's fine. They might not take me seriously because of my age, at first, but once I get up there and sing for them, they'll see they're wrong. As Gram says, you can't judge a firecracker by its size.

My eyes are still a little scratchy, but as far as I know, only one person in this classroom saw me cry at the sign-in table: the girl in the macramé dress. I cringe, thinking of what she might've heard me say about not having money. Maybe when it comes to her, Cline Alden's reputation is a lost cause, but I can at least make a good impression on everyone else.

It's right when I'm looking at the big clock over the dry-erase board that Dr. Johnson stands up and says, "Two minutes after! I'd say that's more than generous to our stragglers."

She walks around to the front of her desk and brings her hands together in a powerful *whap*.

"Hello! My name is Dr. Mireille Johnson. I'm a professor of music here at UK, and it's my pleasure to welcome you to this department's first-ever Young Singer-Songwriter Workshop. We were tremendously impressed by all of your applications, and we're thrilled to have each and every one of you here for this month of Mondays. I'll be your instructor throughout the workshop, and for our final class, we'll be joined by a guest teacher: Kentucky's own Marcia Hayes."

A ripple of excited whispers passes through the room. Dr. Johnson raises her hands to quiet the class, telling us that, to begin, we'll go over some ground rules. She talks about boring stuff first, like where the water fountains are and how often we'll have a bathroom break, and then she moves on to how we need to bring a "spirit of collaboration" to the class.

I get out the composition book I brought along to take down notes as Dr. Johnson tells us that a lot of songwriting is about collaborating with others, hearing their ideas just as much as we share our own. She says she won't tolerate negative talk in the classroom, though she encourages us to give each other "constructive criticism"—suggestions meant to build each other up.

All that sounds good to me. I listen closely as Dr. Johnson continues, explaining the "vision" of this class: it's a chance for a new generation of musicians—that's us—to learn about songwriting, take creative risks, and express ourselves. Dr. Johnson's talking to us about being "proactive"—seeking out ways to learn and better ourselves in class—and I'm taking down notes as fast as I can, when she suddenly says, "You in the back? In the green top."

I stop. Stare. I'm in the back. I'm wearing a green top. Does Dr. Johnson mean *me*?

"Erm," I garble out. "I'm Cline."

"What's that?" Dr. Johnson asks.

I clear my throat and shout, "CLINE."

"Excellent. Now, see? Cline here is a fine example of a proactive student. We didn't ask for you to bring instruments with you, but she's brought her guitar. She's ready for whatever lessons may lie ahead."

I feel itchy all over, with the eyes of so many people on me. I watch as the girl named Veronica leans over to her friend—the one she was saving that seat for—and whispers, loud enough for me to hear, "She's precious."

I glance around to see that *no one* else in the classroom brought a guitar, or any other instrument, for that matter. It's just me.

Does that make me a Goody Two-shoes? Or *precious*? I grimace. Is that what these other kids think of me? That I'm too young and clueless?

I'm so stuck in my thoughts that at first I don't hear what Dr. Johnson says to send the classroom into another frenzy of whispers. I look to the dry-erase board, where she's writing out words:

Daylight Saving Bluegrass Festival
March 12–14
Auditions: Saturday, October 24

Right away, I tune back in.

"Holding auditions for the local talent preshow," Dr. Johnson is saying. "I can't think of a better opportunity for you all to use the skills you learn in this class. I know for some of you, bluegrass may not be your cup of tea. It may be jazz that brought you here, or rock. The preshow selection committee is open to any and all genres, provided you play acoustically. That's why I'd like to use these upcoming auditions as a goal. Think of these four classes as stepping-stones, leading up to audition day. I'll be there to encourage any students who choose to submit their act."

A bluegrass festival, here in Lexington. I write down the website address Dr. Johnson puts on the board, champing at the bit to look up the details. I wonder if anyone famous will be playing. I wonder if, come March, *I* could be playing my guitar on the same stage. This is the best news I've heard, and we're only fifteen minutes into class. I can't wait to see what else Dr. Johnson has up those billowing sleeves of hers.

"I see a lot of rabid faces out there," she says, "daydreaming about how you plan to crush that audition. Am I right?"

There's a murmur of laughter in the room. I laugh along,

feeling like my skin's gone clear and Dr. Johnson can see straight through to my heart.

"Well, take a word of advice from me, if you will," says Dr. Johnson. "Maybe wait a week or two, and see what you learn from this workshop. You might see fit to incorporate some of our lessons into your performances."

I write that down in my composition book: *Incorporate lessons into performances.*

My spine tingles at the officialness of the words. Here I am in a college classroom, listening to a real professor who takes music as seriously as I do. No *Cline, be responsible* lectures here.

"All right!" Dr. Johnson claps her hands again: *whap.* "To begin, I'm going to divide the classroom into pairs."

There's a new flurry of whispers, and chairs around me scrape across the floor, but Dr. Johnson shouts over us, "*Not* self-assigned. I know some of you came here with friends, but I'm going to split you up. The purpose of this workshop is to better our craft, *not* to socialize. I've written down everyone's names right here." She waves a sheet of paper. "First up, we have—well, look at that. The proactive *Cline Alden.*"

Dr. Johnson looks my way, and I feel it in my bones: this is a moment that's going to shake things up. I'm getting paired with another musician. This could be the start of a story. A legendary partnership.

I wait with bated breath as Dr. Johnson calls out the name that might change everything: "Sylvie Sharpe!"

I look across the classroom as Dr. Johnson tells my partner to join me where I sit. Then the girl named Sylvie stands, and my heart sinks.

'Cause it's *her*. The girl in the macramé dress. The one who saw me cry.

13

SYLVIE SHARPE ABSOLUTELY, positively does not want to be here.

For one thing, she's wearing sunglasses *indoors*, like she's too cool for school; and for another, she hasn't uncrossed her arms since she plopped into the chair beside me and said, "Okay, let's get this over with."

Get *my dream* over with?

I don't think so.

I had high hopes for my partner. "Sylvie Sharpe" sounds like a bright, happy name. Only, the girl sitting across from me is anything but happy. She looks around my age, but it's hard to know for sure, what with the sunglasses covering a good chunk of her face. She's fiddling with the fringe of her dress rather than paying attention as Dr. Johnson gives us instructions on what to do next: learn three facts about each other to share with the class.

When I start telling Sylvie my facts, she cuts me off mid-sentence, right as I'm explaining how Mama chose my name.

"Could you *not* talk so loud?"

I gape at her like a goldfish. I know I haven't been talking louder than other folks around us. All I'm trying to do is follow Dr. Johnson's instructions.

When I speak again, I make a point of not only talking soft, I right-out whisper my third fact. That doesn't put Sylvie in a better mood. When she's through untangling her fringe, she starts on the ends of her long, brown hair, braiding a strand behind her ear.

When I'm through with my facts, I ask, "What about you?"

Sylvie looks at me. At least, I *think* that's what she's doing, but it's hard to tell with those giant shades of hers. "What about me, *what*?"

I've just about lost my patience. "Your three facts," I say, through gritted teeth. "What are they?"

Sylvie leans across her desk, getting close to me.

"Look," she says, "my mom made me come today. Anything other than keeping my butt in this chair? Far as I'm concerned, that's optional."

"But your *three facts*." I feel like a broken record, but Sylvie doesn't pay me any mind. She lays her head down on her desk, for anyone to see. Taking a *nap* in the middle of our workshop. Who does she think she is?

With her head tilted to one side, the hair falls away from Sylvie's left ear, revealing three piercings: two studs in the lobe and a ring way up top, in her cartilage.

I try imagining what it's like to be Sylvie, with parents who are cool with you getting your ears pierced and who actually want you to go to a music workshop and can pay for it upfront, and who drive you to class, no questions asked, only for you to *sleep* through it.

Thinking that way gets me real upset with Sylvie. In fact, I'm mad as a wet hen by the time Dr. Johnson asks everyone to share what they've learned. Sylvie pops her head up then, readjusting her sunglasses as though she wasn't slacking off.

If Sylvie won't tell me facts about herself, I decide, I'll make them up. When Dr. Johnson calls on us—third up in our group of sixteen pairs—I stand and say, "This is Sylvie Sharpe. She's sensitive to fluorescent lights, she has a cartilage piercing, and she *really* likes naps."

When I take my seat, I don't dare look Sylvie's way. Sure, I was sassy, but she deserved it. When she stands, I wonder what the heck she's going to say about me. It didn't seem like she was paying attention when I talked. What if she makes up her own facts, too?

Cline Alden is a Goody Two-shoes who brought a guitar to class.

She talks way too loud.

And she cried at the check-in desk, 'cause she can't afford this workshop.

Nope. No way. She wouldn't tell that secret.

Would she?

"This is Cline Alden," Sylvie announces to the class, in a clear voice that startles me. "She's named after the country singer Patsy Cline. Her favorite *old* musical artist is Emmylou Harris, her favorite *new* one is Brandi Carlile, and Cline's been teaching herself guitar since she was nine years old."

I can only stare at Sylvie as she takes her seat. She was listening, after all.

Now Sylvie looks suave and prepared, and *I* look like the bumbling one. What kind of fact was *"She really likes naps"*? I feel hot around the neck as Dr. Johnson calls on the next pair. I don't get to feeling better, either, as I listen to other people's facts.

Almost all the high schoolers have made it to All-State Chorus or Orchestra, which is a big deal. Others have started their own bands. A girl named Cassidy has been classically trained in piano, violin, and guitar for fourteen years *and* recorded an EP in a Nashville studio.

I want to shut myself into my guitar case and hide away. I haven't done any of the things everyone else is mentioning: professional voice training, summer music camps, and instrument lessons. Here I've been, thinking that I can stand out from the crowd just 'cause I want it more than anyone else. Well, how bigheaded am I? Sure, I want to become a singer more than my friends do, but that's only because they don't have the same dream as me. Now, for the first time, I'm in a room with folks who *do*.

Mama's words return to me, right when I wish they wouldn't: *Those musicians of yours are one in a million. The odds won't be kind to you.*

Just because Gram believes in me and because my name is Cline, that doesn't mean I'm destined to become a great musician. These folks? Some of them have been taking music lessons since they were five. That means I'm eight years behind, right from the get-go. Not to mention, it's clear that most people in here have money. You've got to, if you can afford lessons and stay-away summer camps, or, like Cassidy, studio time on Music Row.

What have I, Cline Alden, got? A secondhand guitar and a workshop layaway plan.

By the time everyone's through sharing, I feel like trampled-down dirt. I try my best to concentrate on Dr. Johnson's teaching, writing in my composition book about song structures: *verse, chorus, verse, chorus, bridge, reprise.*

When we take a midclass break, I hang back by the water fountains, listening to some of the high schoolers talk about what colleges they're applying to. Veronica has her sights set on Belmont in Nashville. Her friend, whose name is Chris, gushes about the Cleveland Institute of Music, and Chris's workshop partner, a boy named Jamal, plans to audition for Juilliard. As I listen to them talk, I feel like I'm shrinking in size. I'm afraid, like before, that these people will look down their noses at me.

Only now I think they've got a good reason to.

Sylvie doesn't talk to me for the rest of class, and that's fine by me. It's clear she's in no mood to learn, and even though I take down notes from Dr. Johnson's lecture about harmonies and lyrical hooks, I don't feel much in a learning mood, either.

I mean to go up to Dr. Johnson after the lecture and ask if we'll be swapping partners next week. When she closes out class, though, Dr. Johnson answers my question: "You'll stay with your assigned partner throughout the workshop," she tells us. "Next week, class will be far less lecture heavy and more focused on getting your hands dirty. Your homework for the coming week is to come up with an original song on your own. No old compositions. Something completely new. Then, next class, you and your partner will share those songs with each other."

So there's that. A real punch to the gut. *Surprise, Cline. You're stuck with Sylvie I-Don't-Want-to-Be-Here Sharpe.*

For the hundredth time tonight, I feel like crying, and since Delia warned she'd be late picking me up, I don't follow the rest of the class outside. Instead, I lock myself in a bathroom stall and stand there with my thoughts galloping.

Today turned out so different from what I expected, and I'm not sure the next three weeks are going to get any better. How am I supposed to work with Sylvie for a whole *month*? And next week, will I have to share my original song with the entire class? Before, a prospect like that would excite me, but now I'm worried sick. Practically everyone else here has professional training, which makes me think that, when performance time rolls around, my song's going to sound like "Ring Around the Rosie" compared to their "Ring of Fire."

Even after I come out of the bathroom, it's another twenty minutes before Delia shows up at the building's side door. I guess I'm not so good at scrubbing the feelings from my face, because the first thing she says when I climb inside the Chevy is, "Who died?"

My dream, I feel like saying, but I guess that'd be dramatic.

"Delia," I say instead, "I don't think I'm right for this class."

"Nonsense," Delia replies. "Brenda and I won't abide such talk."

"But it's *true*. Everyone else in there is way more experienced."

"You know that for a fact, do you?"

"Yes," I insist. "They've done lessons and camps and All-State and—"

"So what if they have?" Delia cuts me off, turning left at an intersection. "Experience can only get you so far. Do you know that they've got more talent or drive? Hell, Cline, you've only spent three hours with those kids."

I fold my arms, defensive. Delia's my getaway driver. She's supposed to be on my side.

"I'm *telling you*," I say, "I don't belong."

Delia says nothing for a spell. She drives till we're on Paris Pike, Brenda's headlights illuminating black wooden fences and rolling bluegrass fields.

"Hey." Delia's voice cuts through the silence, startling me. "Did you know I barely graduated high school? By the skin of my teeth. One decimal lower on my GPA, and no diploma for me."

That's news. I never pegged Delia for a bad student.

"Learning is what you make of it," Delia goes on. "You, and you alone. It's not worth comparing yourself to other folks, which is what I did in high school. This time around, I'm not beating myself up for not making the best grade. I just tell myself, 'Delia, you're doing good for *you*.' That's what matters, in the end. You ask yourself, 'Am I doing good for me?'"

"Well, I *am* learning new stuff," I admit, thinking of the notes I took. "And Dr. Johnson said I was proactive."

Delia nods. "So why do you feel like you don't belong in that class?"

"I'm the youngest one there." I stare at my Keds—two bleached ghosts on the floorboard. "I feel . . . unprepared. Not good enough."

"That's not the same as *belonging*, though."

My mouth twists up. "Guess not."

When Delia drops me off at home, she calls out, "Till next time!"

I know she's really saying, *Don't give up.*

The house is dark and silent. Mama won't be home from work till after midnight, and when I creak open Gram's bedroom door, I find her fast asleep in bed. Gram's given up a lot for me, including those one hundred dollars. I think about how hard I've worked to get into the workshop. I think about the notes I took tonight and Dr. Johnson calling me "proactive." I ask myself Delia's question: "Am I doing good for me?"

I guess I am.

So I won't give up yet, I decide. Next week's class is going to be better. It *has* to be, even if I'm paired with the likes of Sylvie Sharpe.

14

I'VE BEEN PLAYING "Cline Kicks the World's Butt" nonstop. I play it Tuesday morning as I pull on my clothes—jacket and corduroy pants, now the weather's gone crisp. I play it in the afternoon, as I walk home from Hollie's place. I even play it in the evening, as I set the supper table for me, Mama, and Gram.

My confidence has been shaky since Monday night. But my favorite singing ladies? They've got confidence I can borrow. When Connie Smith demands to know where her castle is, I ask right along. When Loretta Lynn sasses about rivals stepping over her dead body, I tell myself I'm that brave, too.

After supper on Tuesday, I sneak into Gram's room to tell her about the workshop. I haven't had the chance till now, and I guess that's for the best. I've had a day to regain my courage, so Gram won't see the uncertain side of me. I don't share all the stuff I told Delia on the ride home, because I don't want Gram fretting that

I'm wasting her rainy-day fund. Instead, I focus on the positives, like the new musical terms Dr. Johnson taught me and how I'll be writing a song for next week's class.

"Got any ideas?" Gram asks.

"Not really," I admit. "The stuff I've written before has all been based on *other* songs."

"Well, that's not a bad place to start," Gram tells me. "Your daddy had a gift like that. We'd be eating at a restaurant, and out of nowhere he'd start singing words he'd made up along to whatever was on the radio. Once, he changed 'Always on My Mind' to 'Always on the Rind.' A *love song*, devoted to the watermelon slice on his plate. And your mama, she got so embarrassed. She waved her hands and told him to quit, but he went right on singing till she nearly bust her gut laughing."

Gram's told me this story plenty of times, but I'd never seen it in this light before. Maybe rewriting songs was a joke to Dad, but it *was* songwriting, all the same. Is that a gift I got from him?

I smile, thinking about Dad being goofy. Being *alive*. I like when Mama and Gram talk like this. It makes me feel a little more like Dad is part of my life, in the here and now.

⌘

Maybe it's the music or Delia's advice or Gram's story, but by Wednesday afternoon, I'm feeling better about the workshop. I sit at lunch with my friends, the five of us chowing down on mac and cheese as Darlene tells us how her family is planning on going to Dollywood over winter break.

"I hear they light up the whole park like the North Pole," she tells us.

"Oh man," I say wistfully. "Dollywood."

I've never been, but it sure seems like a dream. A whole theme park inspired by Dolly Parton herself? They say the shows are one of a kind, jam-packed with country music, bluegrass bands, and old-fashioned hymns. That's my idea of heaven.

"I've got conflicted feelings about a place like that," says Ava. "Dolly seems great, but . . . is it super cheesy?"

"All theme parks are cheesy," says Kenzie. "Where else are we cool with a person running around in giant mouse costume, handing out balloons?"

"That makes it sound creepy," Hollie says, frowning.

"Oh, no. It's definitely not creepy," Ava says in an airy, monotone voice. *"Nooo."*

I crack a smile, just as I hear a voice at my back say, "Hey, Cline."

I look up to see none other than Trevor Larson standing at our table. His hands are in his pockets, and there's a funny look on his face.

"Uh, hey, Trevor." I try to stay friendly, but I'm worried he's come to flirt again.

"Hey," Trevor repeats. He tugs a hand from his pocket only to wrap it around the back of his neck. Then he says, "Cline, would you go to the Harvest Dance with me?"

I breathe in real deep and slow. Trevor Larson is asking me to the Harvest Dance. *Me.* Cline Alden. The one girl at this table who hasn't talked about what boy she'd like to buy her a corsage come Halloween night.

I'm staring at Trevor like my brains have liquefied and leaked out my ears. I don't know what to do. Maybe I shouldn't have told Trevor how *Lauper* would make a good name two weeks ago. I was trying to make him feel better, but I guess he took that as encouragement. Maybe there wasn't *any* way I could keep Trevor from asking this question outside of telling him flat out, "I don't want to go to the dance with you." Even now, I don't feel like I can say *that*.

"Uh," I say instead. Then I manage to add, "I've got something going on that night."

Across the table, Kenzie says, "What? You never told us that."

Which is *not* helpful. My face feels hot, so I know it's turning red. Trevor looks embarrassed, too. He's rubbing so hard at his neck, I'm afraid he'll wipe his skin clean off.

"Thank you, though?" I squeak.

"Yeah, um . . . no problem," Trevor mumbles.

Then he's gone.

Darlene's big-eyed and Ava is pressing her lips together. Kenzie says, "What the heck just happened?"

I'm not paying much attention to them, though. I'm looking at Hollie, who's staring at her lunch tray, even though she's finished her mac and cheese.

I want her to tell me not to feel bad.

I want her to say everything's fine.

But Hollie doesn't speak.

The school bell sounds, and I grab my tray and get to my feet along with the others, ignoring the fact that Ava and Darlene are whispering to each other. Kenzie nudges my elbow and asks again, "What happened?"

"I told Trevor I couldn't go to the dance." I feel weak and weird all over as I say it.

"I caught that much," says Kenzie, as we file into the hallway. "But *why?*"

I can't answer that. I look to Hollie again, but she shoves past us, clacking down the hall in her heeled boots, not once looking back.

⌖

Darlene, Kenzie, and Ava take a different bus—one that goes to the east side of town. (So does Trevor Larson, thank heavens.) That means it's just me and Hollie on the ride to her house, sharing a seat but nothing else.

I can tell Hollie's angry. She glares out the window, turned away from me. She didn't say a word between class periods, either, going out of her way to talk to the other girls but not me. I want so badly to ask her what's wrong, but not in front of other people. It's torture, waiting the ten minutes it takes to get to her place, but once we're off the bus and out of earshot of anyone else, I ask the question that's burning me up inside: "Are you mad I turned down Trevor?"

For the first time since lunch, Hollie meets my eyes. "Why would I be mad?" she says.

"I dunno. Why would you be?"

"Well, if *you* can't tell me." Hollie sniffs, turning around so fast that her backpack jostles, and a key chain comes loose from the zipper, clattering to the ground.

I hurry to pick it up. It's a squishy, sequined cat face. I was with Hollie when she bought this on a weekend trip to Hamburg Place, in Lexington. I stare at the cat's pink button nose, wishing we could go back to that Saturday when we went shopping and ate Hawaiian shave ices. When nothing was wrong.

Hollie turns around, hand outstretched, like she expects me to give the key chain back. I don't, though. I hold on, thinking maybe if I do, she'll have to listen to me.

"I told you before," I say. "I'm not all that interested in the Harvest Dance."

Hollie shakes her head, like I'm a robot talking in boops and beeps. "I thought you were just saying that so it wouldn't look bad if you didn't get asked."

I frown, thinking maybe I should be offended. "I meant it," I insist. "I don't like any of the boys at DMS. Not that way."

"That can't be true, though. What about Jared, or Keith? *Every* girl likes those boys."

I don't know what to say. How do I tell Hollie that I'm not like *every* girl?

"Please," I say, offering her the key chain. "Don't be mad."

She snatches it from me. "I don't get you sometimes. You know, some girls don't get asked out to dances at all. Then Trevor, who's cute and a great guy, asks you out, and you tell him *no*? What point are you trying to prove?"

I don't know how to answer. Hollie's questions have stopped making sense. I hate this conversation. I hate the Harvest Dance. I want Trevor Larson to have never asked me out, and for me and Hollie to be having a normal afternoon, where we'll jump on the trampoline and watch TV for a while.

It's clear there's no chance of that, though. Not today.

"You know what?" Hollie says. "I'm not feeling so good. Maybe you should head on home."

"Yeah, maybe I should."

I turn my back before Hollie can see my tears. Only after I hear her front door slam shut do I yank out my phone and plug in the earbuds. I hit Play on "Cline Kicks the World's Butt"; and it's Linda Ronstadt midchorus, singing about how love is tricky, and if you go after it, you'll come up with nothing but a handful of thorns.

Linda's voice is sweet like syrup and mighty as dynamite. Most days, a song of hers would cheer me up. Today, though, it's only making me angrier and sadder and, more than anything, confused.

Why is Hollie mad at me? How does me turning down Trevor

have anything to do with *her*? I can't help but think this would be way easier if Hollie knew the truth. If she knew that I liked girls instead of guys, this would all make sense to her, wouldn't it?

I guess I've been hoping that maybe, on account of us being best friends, Hollie would just *pick up* on who I like. She's always had my back before, when the other girls teased me about guys. I'm almost positive she'd understand if I told her right out about me liking girls.

Only, I don't feel like telling Hollie *anything* right now.

I head home, hoping each step will take me farther away from my bad feelings. That they'll stay right there on Hollie Kendall's front lawn and, like weeds, wither up and die.

⁓

Here's a nice thing about the Elephant room: no one there asks how you feel about boys. They mostly want to know if they can have more Cheerios.

It's my third week working in the nursery, and though Morgan and I aren't what you'd call best buddies, we've reached a truce. She doesn't nag me about rules as often, and I let her feel like she's in control.

Tonight, it's me, not the little kids, who makes a mess. A strand of my hair drops into an open jar of finger paint, but I'm too lost in my thoughts to notice at first. All night, I've been worrying about Hollie. Trevor Larson, too. As I wash out my hair in the sink, I wonder if I could've turned down Trevor in a better way—maybe asked to talk to him privately after school. But it's too late for *would've*s and *should've*s now.

When we've checked out the very last kid from the room, I take my fifteen dollars and run for the door. I'm hoping Hollie will be in a better mood, and when we see each other on the church lawn, we can pretend today's fight didn't happen. I burst outside into chilly autumn air, but when I get to the lawn, I stop short, my heart sinking fast.

Hollie's not here. Neither are Livy, Emma, or Scott. I check the time, but it's not any later than usual. We've hung out in this same spot two weeks in a row. I sit in the grass, waiting, but the others don't show—not after one minute, three, or five. I tell myself that maybe youth group ran long, but I wonder if Hollie is staying inside on purpose, so she won't have to see me. *Why* is she so mad, though? And how can I make things better if Hollie won't talk to me?

Mama picks me up and drives me home. I get ready for bed and kiss Gram good night, but afterward, I can't fall asleep. Hollie's words from earlier are slicing through my head, each syllable sharp as a knife: *Every girl likes those boys.*

Who gets to decide what every girl wants? Is there a committee, same as there is for the CMAs? A set of judges who hand out trophies and determine the rules? Well, they sure didn't consult Cline Alden.

Then I remember something else Hollie told me: *some girls don't get asked out to dances.*

Could it be that Hollie's . . . jealous? Maybe she wanted Trevor to ask *her* to the dance, and me turning him down felt like a slap in the face. I hadn't thought of that. Truth be told, I've never considered that Hollie could be jealous of me. She's the one with the big house and more money. She has plenty of friends, and she does better in school than I do. But if Hollie *is* jealous, that would at least explain why she's upset.

So, that settles it. Tomorrow, I'll make up with Hollie. I'll tell her I'm sorry, just to be sure we're good. I can't make Trevor Larson feel any better, but I can do that for my best friend, at least.

15

I'D BE LYING if I said I haven't considered ducking my tail between my legs and never going back to the Young Singer-Songwriter Workshop. But every time this week that I've thought about chickening out, I remember the music—what got me into this workshop to begin with.

Dr. Johnson's homework from our first class was to come up with an original song. No fudging. No song you've written before. Something *wholly* new, in one week's time. If you ask me, that's less homework and more challenge, and Cline Louise Alden does not back down from a challenge.

On Thursday, I tracked down Hollie at school first thing and told her I was sorry about our fight. She said it was all right, and that afternoon we hung out at her place like nothing had changed. Hollie didn't bring up Trevor, but I'm pretty sure now that's what our fight was about.

I guess it's on me for not realizing my best friend had a crush on a boy. But it's on *Hollie* for assuming who I like. What she said about every girl liking boys makes me want to shout, "See *all* of who I am." Then again, I'm not sure how to show who I am in words. It's not as simple as telling Hollie, "Hey, the way you like Trevor? That's the way I felt about Brandi Carlile when I was in seventh grade."

Those thoughts pester me all weekend, even on Saturday night as I sit in bed, composition book atop my crossed legs. I've been staring at a blank page for fifteen minutes, as Dr. Johnson's words about rhyme schemes and musical theory swirl around in my head. I've composed a few songs before—fun, strummy melodies based on the hits of my favorite ladies. Like Gram said, maybe I got that inclination from Dad. This time, though? I want to write something personal. Something that's really *Cline*.

I poke my tongue against my cheek, looking up from the blank page to the old mason jar on my dresser, where I used to store my babysitting money. These days, I keep my nursery earnings in an envelope, stashed in the top drawer of my nightstand. The envelope's already labeled with the workshop's mailing address, as a reminder of where my money's headed. But the mason jar—I emptied that for the application fee. All that remains is a quarter and single, shiny penny.

Staring at that penny, an idea comes to me. I put my pen to paper, scratching out words:

I'd give a penny for your thoughts,
and I'd give a million for your love.
I know a heart's a thing that can't be bought,
But just know you're the one I'm thinking of.

They're good lyrics, I think, but they're not exactly right. They're not completely me. I stare at the last line, chewing so hard on my lip that I taste blood. I scritch out a word with my pen, then chew harder. My whole mouth's starting to taste like metal when I press the pen on the page and write in a newer, better word. Now the last line reads like so:

But just know you're the girl I'm thinking of.

I stare at the change a good long while. It's the first time I've put down in writing the way I really feel. It's scary. But it also feels good—like I've finally dropped a fifty-pound bag of flour I've been hauling around town. I tap the paper with my pen, saying the words out loud: "You're the girl I'm thinking of."

Goose bumps run up my arms, and I lose my breath. That's when I realize something: I can't say the words I want, but maybe I could *sing* them. The workshop is plenty intimidating, sure, but it's also a good twenty miles from Paris, and those twenty miles? They make a big difference. There's no one in that workshop who knows me. In Lexington, I'm not Cline, daughter of Judy and granddaughter of Cynthia. I'm not some girl who hangs around the Goldenrod or who tripped down the stairs once at DMS and got a bloody nose. Maybe I can't be *all* Cline at school, or with Mama or even with Hollie. I can be myself in this song, though.

The next line comes to me easy as pie, and the next, and the *next*. At first, I thought those first four lines would be a verse, but soon it's clear that they're made to be the chorus. I fiddle with the bridge and revise the lyrics until the song is just so. Then, it's a matter of music. I pull out my guitar and start working and reworking my fingers on the frets, humming out different melodies until I find the right one. The first time I sing the chorus all the way through, a whoosh runs down my spine, and it feels like magic.

It's not until I'm through composing that I realize I haven't once thought about those other kids in the workshop, with their training and qualifications and big plans for music school. I remember what Delia told me on the ride home from Lexington: it's not worth comparing yourself to other folks. You ask yourself, "Am I doing good for me?"

Tonight, I can answer that question with a big, undeniable *yes*.

⌒∞⌒

On Monday night, I jump into Delia's truck, full of tingling nerves. This time around, traffic is light, which means I show up to class a good fifteen minutes early. I decide to take a seat closer to the front of the classroom. I haven't brought my guitar, since Dr.

Johnson told us we won't be working on musical accompaniment till our third class, and there's a line between being "proactive" and being plain dense.

Students file in around me and take seats next to their partners. Most of them are exchanging notebooks, gabbing about their songs. One row over, Chris and Jamal are joking around and harmonizing the chorus of "Ain't No Sunshine" by Bill Withers. Veronica is talking to her partner, Gia, about her admissions essay to Belmont. There's excitement buzzing all around as I open my composition book to my song, which I've titled, "Penny for Your Love."

I'm humming the melody to myself, tapping my pencil eraser on the page, when someone takes a seat at the desk beside me. I look up, startled.

It's Sylvie. This time without the sunglasses.

Her eyes, turns out, are mostly brown, with green rings around the pupils, and she's got eyelashes longer than a mile.

"Hey," she says to me.

"Uh . . . hey?"

Sylvie takes out a notebook from her backpack, placing it on the desk. Then she looks me right in the eye and says, "I want to apologize for how I acted last week."

I stare at Sylvie in shock. I can't think of anything to say.

"I get these migraines," Sylvie goes on. "They're super bad. When I have one, I feel like I'm gonna *die*. I felt one coming on before my mom brought me here last week, but she thought I was chickening out of the workshop and made me come anyway. Wow, did she feel bad when she picked me up." Sylvie rolls her eyes. "Anyway, that's why I was wearing sunglasses. Light makes the migraines worse." She smirks a little. "Especially fluorescents, like you said."

Oh man. I did say that, didn't I?

"I was pretty awful to you," Sylvie admits, like she's giving my three bad facts about her a pass. "It's just, *everything* seems bright and loud with my migraines, and I could barely sit up straight, let alone talk. So, you don't have to forgive me, or anything. I dunno if I'd forgive me, if I were you. Probably seems like a made-up excuse. But there it is."

Huh. That's a whole lot to think about. Maybe Sylvie isn't a jerk. Maybe she really was sick. She's right, though: it does sort of sound like a made-up excuse. I've heard of migraines before on TV ads for medicine, and they don't seem great, but I think a person's capable of feeling sick without being downright *rude*.

Though . . . I guess that's what Sylvie's apologizing for, isn't it? The rude part.

"Okay," I say. "I forgive you."

Sylvie looks relieved. "I was wondering if we could start over. Pretend *this* is our first day as partners? I promise I'll make a better impression."

I think about my tears at the sign-in table last week and the way I rambled at that poor woman, Jocelyn. Sylvie hasn't brought that up once, even though I *know* she saw, and I do appreciate that. Maybe Sylvie's heart really is in the right place.

I say, "I think I can make a better impression, too."

"Cool." Sylvie opens the notebook at her desk. "So, what do you think Dr. Johnson's going to have us do with these songs? She said today's about collaboration, so I bet she'll have us mash them together. You know, Frankenstein-style."

I stare at the page Sylvie's opened her notebook to. There's a title—"Serenity"—and words scrawled beneath it. Turns out Sylvie did her homework, too. Will wonders never cease?

"I thought you didn't want to be here," I say.

"Huh?" Sylvie looks up.

"Last week, you said your parents forced you to come."

"Well, yeah. Like I said, my mom didn't believe me about my migraine. And, like, I don't blame her. I can be dramatic. I faked one *once* to get out of this test last year? It's been the boy who cried wolf ever since."

I stare at Sylvie, who starts looking uncomfortable.

"I just didn't want you thinking I had terrible parents, or something," she adds.

"Wait," I say, 'cause I'm still trying to make sense. "You *do* want to take this class?"

Sylvie leans back in her chair, folding her arms, though it's not like last time, when she seemed annoyed. "Well, yes and no. Singer-songwriter stuff tends to be folksy, and I'm not into folk or country crap. But I *do* write and play my own songs, so when my mom read about the workshop, she convinced me to apply.

What I'd *really* like is to go to a summer rock camp. There's this awesome one in Nashville, but my mom doesn't like that it's so far away. So this workshop was, like, a consolation prize."

This girl keeps getting stranger. Five minutes ago, I thought she was one person, and it turns out she's completely different. But now we've got a whole new problem on our hands.

"You don't like country music?" I ask.

Sylvie shrugs. "It all sounds like the same song, over and over."

My jaw unhinges. "I could say the same thing about rock 'n' roll."

Sylvie balks. "You could not."

I shake my head at her. "You don't know country."

"Well, maybe *you* don't know *rock*."

It's clear we're having a fight, but we're both smiling about it. It's not like last time, when Sylvie made me want to pull my hair out from its roots.

Speaking of hair, I've been looking at Sylvie's this whole time: long and brown as a hickory nut, done up in a neat ponytail. Spick-and-span, no flyaways in sight. Today, instead of a macramé dress, she's wearing blue jeans and a leather jacket, and her cartilage piercing is a little rose gold stud. Even without the sunglasses, she looks effortlessly cool.

Me? Sitting here in my corduroys and my favorite but *old* turtleneck, I get to feeling frumpy.

"How old are you?" I ask.

Sylvie arches a brow. "Lucky thirteen."

"Same."

"Yeah, I remember."

That's right. I told Sylvie plenty about myself last week. Turns out, she was listening to every last bit.

"So, you're in seventh grade?" I ask. "Or eighth?"

"Eighth." Sylvie squints at the ceiling. "Gotta say, it's not my favorite. I hear people say stuff gets better in high school, but I've got this feeling they're just lying to keep us under control."

"I hadn't thought of it that way," I say, because I really hadn't.

"Think about it," Sylvie goes on. "There are studies about how teenagers need at least nine hours of sleep per night, but then society is like, 'You have to get up at seven to go to school *and* stay up till midnight with extracurriculars and homework, or whatever.' They're keeping us sleep-deprived with pointless hoop jumping, when think what we could be doing instead. Greta Thunberg dropped out of school to save the planet when she was fifteen. Joan of Arc was leading a freaking *army*."

I hadn't considered any of that, either. The way Sylvie's talking has got me a little slack-jawed. I'm almost too nervous to say what I do next, but I figure it's on topic.

"Patsy Cline got herself an audition for the Grand Ole Opry in high school."

"Yeah!" Sylvie nods appreciatively. "You get what I'm saying. Like, why do we think one size fits all? Who says we have to do Model UN and AP classes and, like, go to college? Maybe that's not what some of us *want*. It's like the myth of Procrustes, stretching everyone out to fit the mold. No, thanks."

"Um," I say uncertainly. "Yeah."

Sylvie might be my age, but in some ways, she seems older—like she's thought thoughts and done things I haven't. She talks with passion, like she's reporting breaking news. And she's got a cartilage piercing, for land sakes.

I'm about to ask how bad it hurts to pierce your upper ear when Dr. Johnson enters the classroom, striding to her desk and saying, "All right, musicians! Let's get started."

So we do.

Dr. Johnson begins by telling us, "Collaboration is at the heart of the songwriting experience. So often, music is what connects us to others. It's about finding common ground and turning our hopes, dreams, and fears into universal ideas."

Then she gives us a history lesson on how musical performance is often a "group project," from the concertos of Johann Sebastian Bach to the hits of Simon and Garfunkel—this band I haven't heard of but mean to look up once I get home.

For the second half of class, Dr. Johnson has us swap our homework with our partner's. Sylvie's guess was right on the money: we have to come up with one song that combines elements of both our compositions.

Sylvie's composition isn't a love song. It's about taking a break when times get tough. So, it's different from mine, but it's also good. Her chorus goes like this:

Hands folded, fingers crossed,
Alone in a room, wondering—
Face molded, teeth flossed,
Could I have serenity then?

They seem like lyrics for a soft, slow song, but Sylvie says it's supposed to be fast, complete with electric guitar.

I'm a little nervous when it's time to share my song. A *lot* nervous, actually. After all, I've put right there in the lyrics, *You're the girl I'm thinking of.* As Sylvie reads my words, I watch her closely, waiting to see if she'll look surprised or frown or ask a question. All she says, though, is "This is really good."

I break into a smile, relieved. That wasn't so bad. I was hoping I could be myself here, and so far, it turns out I can.

It takes a lot of talking back and forth about lyrics and instrumentation and what Dr. Johnson calls a "cohesive vision," but in the end, Sylvie and I come up with a song—our Frankenstein's monster, as Sylvie put it. This new song is titled "Penny for Serenity." It's a medium tempo, to be played by an acoustic guitar and, at Sylvie's suggestion, a piano. Our new lyrics are a love song, like mine was, but they're also about Sylvie's serenity:

Could I find serenity with you?
We'll get lost in each other's thoughts
And wind up someplace new.

Guess it's crystal clear just from my face
That you're the girl I'm thinking of,
And you make my heart race.

When your hand is folded into mine,
A darkened night lights up with sparks,
And look how bright we shine.

Before I know it, Dr. Johnson is announcing that it's nine o'clock—the end of class. Folks talk about time flying by, but tonight? It went at turbojet speed.

Sylvie and I aren't completely happy with our song.

"It's too mushy," Sylvie concludes, when we read over it together, and I agree. But she doesn't suggest we take out the line about thinking of a girl. She hasn't suggested we change that part—not once.

Dr. Johnson's told us that this song of ours is our "baby" for next week's class. That's when she wants us to put it to music. We'll have more chances to revise what we've written then, since according to her, "songcraft is more about *re*writing than writing." She also says we're welcome to collaborate outside of class time, if we want.

I'm shivering as we leave the Fine Arts Building, but I don't think it's owing to the crisp October wind. I'm shaking with *excitement.* Today was about the music, pure and simple.

Ready whenever, I text Delia.

Other students have been leaving the building one by one, some heading to their parked cars and others to parents waiting for them on the street. Now that the rush has died down, I'm left sitting on a stone wall near the side door, my legs dangling. I keep an eye out for Delia as I listen to "Cline Kicks the World's Butt" all alone.

"You waiting around, too?"

At least, I *thought* I was alone.

I drop my phone in my lap, turning to see Sylvie at the door.

"Oh!" I sort of shout. "I thought you'd already left."

"Nope," Sylvie says, coming outside. She hoists herself up on the wall next to me. "Mom's got Zumba class Monday nights. She usually runs late, talking to friends."

Sylvie starts rolling her eyes, but catches herself. "She *isn't* a terrible parent, though."

I laugh. "I get it, don't worry. My mama doesn't even know I'm here."

Welp. I didn't know I was going to share that secret with Sylvie. But I don't feel panicked about it, the way I would if I slipped up with Hollie and the girls at school. Sylvie lives here in Lexington. There's no chance she'd run into my mom. This secret's safe with her.

"Whoa," Sylvie says. "For real?"

"Mama doesn't think music's practical. She says it won't pay the bills."

"Aw, that sucks. My mom grew up in Mexico City, where she went to this conservatory as a cellist? So she's all for musical *anything*."

I nod. "I mean, my mama *used* to like music. She was actually really great at piano. But then, I don't know. She just . . . stopped."

Sylvie scrunches her nose sympathetically. "Do you have another parent? What do they think?"

"My dad's passed away," I say, swallowing the throat pang I get most times I bring up Dad.

"I'm sorry." Sylvie's quiet a while before she says, "So, you decided to come to this workshop on your own."

I nod.

"Badass." Sylvie's looking me over like she's got newfound respect, and my insides suddenly feel like they're aglow. "So, uh . . . is that what the money thing was about last week?"

Like that, the glow inside me flickers out. I lower my head, embarrassed, and say, "Yeah."

"Hey." Sylvie knocks her knee against mine. "Nothing to be ashamed of. That's impressive, you coming up with the money on your own. I don't have three hundred dollars. That was all my parents."

It's nice of Sylvie to try to cheer me up, but I don't want to be thinking about the workshop's tuition, or how I've only got fifteen

129

dollars more than I did last week, when I need *one hundred and sixty-five*. I agreed to Jocelyn's terms 'cause I was so desperate to get to the first class. But I'm not going to make that new October deadline. I'll have to write the workshop folks a letter next week and send it along with the money I do have, asking for another extension. They'll see, like they did before, that I'm good for it. I'll have paid them forty-five more dollars, and that's progress. Anyway, UK is a big, rich university. They can wait a while longer for the rest of my tuition. That's what I hope, anyway, but if I think about it too long, it'll put me in a mood as sour as one of *Mama's* money moods.

Instead, I ask Sylvie something else that's been bugging me: "Do you really think all country music sounds the same?"

Sylvie smiles slyly. She raises her hands to her chest, clutches at her heart, and scrunches her face into a moping expression. Then, in a perfect imitation of a Tim McGraw drawl, she belts out, loud as anything, "My boots are tarnished by your no-good, two-timing cheating heaaart! I'm gonna drive my pickup a hundred miles till we're apaaart!"

I start to laugh—I can't help it—as I look around and see that Sylvie's caught the attention of a passing pair of college kids. They're grinning, and one even lets out a hoot of approval. Sylvie pays them no mind, though. She's still in performance mode. Now, instead of made-up lyrics, she's doing a dead-on impression of a pedal steel guitar, imitating its wail while plucking and sliding her fingers along invisible strings.

Sylvie's *good* at impressions. So much so that when she's through, I have to clap.

Sylvie bows solemnly, waving her hand in a flourish. Only, I can't let her have the last word—or *note*, as the case may be. Good as she is, Sylvie's got it all wrong.

"I'm not talking about *that* country," I tell her. "I barely listen to guy singers at all."

Now that Sylvie's back to her usual self—not fake Tim McGraw—she eyes me skeptically.

"What I love about country," I explain, "and folk and blue-grass, too, is how many good women singers there are."

Sylvie's brows shoot up. "Well, that's what I like about *rock*."

"How do you mean?"

I don't know much about rock 'n' roll, but what comes to mind is sweaty men in T-shirts, jamming on electric guitars.

Sylvie gives me this look, like I'm pulling her leg. Then her eyes get wide. "Oh man, you're *serious*. C'mon. Joan Jett? Debbie Harry? Patti Smith? Tina Turner? Any of those ring a bell?"

Sylvie gets a big blank stare from me.

In response, she starts slapping one hand rhythmically on the wall. She sings again, only this time her voice is alto and packed with gravel as she belts unfamiliar lyrics about putting dimes into jukeboxes and loving rock 'n' roll. As I stare at her, I realize that these impressions of Sylvie's aren't meant to show off. They're meant to make me laugh. And I do.

"Sorry," I say, giggling. "Doesn't ring a bell."

Truth is, I don't recognize a single one of the names Sylvie said, but her listing them off has got me thinking.

"I have an idea," I say, taking out my composition book and ripping a sheet from it. I tear that paper in two, handing Sylvie one half and keeping the other. Then I rummage through my backpack till I find two pencils—one for me and one for her.

"You write down those names," I tell Sylvie. "Your top five favorite rockers. And *I'll* write down my five country favorites. We'll listen to them this week, and next class, we can report back."

Sylvie gives me a look. "You're funny, you know that?"

I gulp, wondering if maybe this was a bad idea. But then Sylvie takes the pencil from me and adds, "The *good* kind of funny."

As she starts scribbling down names, I make my own list:

Emmylou Harris
Dolly Parton
Linda Ronstadt
Loretta Lynn

I think hard on number five, wondering if I should make it Patsy Cline, or if that would seem egoistical, seeing as how I'm her namesake. In the end, I decide on Brandi Carlile. Even though she's not technically country, I think Brandi's got a sound like country ladies of the past.

I'm about to announce that my list's complete when a car horn blasts from the street. I look up to see Delia there, waiting for me in Brenda. There's an SUV behind her, and from it, a woman in a workout top with brown skin and long, curly hair calls through her open window, "Sylvie, babe! Let's go!"

"Whoops," says Sylvie. "Guess we lost track of time."

I hand my paper to Sylvie, and she hands me hers.

"It's a pact," I tell her, as we hop off the stone wall. "You gotta listen, okay?"

Sylvie throws out her hand, tiniest finger extended. "Pinkie promise."

Grinning, I link my pinkie around hers. We kiss our knuckles, sealing the deal, and then break apart, heading to our rides.

"Oh, hey! Cline!" Sylvie calls out, right as I'm opening Delia's passenger door.

"Yeah?"

Sylvie hangs out the window of her mom's SUV. "That audition on the twenty-fourth? Maybe, if we like our collaboration, or whatever, we could audition together."

I *thought* I was already grinning, but now I really am. I say, "That could be fun."

Sylvie nods and waves goodbye. Then her mom drives off, and I climb into Brenda's cab.

Delia's giving me a sidelong smirk.

"Better day?" she asks, like she knew it would be.

I stick out my tongue, and Delia places a hand on her chest.

"*That's* how you treat your getaway driver?"

I only laugh as she turns up her music—Kacey Musgraves singing "Pageant Material."

I unfold the paper in my hand. That's when I see that, beneath her list of five favorite rockers, Sylvie's written out ten digits. Her phone number.

I keep right on grinning.

⌒⟡⌒

Gram is still awake when I get home.

When she calls me into her bedroom, I come bounding in, letting out all my news about songwriting with Sylvie and the Daylight Saving Bluegrass Festival audition.

"Well, sweetie, this sounds like it could be your big break!" Gram says.

I pause, considering. I hadn't thought about the audition that way. Up till now, it's just seemed like a chance to show what I've learned in the workshop, like a kind of final exam.

Now that I'm not in the worried state I was last week, though, and auditioning with Sylvie is a possibility, I really think it through. I guess the audition *could* be my big break. Who knows who could be there, watching me play? And if Sylvie and I get chosen to perform in the festival preshow, who knows who could be watching us *then*? All my favorite singing ladies got discovered somewhere, some way. Well, what if the Daylight Saving Bluegrass Festival is how Cline Alden catches some Nashville producer's attention? It could be the start of my singing career.

"You're right," I tell Gram, losing myself to a dreamy haze.

Gram nods, like my saying so has decided the matter: the audition *will* be my big break.

Well, the way I'm feeling tonight? I think that might really be true.

16

"NOW, HANK, I'VE got their quote right here in front of me."

Mama's on the phone in the kitchen, talking dollars and cents to Hank at Gilchrist Pharmacy.

We Aldens are no strangers to the ol' pharmacy haggle. Ever since Dr. Windisch started prescribing Gram more pills, it seems Mama's taken on more and more hours at the Goldenrod. But no matter which way Mama cuts our monthly budget, there doesn't ever seem to be enough money to cover all Gram's prescriptions. It's especially bad now that those Cleveland doctors have put her on two new medicines. I know the new pills are for the best. They're going to keep Gram's memory in good shape. All the same, they sure could cost less.

Every week, Mama splits the pills of Gram's that can be safely halved, so as to spread the medicine out and make it last longer. And every so often, like now, she'll hop on the phone with Hank to let him know about a better deal she's found at a pharmacy out of town.

"I've known your daddy how long, Hank?" Mama asks, tapping her nails on the kitchen counter.

You *know* Mama means business when she brings up Hank's daddy, Chester Gilchrist.

I hear Hank tell Mama on speaker phone, "Our families have known each other a long while, Judy. That's why you've got to understand, we're a small family business. Sometimes, we just can't cut costs like these big box stores do."

"So, I suppose I'll have to take my business to them?"

That's it: Mama's ace. I don't think it's nice, threatening to bail on the Gilchrists like that. I get squirmy every time Mama does it in front of me, but she says when it comes to haggling, it's business, not personal.

Bringing up Hank's daddy, though—seems personal to me.

I wince at the long silence as Hank tries to come up with an answer to Mama's burning question. Mama and Hank both know she doesn't have the time or gas money to drive to a big pharmacy in Lexington every time Gram needs her pills refilled. One of these days, I think Hank will call Mama's bluff. Put his foot down and refuse her flat out.

Today isn't that day, though.

"I tell you what," says Hank. "I'll bring down the donepezil by five, but that's as low as we can go."

"That's *not* a match to—"

"I hear that, Judy. I'm just telling you what I can do."

Mama tip-taps her nails on the counter, not saying a word. This is a form of haggling she calls "smoking out the fox"—waiting to see if the silence gets so uncomfortable the other party budges.

The pharmacy line stays dead silent, though. Hank's not budging today.

"Well, it's highway robbery," Mama finally concludes. "I don't see how these Big Pharma folks can sleep at night."

"Nor can I, but I'll remind you again: Big Pharma we ain't."

Once Mama's hung up, she snorts and says, "You ain't Big Pharma, but I've seen the car you drive, Mr. Pharmacist Fancypants."

I smile into my orange juice glass, relieved the haggling's over. A twenty-minute conversation on a nice Saturday morning, and for what? Five bucks off one of Gram's medicines. It's so much effort for so little money.

I get a stabbing feeling, close to my heart—guilt about the hundred dollars I took from Gram. I know she's happy I'm spending her rainy-day money. But looking at it another way, you could say that hundred bucks is worth *twenty* of Mama's phone calls to Hank.

"Now then, Cline," says Mama, joining me and Gram at the breakfast table. "What's the plan for this evening? You're heading straight to the lock-in from Hollie's?"

I nod around my mouthful of cereal, thinking how glad I am

that Hollie and I aren't fighting anymore. We haven't been able to spend much time together the past few days, but I'm hoping we can do that at the lock-in.

"Mrs. Kendall will be able to bring you home after church, right?" Mama asks. "I'll be at the Goldenrod till five tomorrow."

"Yep," I say.

Mama arches a brow. "I don't like the sound of this lock-in. A giant slumber party seems like a recipe for disaster."

"Who's having a slumber party?" asks Gram, looking up from her buttered toast.

There's a funny look in her eyes, like they're clouded up and trying to catch hold of sunlight.

"Mine, Gram," I say. "The lock-in at New Hope tonight."

I'm hoping Gram will nod along and say she remembers. Instead, she drops her butter knife to the floor.

"That's okay!" I say, hopping from my chair and grabbing the fallen knife. I take it to the sink and fetch a new one for her. By the time I reach Gram's side, though, her sun-searching eyes have filled with tears.

"Gram," I say, setting the knife by her plate, "what's wrong?"

Mama's giving me a warning look, like I ought not pester Gram in this state. I want to be sure she's all right, though. Gram's chest is heaving, and her breath starts coming out in rasps.

"Roger," she says. "When's Roger coming home?"

I get real still, watching as Gram touches the gold band on her ring finger. Gram brings up Papaw every so often, but only to talk about how life used to be: how Papaw played with a band on Friday nights, fished in Lake Julian, and planted zinnias and dahlias in the garden. *Played, fished, planted.* All past tense. Never present, as though Papaw is still with us.

"Mother," says Mama, placing a hand atop Gram's, "you're back in Paris now. Papaw isn't here."

Gram's eyes get cloudier than ever. No sun in sight.

This is bad. Scary, even. Gram is sad and confused, and I can't stand to see her like this.

I want to rewind to five minutes ago, when we were having a normal breakfast, same as any other morning. I want to crawl into Gram's brain and sweep all the corners that need dusting, put everything back in its rightful place. I want to shout, "NO! You're *not* sick," and have it be true.

I can't do any of that, though.

So instead, I run from the room, leaving behind Gram's tears and a half-finished glass of orange juice.

⁓

Alone in my room, I curl onto my side on the bed, trying to get my thoughts straight. I've been so sure that Gram is okay. I know her best—better than any doctor—and I haven't noticed her memory slipping. Now, though? I feel like my certainty's getting shot down skeet-style, shattering into pieces of broken clay.

I don't want to even consider the possibility, but . . . it could be those doctors in Cleveland didn't give Mama good news, after all.

Maybe Gram really is losing some of her memories. Because how could she not remember the week in the hospital after Papaw's heart attack, when we thought he'd pull through the bypass surgery but didn't? I was only six, but the memory of that waiting room is seared into my mind.

I tell myself that maybe it's *partly* true. Maybe Gram has a bit of Alzheimer's. But she's taking those pills, and pills make you better, don't they? Mama's comforting Gram right now, reminding her of what's real. Soon, Gram will be back to her usual self, and this won't happen again. She's taking the medicine. Nothing else is going to change.

All the same, worry keeps nibbling at me. Biting. *Chomping.* I need a distraction from it.

A real good one.

My eyes land on the folded-up paper on my nightstand—Sylvie's list of her top five rocker ladies. I grab the paper, open it up, and read over the newly familiar names:

In no particular order, listen to

Joan Jett
Stevie Nicks
Brittany Howard
Janis Joplin
Courtney Love

Sylvie wrote "no particular order," so I started by listening to Courtney Love on Monday night. Courtney was the lead singer of a band named Hole, and she screams *a lot* in her songs. It was so hard to make out the lyrics at first, I had to look them up online to be sure I got them right.

Courtney sure doesn't sound like Emmylou. I don't much care for how raspy her voice is, or the loud guitars and smashing drums. But I told Sylvie I'd give her music a fair listen. So I kept on listening, and actually? Some songs grew on me. There's one I particularly liked, named "Violet." It starts strummy and haunting, like a starlit dream. The screaming in the middle I could do without, but in the end, I'd say Courtney's talented.

Same goes for Brittany, Stevie, Janis, Joan, and their bands. I really like Joan's song "Bad Reputation," which is about girls doing whatever the heck they want, and I'm looking forward to telling Sylvie that there are plenty of Stevie Nicks songs that sound a whole lot like folk music.

I haven't forgotten about Sylvie's number, scrawled at the bottom of her list. I've thought about texting her my thoughts on the music, but every time I open my messages, I get nervous. Sylvie seems so cool, and I don't want to write something that will make her think I'm *not*. We got along great last class, and I want to keep it that way. If Sylvie starts thinking I'm not as sophisticated as her, maybe she'll regret giving me her number.

So I don't text Sylvie, but I do keep listening to her favorite music. I put "Violet" on repeat, listening again and again. Today,

I don't mind the screaming so much—maybe because I feel like screaming myself. It's an hour later when I put away my phone and slip out into the hall. Gram's bedroom door is shut, but not closed all the way, and I look in to see her tucked into bed, asleep.

This morning was bad, I tell myself, *but that was the worst of it. Gram's going to be okay from here on out.*

I slink farther down the hallway but stop when I hear Mama's sniffling. I can see her over the kitchen counter, though she can't see me. She's facing the window, back turned to the hall, and when she raises a hand to her face, I know she's crying.

Mama's so hard at times, with nothing but rules and stern tones for me. I've wondered before if her heart has toughened up over the years and isn't soft in the same places as mine and Gram's. If *that's* why she stopped loving music. As I watch her in the kitchen, though, I realize Mama's heart is still plenty soft. She just doesn't let me see.

17

IT'S ALMOST SIX o'clock when I show up at the Kendalls' house, ready to carpool to the New Hope lock-in.

"Cline!" Hollie calls from the top of the stairs. She's got a purple duffel bag slung over one shoulder, and it takes me a good second to figure out what's different about her. As she comes down the stairs, I put it together: she's wearing *makeup*. Not a whole lot—mascara on her lashes and pink lipstick. Still, it's new.

"What do you think?" she asks, when she reaches the base of the stairs. "Mom and I went to one of Mrs. Yune's makeup parties last week, and Mom says I can start wearing a little."

"It's great," I tell Hollie, getting a funny feeling. I think it's . . . well, jealousy. I wish Mama were as cool as Mrs. Kendall and let me wear makeup, but she's told me flat out that I can't use anything but lip gloss, *and* I can't get my ears pierced till I'm sixteen.

"I thought tonight would be a good mascara premiere, you

know?" Hollie says, bouncing up and down.

Her excitement's contagious. Maybe I'm not allowed to wear makeup, but I *am* going to my first ever lock-in. By the time we reach the church, I'm busting with enthusiasm. Tonight, the youth center's doors are wide open, and the place is flooded with light. Balloons and streamers hang from the ceiling, and a banner overhead reads *Shine Your Light*.

Hollie explained on the ride here that youth group is divided into middle and high school. She said that tonight's lock-in is just for middle schoolers, so I figured there wouldn't be too many kids. There are *lots* of people here, though. I recognize a couple of faces from Dunbar Middle, but no one I'm friends with, and I get nervous when I realize that Hollie is the only person here I really know. I wish Ava were here to crack a joke or Darlene and Kenzie were by my side, talking about their newest alien theory. But I tell myself to be brave. This is a chance for me to hang out with *new* friends: Livy, Emma, and Scott. Tonight's going to be great.

The kids in the youth center are talking over music I don't recognize but Hollie tells me is by a band named Hillsong. There are some adults walking around, wearing name tags and popping in on conversations. Most look pretty young, like they're in college. One of them—a lanky, white guy with a name tag that says *Tyler*—is tossing silver balloons into the crowd for kids to bounce around in the air like beach balls.

"That's our youth pastor," Hollie tells me, right as someone taps her shoulder. We both turn around to see that it's Emma.

"Hey, girls!" she says. "Did you hear there's going to be pizza?"

Hollie lets out a big, relieved sigh, as Emma tells me, "We were worried it'd be Lenny's Barbecue. They catered the last lock-in, and Livy found a *bone* in her pulled pork sandwich. Not to mention, it's sweet sauce–based, not vinegar, and anyone who's got taste knows that vinegar's the only way to— Oh, there are the others!"

Sure enough, Livy and Scott are headed our way through the crowd.

Hollie frowns in their direction. "Did they get a ride here together, or something?"

Emma shrugs. "Well, they both live over in Lakewood."

Aside from Hollie's neighborhood, Lakewood is the nicest subdivision in town. I pull my jacket close, feeling kind of grateful none of Hollie's friends have asked me where I live. I'm pretty sure my house is half the size of theirs, and it's *not* in some fancy neighborhood with its own tennis court and pool.

"Did you hear?" Scott asks us. "It's a pizza night."

"Uh, yeah." Emma laughs. "Already covered that."

Scott acts like he's offended. He's right about to say something when the music cuts out and a man's voice blares through the speakers.

"Welcome, welcome! Everyone take a seat."

That guy named Tyler stands on the stage, speaking into a

microphone as we shuffle down a row of seats. I'm planning on sitting next to Hollie, but then she skips ahead, past Livy, to sit between her and Scott. I take a seat beside Emma instead and try not to feel miffed. I'm sure Hollie didn't mean anything by it. Anyway, Emma's plenty nice. She whispers to me, "I'm really glad you could make it."

"All right, ladies and gentlemen!" Tyler shouts from the stage, like a game show announcer. "Are you ready for the main event?"

Kids around me cheer and clap their hands.

Youth group is different from what I expected. I thought it'd be mostly talk about God and the Bible, but so far it's more like a party. We play a whole bunch of games: shoe shuffle, circle untangle, cup stack relay, and naturally, chubby bunny. The pizza shows up piping hot, and we scarf it down along with gulps of Dr Pepper.

It's only after supper that we break for "the message," which is when Tyler gets back onstage and actually talks religion. He reads a long passage from a weird-named book in the Bible, and I feel a little uncomfortable when most of the folks around me—Hollie and Livy included—pull out Bibles they've brought along. Emma doesn't have one, though, and she nudges me midway through Tyler's talk, feigning a long yawn.

I giggle softly, but then I go back to paying attention to Tyler. I figure if I can make sense of his "message," I'll understand more about Christianity. Before, at my visits to Hollie's church, the pastor's sermons were *really* worth yawning over. Tyler's preaching is different, though. He tells stories about his college days in Georgia and brings up *The Avengers* and waves his hands around like he's an actor in a play. I don't exactly get why he keeps saying stuff like "the outside world" and "the lost." He makes it sound like anyone who isn't a Christian is wandering around like a zombie in the dark, and only folks who believe the Bible have "the light." That kind of freaks me out.

Then again . . . I get to thinking, what if Tyler is right about this stuff? What if I, Cline Alden, *have* been wandering around in the dark? Maybe it's better to be a Christian. Scott, Livy, and Emma all seem really happy, and I know Hollie is. Maybe they have something I don't.

But does Hollie think of *me* as "lost"? Does she think I'm not going to heaven or that I'm living my life the wrong way? I'd never considered that before, and she's never said as much. Maybe Hollie thinks differently than Tyler about all this "light" and "dark" stuff. Maybe she finds the message as boring as Emma does, and she's just reading along in her Bible 'cause that's what you're supposed to do.

I want to ask Hollie about all this, but I don't have chance, because right after the message ends, we get back to games. When one of the assistants, a girl named Chloe, announces that we're going to play Romans and Christians, the youth center bursts into cheers.

"What's that?" I whisper to Emma.

She replies, "You'll find out soon enough."

Turns out, Romans and Christians is just a church way of saying "capture the flag," with a little hide-and-seek thrown in. We're split into two groups, and the Christians are supposed to hide all over church, while the Romans look for them. If a Roman finds a Christian, they have to tag them and take them away to "prison." Meantime, some of the Christians try stealing the Romans' torch—a big, yellow flashlight. The game ends when either all the Christians are locked up or the Romans' torch is stolen and brought to the Christians' "secret church," here in the youth center.

Chloe tells us that no place in the church is off-limits, except for the administrative offices. Which is pretty cool. In a building this big? The hiding possibilities are endless. I guess that's why everyone's so pumped, and I get real excited when Hollie and I end up on the same team: Christians.

Scott, Livy, and Emma wind up on the Romans side, and before we split up in the church hallway, Scott tells us, "Better watch your backs, or we'll feed you to the lions!"

"Sheesh," I tell Hollie, as they walk away, "that's messed up."

Hollie shrugs. "It's what happened to Christians back then."

She looks disappointed, and I guess it's because our whole group couldn't stick together.

"Don't worry," I tell her. "We're gonna whoop their butts."

We join up with the rest of the Christians, where some folks are already hatching a plan to steal the Romans' torch. I'm listening in and about to raise my hand to volunteer as a spy, when Hollie tugs on my sleeve, gesturing like she wants to break off from the group.

I step away, following her down the dark hallway and into a big, empty room.

"Oh, whoa," I say, when we step inside. "Cool."

I can see now why Hollie wanted me to see this place. There's a grand piano and a drum set here. Stacks of sheet music sit on a nearby music stand, and the best sight of all is a couple of acoustic guitars in the corner.

"This is where the church choir practices," Hollie tells me. "Emma says the school uses it for band practice, too."

That's right. I'd forgotten about New Hope Christian School. It's weird to think about a church *also* being your school. No, thank you. I'm fine seeing the inside of DMS only five days a week.

"So, uh . . . do you wanna hide here?" I ask Hollie.

I'm looking around, but there aren't really any hiding places. It's mostly folding chairs and music stands, and a Roman would spot us under the piano first thing.

"Oh," Hollie says, like she's surprised. "Do you want to play that game?"

"I dunno," I say. "It seemed like fun."

Hollie blows out some air and says, "I guess. I liked it okay when I first started youth group, but it's gotten old. You know? It's more for the sixth graders."

I feel silly now for getting so excited. "Yeah, I guess it is."

"I thought we could just hang out," Hollie goes on, taking a seat on the piano bench.

I brighten up at that. Ever since Hollie's and my fight, things haven't felt completely back to normal. I've wanted more alone time with her, to be sure we're really okay. It's nice to think that Hollie wants that, too. I sit across from her on one of the folding chairs, crossing my legs atop the cold metal. I'm thinking of asking Hollie what she made of Tyler's message and how she feels about all that talk of the "outside world." Hollie speaks first, though.

"Cline," she says. "I don't know what to *do*."

Hollie doesn't sound like her usual self, and when I ask what's the matter, she drops her face in her hands. She doesn't talk for what feels like a whole minute. When she pulls her head up, her cheeks are flushed all over.

"How the heck do you tell someone that you like them? I mean, *like* them. Now's about the time I wish I had an older sister. There's got to be a method older girls have they're not telling us about."

I blink at Hollie. "You like someone?"

She buries her head again and lets out a muffled squeal.

Well, there it is. Now I know for sure that this is what Hollie was so upset about last week. She likes Trevor Larson, and now she's working up the nerve to tell me so.

That thought sends a pang straight through my heart. Hollie's being so honest. What about me, though? I haven't told her who *I* like.

My heart is zooming laps when I ask, "Do you wanna talk about it more?"

Hollie shakes her head, keeping her face hidden. That leaves me to think about her question: How the heck *do* you tell someone you like them?

I glance to the corner of the room, at those acoustic guitars. I'm remembering something Dr. Johnson said in class last week: "Music is what connects us to others."

Then I'm thinking of "Penny for Your Love."

What if I shared my song with Hollie?

That would mean taking a risk. A big one. That song is personal. It's about liking a girl, and this isn't the workshop, where I can show my music to people who don't know me that well. This is my *best friend*.

My legs feel funny as I get up and cross the room, picking up the nearest guitar. Playing my song could be a huge mistake. Or it could be the best thing I've ever done. 'Cause this is what friends are for, isn't it? If Hollie's had a tough time admitting who she likes, she'll feel so much better when she knows I've gone through something similar. We'll understand each other better, which means we won't get into pointless fights like the one we had last week.

It's more than that, too. I want to be as brave here in Paris as I've been in Lexington. I want to open up about what's been on my heart for what feels like *ages*. I've been asking myself lately if it's the right time to share this part of myself with Hollie. And tonight? It sure feels like it is.

I take a seat, guitar in hand, and pluck the strings one by one. The guitar's perfectly tuned, and I figure that's a sign.

"Here," I tell Hollie, who still won't look up. "I want to play you a song I wrote."

I don't think twice after that. I get to strumming, and I sing Hollie "Penny for Your Love."

I only mess up the notes once, on the bridge, but I sort myself back out. And even though my insides have started to shake, my voice stays steady. I sing each word of the chorus loud and clear:

I'd give a penny for your thoughts,
and I'd give a million for your love.
I know a heart's a thing that can't be bought,
But just know you're the girl I'm thinking of.

Hollie raises her head midway through, her eyes fixed on me till the song's end. As the last chord rings out in the room, I start to feel nervous. I study the guitar's pick guard, waiting for Hollie to say something. Anything at all.

"I don't get it," she finally says.

I look up quick, meeting Hollie's gaze, but I can't tell what's going on in her head.

"You said it's a song *you* wrote, right?" Hollie asks.

I chew my lip. "Yeah. It is."

"Then why'd you say, 'the *girl* I'm thinking of'?"

I try to swallow, but that's tough, since my throat feels dry as a Texas desert. Still, I decided to be brave, and I'm not stopping now.

"It *is* a girl I'm thinking of," I explain. "Not anyone in particular. But when I think about crushes? Like, the way the girls talk about boys at lunch. I . . . feel that way about girls."

There. It's done. I said it in a song first, and now I've said it for real.

The look on Hollie's face is changing. At first, she seems confused. Then she seems . . . worse than that. *Upset.*

"But that isn't . . ." Now Hollie's outright scowling at me, like I've done something wrong. "Wait. Do you have a crush on *me*?"

I shake my head. *No.* Hollie doesn't get it.

"The song isn't about you," I say, trying to get her to see. "It's just about being nervous in general and telling people how you feel. I thought you could relate. That it'd make you feel better?"

"How would I relate to *that*?" Hollie asks. "When I was talking about liking someone, I meant Scott. I want to ask him to the Harvest Dance, but I don't know how. That's not anything like getting a crush on a *girl*. I mean, that's not . . . Cline, that's not normal."

Like that, my race car heart smashes into my ribs—a head-on collision.

No, no, *no*. I stare at Hollie, stunned.

What did she just say?

Did she really say *that*?

Tears well in my eyes, and my gut starts to burn like it's filled with sizzling acid. I clench my fists and shake my head, as though doing that will get rid of the words ringing in my ears.

I thought Hollie would understand, see how we both have the same problem in different ways. I thought maybe she'd even give me a hug and tell me thanks for being brave. Instead, she's acting like *this*.

Even though I feel like shouting, I keep quiet, lips stitched. I've said—and sung—more than enough for tonight.

"GOT YOU, CHRISTIANS!"

The door to the music room flies open, and a flashlight beam shines on my face.

Two guys are standing there, looking smug as anything.

"If you didn't want to get caught," says one, "you shouldn't have been singing those hymns."

The other one laughs. "That's right! Now off to prison with you."

⁂

Hollie won't speak to me. Not even in "prison," which happens to be the church nursery. She turns her back on me whenever I get close, talking instead to some girl named Elodie. A few minutes after we're locked away, our only guard runs off to catch another Christian running by.

Elodie yells, "Prison break!", and all the other prisoners go running.

I don't follow Hollie, though. It's clear she doesn't want me around after what I told her. That's what I get for paying a penny for Hollie Kendall's thoughts.

Before the prison guard returns, I slip into the Elephant room. It's dark in here, but I know my way around. I take a seat in the corner, in one of the toddler-sized chairs, and eat straight from a carton of Goldfish.

I feel so small. I don't want to be here at New Hope anymore. I want to be back home, in my bed, with Emmylou singing me to sleep. I could call Mama and tell her I'm not feeling good. It's nearly midnight though, and I know she'll be exhausted from her shift. It wouldn't be right, waking her up to come fetch me. So I stay in the Elephant room until I hear a guy yelling down the hall, "Game's over! Report to the secret church!"

Only then do I make my way back to the youth center, where I find Hollie sitting with the others, like before. Now I get why she wanted to sit next to Scott so badly. Why she's wearing makeup. Why she cared about Scott riding here with Livy. She's been crushing hard on a boy. Not Trevor, like I thought before, but *Scott*.

And what did I do?

I went and told Hollie how I like girls.

I just can't believe she would tell me that I'm *not normal*. Is that what she really thinks? How could she? I'm the same Cline I was an hour ago as I am right now. How does me liking girls make me any different?

I get to thinking again of Tyler's message. What if Hollie *does* believe the stuff he said? All this time, has she thought that I'm different from her? I'm lost, while she's found? I'm in the dark, while she's got the light? And now I'm not normal, but she is.

I don't want to be near Hollie right now, but I don't want to sit next to strangers, either. So I squeeze in next to Emma just as Tyler announces that it's time for us to split up, boys and girls, into our different overnight rooms. The guys will be staying here, and the girls will be heading to a place called fellowship hall.

"Remember," Tyler tells us, "if girls are red and boys are blue, then there should be *no purple.*"

I make a face, since that's the silliest thing I ever heard, but I follow Emma as we file out of our row, waving good night to Scott, who's already talking to a group of guys in the row behind him. After we've gathered our overnight bags, Chloe and a few other girl leaders take us up a flight of stairs to fellowship hall—a gigantic room with a tall, slanted ceiling and big windows.

Girls start rolling out their sleeping bags on the carpeted floor, and I haven't even had the chance to set down my backpack when Hollie announces, "Livy and Emma, I want to sleep between you two."

I watch as they set up their makeshift beds, Hollie in the middle—away from me—and I feel like curling into a ball and crying my eyes out. Instead, I set up my things next to Emma and crawl into my sleeping bag. Chloe announces lights-out, and soon the room is cast in the blue-gray dimness of night.

Beside me, Emma's whispering excitedly to the others. She pokes my turned back and says, "Cline, don't you think so?"

I give a big yawn and say, "Sorry, I'm *really* tired."

Emma laughs and calls me a party pooper, but after that, I'm left alone.

Only then, in the dark, do I let the tears spill out and soak my pillow.

18

MY EYES ARE so scratchy when I wake, you'd think I'd been dozing on a hay bale. Morning light spills through the windows of fellowship hall, and girls are chattering all around me. At first, my heart feels light.

The lock-in, I remember. *You're at New Hope.*

Then the memories from late last night charge in:

Hollie in the music room.

"Penny for Your Love."

That's not normal.

And I want to go back to sleep for a week.

"All right, girls! The bathrooms are down the hall. Everyone needs to be dressed and ready for morning service by eight!"

I realize it was Chloe who woke me up. She's standing over our sleeping bags, looking cheerful in a plaid dress and boots, giving instructions to girls who run up to her with questions.

I rub sand from my eyes, looking cautiously to my left. Emma and Livy are there, giggling over something on Emma's phone.

"Good morning, sleepyhead," Emma tells me. "For someone who falls asleep so soon at parties, you'd think you'd be an early riser."

Emma's just having fun, but I'm in no mood for teasing. I feel worse than day-old roadkill.

"Where's Hollie?"

As I ask the question, I'm struck with a terrible thought: What if Hollie told the others about my song and what I said about liking girls?

If she did, though, Emma and Livy don't act like anything's different.

Livy says, "Bathroom," her eyes glued to the phone screen.

"Yeah," Emma adds. "She takes more time now that she's got a *beauty routine.*"

Chloe comes over to tell Emma and Livy to put away the phone and get ready. By the time the three of us reach the bathrooms, Hollie isn't there. Emma and Livy speculate that she headed down early to the youth center for what they're calling a prayer service.

I don't want to look ignorant, but eventually I break down and ask Emma what a prayer service is, exactly.

"It's nice," she tells me. "We eat breakfast, and then whoever has something to share—like a prayer request or praise for something good—gets up onstage and tells everyone."

When we get to the youth center, Hollie's there, sure enough. She's sitting in the front row, eating a bagel and talking to Scott.

Emma rolls her eyes. "So *that's* why she ditched us. She is so obsessed with him."

Livy's mouth twists at that, and it's clear to me that Hollie isn't the only one with a crush on Scott. For all I know, Emma has one, too. The only odd one out, it seems, is me.

We're shooed toward a table crammed with breakfast food, but I don't have an appetite. I spoon a few pieces of cantaloupe onto a plate and follow Emma and Livy into the row behind Hollie, since hers has already filled up.

Emma leans forward, between Hollie and Scott, and hisses, "Thanks for saving us seats, losers."

"You snooze, you lose," Scott says, grinning.

Hollie doesn't even turn around.

I stop mid-chew, the cantaloupe souring on my tongue. I can't believe that I thought Hollie would always have my back. Or that I've kept so many secrets she shared with me on her trampoline, but she can't accept this part of who I am.

I glance around the room. Would everyone else at New Hope feel the same way as Hollie, if they knew I liked girls? Would Emma, Livy, and Scott want to stop hanging out with me on Wednesday nights? What about Hollie's family? Are they the ones who told Hollie that people like me aren't normal? And Mrs. Yune—would she feel that way, too?

I try to quiet my thoughts when Tyler gets up onstage. He talks into the microphone about how, as a youth group, we're here to "hold each other accountable" and "lift up our brothers and sisters to the Lord." That's the point of the prayer service, he says: for people to share what's on their hearts.

Then he asks if anyone here has something they'd like to tell the group. A girl behind me raises her hand and, when Tyler calls on her, she walks up to the stage and takes the mic. She tells us that her aunt will be having back surgery on Friday, and she'd appreciate some prayers. Beside me, Livy nods along and writes down "Meghan's aunt" on a blank page in her Bible, under the title *Prayer Requests*.

Emma catches me looking at Livy's list and makes a face. I try smiling, but truth is, my heart's not in it. Meghan's request has got me thinking of Gram and how she cried over Papaw yesterday, thinking he was still alive. I guess that's the sort of thing that would call for a prayer request: "My Gram might have a little bit of Alzheimer's, and I want her new pills to make her better."

Then I'm thinking of Hollie, wondering for the billionth time what I can do to make everything right, like last night didn't happen, and Hollie didn't say what she did. How can I prove to her that I'm not different? I *am* normal. I can't change my liking girls, but I can make myself more like Hollie's friends here. I can keep working at the nursery. I can buy a Bible and write down prayer lists like Livy. I can even start going to church on Sunday mornings. I can share my *own* prayer request.

And just like that, my hand's shooting in the air. Tyler nods when he spots me.

"Yes!" he says, smiling real big. "What's your name?"

My body's buzzing all over and my knees feel rubbery as I stand.

"C-Cline," I stammer. "I'm . . . I'm Hollie's friend."

Because I sure feel like Hollie needs reminding.

"Would you like to come up here, Cline?" Tyler asks, motioning to the stage. "What's your prayer request?"

I gulp. Loudly. My prayer request. Right. If I share one of those, I can show Hollie how I'm a part of this youth group. Only, now that the moment is here and I'm standing up, every eye in the room glued on me, I can't speak.

Something's dawning on me: I don't *want* to share a prayer request. I don't want to tell all these folks about Gram. That's personal, and me sharing about her Alzheimer's? It wouldn't be because I believe God's going to make Gram better. It'd be to prove a point to Hollie.

I've kept an open mind about the whole church thing these past few weeks, wondering about what Hollie and her friends believe and if maybe I could believe that stuff, too. Now, though, I know there's one thing Hollie and I will *never* agree on. And I may not be a full-on godless woman like Mama and Gram, but I don't like Tyler's talk of "light" versus "dark." New Hope's building is nice, and so are plenty of people here, but that doesn't mean I should shift around who I am or what I think to try to belong. I can't do that.

I won't.

Only, I really wish I'd figured that out before I stood up in front of the whole youth group. Heat whooshes into my face, and my freckles feel liable to combust. It takes all the courage I've got to summon my voice again and say, "U-uh, actually, I've changed my mind."

I sit down fast, my butt hitting the chair like it's made of cast iron. Some folks around me snicker. Emma's looking at me, trying to catch my eye, but I can only stare at my hands, clenched into fists on my lap.

"Well, that's fine," Tyler says cheerily into the mic, as though I didn't just utterly humiliate myself. "Who else would like to share?"

I look up in time to see none other than Hollie raising her hand.

Like that, my thoughts spiral. Is something wrong with one of *Hollie's* grandparents?

What sort of prayer request could she have that I don't know about? Now, instead of being mortified, I'm downright mystified.

When Hollie reaches the stage, it's clear she's nervous. Maybe other people wouldn't notice the way she taps her left foot or grips the mic, but I do.

"Um," Hollie says into the microphone. "This isn't easy, but . . . it's been on my heart all night. And I know these prayer services are for us to share what the Holy Spirit stirs in us. So, uh . . ."

Hollie doesn't look out at the audience. Not at me. Her eyes are fixed on her tapping left foot.

"I have this friend," Hollie says, "and she told me recently that she struggles with same-sex attraction."

Dread clamps down on my body, chilling as ice-cold water.

Oh no. Hollie's prayer request is *me*.

"It's been difficult for me to process," Hollie goes on. "It's still so fresh. I guess I'm questioning why God gave her this burden, but I know his plan is perfect. If you all could just . . . keep this friend in your prayers. It could be she's able to fight through whatever she's feeling now and find a godly man in the future."

Hollie's not talking like Hollie anymore—at least, not the Hollie I know. She sounds like she's trying to be an adult, using words that aren't hers. Only they *are* her words, and they're hurting me worse than any stubbed toe or headache I've ever had. Worse, even, than the flu I got last Christmas.

I'm frozen to my seat, not sure I'll ever move again.

That's when Tyler steps up to the mic, whispering something to Hollie that I can't hear. She hands him the microphone but stays where she is onstage, eyes cast down.

"That's a very brave, personal thing Hollie's chosen to share," Tyler tells us. "And it's a tough topic for a lot of people these days. It's been several years now since the government chose to legalize same-sex marriage, and some people think that's a sign that being gay is okay. But as Bible-believing Christians, we have to stay true to what God's word says about homosexuality: it's not part of God's plan for us. It's the sign of a broken world. And we cannot support sinful behavior that grieves the heart of God. We *should* love everyone—including those who struggle with same-sex attraction, like Hollie's friend. Though we cannot support decisions they make to act on those sinful feelings, we can support *them*, encouraging them to walk with the Lord. I'm not saying that's an easy task. There's nothing easy about being a Christian. Think about the very Christians we were pretending to be last night: they were imprisoned for their beliefs. Murdered, thrown to lions. But through it all, those faithful to Christ remained a light in the darkness." Tyler points to the banner overhead. "They *shone their light*." He turns to Hollie, smiling. "And I know you will, too, Hollie."

Tyler keeps talking, but I don't hear what he says. There's a hollowness in my ears, where sound used to be. I watch Hollie leave the stage and approach her row. Right before she takes her seat, her eyes lock on mine, and there's only one word to describe what I see inside of them: *disappointment.*

Like that, my body unfreezes. I don't know what I'm doing. All I know is that I can't stay sitting here any longer. I hop up right in front of everyone, while Tyler's yammering on, and I stumble over Emma and Livy until I reach the end of our row. Then I'm running as fast as I can for the doors. I keep running through the hall, aware that there's music and singing coming from the big auditorium. It's Sunday morning, and everyone's in church.

Well, *not me.*

I shove out the church's front doors before a couple of men in suits can open them for me. I've made up my mind: I'm walking home. I'll do *anything* rather than stick around here.

As I'm headed across the church lawn, toward the street, I hear someone call my name.

It's not Hollie, I know that much. Not anyone my age. It's a grown woman's voice.

"Cline Alden! Hey!"

It only takes a second more to figure it out, and when I turn around, I know who to expect. She's headed toward me in blue checkered pants, the bangles on her wrist clanging: Mrs. Yune.

I don't want to talk to Mrs. Yune, pretending like nothing's wrong, playing the part of the responsible, Safe Sitter–trained nursery worker. Just the thought of that sends me into tears.

Mrs. Yune stops short as I start to sob.

"I—I'm sorry," I hiccup. "I'm sorry. I'm fine."

"Well, *no*. Clearly, you're not."

Mrs. Yune speaks in her no-nonsense voice—the one she uses to tell parents they *must* sign out their child. I'm feeling weak all over, and I figure there's no point in fighting. So I just nod and cry some more.

Mrs. Yune places her bangle-clad hand on my back. "Why don't you come into church with me, and we'll—"

"No!" I shout, stumbling away. "I'm not going back in there."

Then it comes out of me, jumbled up, like I'm dumping out a box of mixed-up puzzle pieces: "Hollie" and "lock-in" and "Tyler" and "same-sex" and "wrong."

Mrs. Yune nods encouragingly to everything I'm saying. I know I should keep my mouth shut, but I don't. Mrs. Yune's been nothing but kind, and I need kindness right now.

When I'm through rambling, she says, "Would you like me to drive you home?"

It's silly, but her asking that makes me burst into tears again.

Mrs. Yune says, "I'll take that as a yes."

I'm bleary-eyed and snot filled as Mrs. Yune leads me across the parking lot to a light pink sedan.

"Right," she says, opening the passenger door for me. "I've got to clear up something in the nursery real quick, but then I'll be back."

She hurries around to the driver side and cranks the engine on, so heat comes out the vents, warming me up. She's about to leave me there when a thought hits me smack in the face.

"My backpack!" I shout hoarsely.

Mrs. Yune pops back in the car. "What's that?"

"My backpack," I repeat, feeling downright miserable. "I left it in the youth center with my sleeping bag."

Mrs. Yune asks what my things look like, and after I tell her, she nods and slams the door shut, leaving me alone.

There's music playing from the speakers, and at first I think I'm hearing wrong. I guess I was expecting hymns or the stuff we heard in the youth center last night—Christian music, for a Sunday morning. That's not what's playing, though. It's Loretta Lynn, and she's singing one of her most famous numbers: "Blue Kentucky Girl." She tells the tale of a lovesick girl whose true love moved out to the big city and left her behind in Kentucky. The banjo melody sounds upbeat, but the words are filled with pining and sadness.

As the music plays, more terrible words come back to me:

Struggling with same-sex attraction.

Sinful behavior.

A broken world.

I cry harder, but as I do, these funny laughs spill out my mouth. 'Cause somehow, though she's years and miles away, Loretta seems to be singing straight at me—one blue Kentucky girl to another.

19

I DON'T SAY a word to Mrs. Yune on the drive home, outside of giving her my address.

The longer we drive, the more rotten I feel. I wish now that I hadn't told Mrs. Yune about the prayer service. What if she's just being nice to me because she thinks I'm "lost"? Is she going to fire me later, because she thinks my liking girls is *sinful*?

I'm embarrassed, but I'm other things, too. Angry. Hurt. Sad.

I want to feel all those things alone in my bedroom, with no one for company but Emmylou, Dolly, and Loretta.

I breathe a sigh of relief when we turn the corner onto my lane and my house comes into view. My seat belt's already off by the time Mrs. Yune stops the car.

"Cline."

It's been quiet so long, Mrs. Yune's voice booms through the air like a cannonball.

"I'm so sorry," she tells me. Her hand is still on the gearshift, nails painted magenta. "What happened in that youth group wasn't right."

I sniff, studying Mrs. Yune's manicure. "You mean, you don't agree with them?"

She's using her no-nonsense voice when she tells me, "I certainly don't."

"But . . ." I frown, trying to understand. "You go to the same church."

"That may be," says Mrs. Yune, "but Tyler Evans and I have *very* different ideas about what kind of God we believe in."

I'm more confused than ever. "Don't all Christians believe in the same God?"

Mrs. Yune shakes her head at me. "I wish I had an easy answer for that. What I can say is this: I believe in a God of love. A God who loves *everyone* and wants them to be exactly who they are."

I manage to look Mrs. Yune in the eye. "Then, you don't think me liking girls is . . . sinful behavior? Or the sign of a broken world?"

I don't think I've seen Mrs. Yune angry before. Stern, sure, when she's giving late parents a talking-to. Never the way she's looking now, though—like she wants to punch out the windows of her nice car.

"Those are horrendous assertions. Not to mention, completely incorrect. There's nothing wrong or broken about you, Cline, understand? You are perfect the way you are, no matter who you love."

"Okay," I mumble.

Mrs. Yune taps her nails on the gearshift, looking out at our tree-shaded lane. "I didn't always understand what I'm telling you now. The church I was raised in taught me to believe what your friend Hollie seems to."

"I didn't know she felt that way," I whisper. "If I had, I wouldn't have told her my secret."

"I had to grow up before I changed my mind," Mrs. Yune tells me. "It may be that Hollie has some mind changing to do yet. But that *doesn't* mean you have to let people treat you bad in the meantime. You can stand up for yourself, or walk away—whatever feels right to you."

I don't want to consider walking away from Hollie. Not after all these years of us being friends. But I'm not sure I can forgive her for what she's done.

I don't know what to say anymore. I want to tell Mrs. Yune thank you, but I'm too humiliated. She's basically my boss, and somehow I've ended up telling her what I haven't told even Mama or Gram: that I like girls.

I think Mrs. Yune understands my predicament, because next thing I know, she's out of the car and unloading my things. I get out and meet her in the driveway.

"Is your mother home?" she asks.

"She's at the Goldenrod. My gram is here, though."

Mrs. Yune nods. "Would you like me to tell her about this?"

I'm not sure which "her" Mrs. Yune means—Gram or

Mama—but, truth is, I don't want her telling either of them. From here on out, I'd like to keep my feelings to myself.

"I'd rather you didn't," I say, and Mrs. Yune nods again—serious and sharp.

She watches as I lug my things up the front porch and let myself in. I wave goodbye to Mrs. Yune, but she doesn't wave back. She's looking out on the road like she's in a trance, and it's not till after I've locked the door and kicked off my boots that I hear her drive off.

◦◦◦

No matter how many times I check my phone, there are no texts from Hollie. No "Are you okay, Cline?" or "How'd you get home?" Nothing. And I sure as heck don't feel like texting *her*.

How did I not know that Hollie felt the way she did? I thought I knew almost everything about my best friend. Now it's like I'm seeing a whole other side to her. Maybe she really does believe I'm in the dark, while she's got the light. But that kind of thinking doesn't make sense to me. Can't we *all* have the light? Why isn't it okay for us to be different? Was Hollie only my friend because she thought I was like her?

I think about how Hollie didn't introduce me to her church friends for two whole years, even when I went to Sunday morning services with her family. The first time I met them for myself was only when I started working at the nursery. And when I got invited to the church lock-in—it wasn't Hollie who suggested it. Nope. That was Livy.

I start to get an awful suspicion: maybe Hollie likes her church friends more than me. Maybe she's felt like she's been outgrowing me—this friend she's had since kindergarten. Maybe she thinks her newer friends are cooler. I know one thing for sure: she cared more about sharing her "prayer request" with her youth group friends than she did about me and my feelings. And then . . .

I wince, remembering this morning. *Then* I ran out of youth group. Leaving the way I did, right after what Hollie and Tyler said, probably made me look like the friend Hollie was talking about. What if everyone in youth group thinks I like girls now? What if that's made Hollie even *more* embarrassed to be my friend?

Everything makes sudden, perfect, *terrible* sense, and all I want to do is cry for days.

When Mama arrives home from the Goldenrod and asks how the lock-in went, I say fine, which is the biggest lie ever told west of Appalachia. I spend the rest of the night moping around the den, watching TV with Gram.

That's one good thing, at least: Gram is back to her old self. She doesn't look confused, and she doesn't cry. She doesn't call me by Mama's name or bring up Papaw. Instead, she laughs at old sitcoms as she works on a cross-stitch of a pumpkin patch, her fingers flying with precision. That means the pills *are* working.

Gram can tell I'm not in a good mood tonight. I feel her watching me from the corner of her eye, and she asks me more than once, "You all right, sweetie?" Every time I lie to her, I feel a little worse. I wish I could tell Gram about the lock-in. It's not that I think she'll judge me. I really think that, of all people, Gram would be okay with the fact that I like girls. It's just that I feel worn thin, like a Sunday dress that's been used every week for years straight. I'm too upset to talk about Hollie and too exhausted to even think about sharing my secret with someone else. I'm nearly too worn out to think, period.

I go to bed early, but I still sleep in till nine o'clock. Dunbar Middle is out for Indigenous Peoples' Day, and I'm real grateful there's no school. I'm not ready to see Hollie. Not today, and maybe not ever.

The Young Singer-Songwriter Workshop follows the university's calendar, though, which means I *do* have songwriting school tonight. I can't be slacking the rest of the day, so I throw off my covers and fetch my composition book and a pen.

At tonight's workshop, we'll be putting our collaborations to music, and I mean to get a head start. Not to mention, songwriting's a good distraction from all the stuff I don't want to think about. First, I fiddle around with the lyrics Sylvie and I came up with last week. They weren't exactly polished, and we agreed to work on them on our own. So I cross out and rearrange words till the chorus comes out right:

> I'd like to find serenity with you,
> Get lost in rambling thoughts
> And end up someplace new.

On the road of life, I don't care when we'll arrive,
Or who's behind the wheel,
If we're together when we drive.

It's a new song entirely when I'm through with it. I've replaced all that money talk from "Penny for Your Love" with big-time road trip imagery. All the same, I keep the line about having a girl on my mind, moving it from the old chorus to the new second verse:

I've been traveling miles,
Picking up scars and smiles,
Singing along to the radio,
Speeding up, never going slow.

Now when I sing those songs,
I wish you were here, riding along,
So you'd know that I'm singing with love,
And that you're the girl I'm thinking of.

At first, I thought that line was best suited to the chorus. Now, though, I see that it's right where it belongs. In fact, I think it means *more* for me to sing those words just once, before the chorus. After seven lines of buildup, they're the real lyrical punch. My gut twists when I read the full verse back, and I can't help thinking of Saturday night. But I'm not letting what Hollie said to me then change the heart of my song.

I remind myself what Mrs. Yune told me yesterday: *You are perfect the way you are.*

Thing is, I know I'm not perfect, but I've never thought that I'm not okay, either. I still don't. Hollie was wrong to call me *not normal*, just like Tyler was wrong to call my liking girls a sin. I don't feel guilty for writing songs about girls or having a crush on Brandi Carlile in seventh grade. That isn't why I've kept my feelings a secret. I kept my secret because I was afraid of folks treating me bad. I just never thought one of those folks would be my best friend.

I start feeling low, thinking like that, so I find another distraction: I write the spruced-up lyrics on a new page, without any of the chicken scratch. Then I get to thinking up a new title, since "Penny for Serenity" won't work anymore. I try "On the Road" and "Someplace New" and "Let's Get Lost Together," but nothing sticks. They all sound . . . bleh.

I've just about given up when I remember Sylvie's top-five list. She wouldn't have given me her number if she didn't want me to text, and Dr. Johnson said we were welcome to collaborate outside class. That doesn't keep me from nervously staring at my phone for a long, hard minute, though.

I know I shouldn't be so worried about Sylvie thinking I'm uncool. Dolly Parton sings about wearing a homemade coat of many colors to school, and *she* didn't care what the other kids thought. So I guess I'll make like Dolly and keep my chin held high.

I grab Sylvie's note from my dresser, tap in her number, and write a text:

Hey! It's Cline from the workshop. Do you

I stop. I don't need to write "from the workshop." How many Clines does Sylvie know?

Hey! It's Cline. Do you want to talk about music stuff?

I frown. Music *stuff*?

Hey! It's Cline. Do you want to talk about our song?

Welp. That's as good as it's going to get. Before I can second-guess myself again, I send the text.

I stare at my splintered phone screen, wondering if Sylvie will answer anytime soon. Maybe she doesn't have the day off like me, or maybe she *does* and she's spending it out with friends. Then I start thinking of Sylvie's friends and how they probably dress edgy and listen to rock like her, and—

My phone lights up, blasting a ringtone and cutting my thoughts short. I squint in disbelief at the name on the screen.

It's Sylvie.

She's calling me.

I am *not* prepared for this.

But I just texted her, so she knows I'm here. I have to pick up.

I steel myself and answer the phone.

"Hello?"

"Hey, Cline!" Sylvie's voice is bright and cheery. "My answer is *yes*."

"O-oh," I say. Then, "Wait. What was the question?"

"If I wanted to talk about our song."

"Oh, right," I say real fast, grimacing at myself in my bedroom mirror. *Duh, Cline.* "I . . . didn't think you'd call."

"You said *talk* about the song, didn't you?"

"I guess so," I say, starting to smile.

"Well, it took you long enough to text. Figured I'd catch you while I could."

Sylvie sounds like she's joking, but my stomach does a flip. Was she expecting me to text? Like, she *wanted* me to?

"It was a busy weekend," I tell her, trying to sound more chill, like I talk to random rocker girls on the phone all the time.

"Oh yeah?" Sylvie sounds intrigued. "I'm jealous. I spent mine eating hummus and watching Netflix. I didn't change out of my sweatpants for, like, two days."

That's a surprise. I figured Sylvie was the kind of girl who went to concerts and hung out at the movies. I didn't take her for the sweatpants at home type.

She adds, "I did have a migraine Saturday night, so that didn't help."

I wince. "That sucks."

"Yeah," Sylvie agrees.

"Are you feeling better?"

"Mostly. Sometimes I feel kind of . . . *off* afterward, if that makes sense."

"Like, when your stomach feels weird after you have food poisoning?"

"Not exactly. It's hard to explain to someone who doesn't get them. *Anyway*, I'm sure you're bored to tears, talking about my health problems."

I smile a little. Truth is, I haven't been bored at all.

"So, you have school off, too?" I ask.

"Yeah. I'm glad about that, at least."

"Me, too," I say, my mind flashing to Hollie.

"I've been working on this project for my earth science class," Sylvie says, "about climate change and eating a plant-based diet?"

"I thought you weren't a fan of school," I say.

"Really?" Sylvie sounds surprised. "Well, I sort of word-barfed on you the other night. I do that a lot. Mom says it's good to have passion, but you also have to have, like, clarity of speech. That's my Achilles' heel. I'm working on it."

"Sure," I say, thinking again of Hollie. "Sometimes I wish I'd said stuff differently, too."

"I'm fine with school," Sylvie explains. "It's more like, you know, *the system*. How adults try to make us all follow the same path and then, like, put us in tons of debt. But that's more a problem of, you know, the illusion of meritocracy. Also, the underfunding of the education system. Like, come on. Pay our teachers more, right?"

"R-right," I stammer. I'm still processing Sylvie's words, but I *think* I agree with everything she's said. I, for one, am all for paying teachers more money. I think of what my life would be like if Ms. Khatri hadn't told me about the YouTube channels where I could learn to play guitar for free. She deserves the best salary in the world.

"Anyway," Sylvie goes on, "my project is about school lunches and how government regulation here won't let cafeteria workers offer students plant-based milk, even if they're lactose intolerant, which plenty of people are. Not to mention, our school milk comes from cows that are treated *terribly*. I wanted to give everyone in class the chance to drink three different kinds of plant milks, to show what a good alternative they are, but then I found out I *can't* do that because of classroom food rules. And then I got my migraine, so I'm more behind, and the presentation is Wednesday. It's . . . a lot."

That *is* a lot, and I'm still hung up on the fact that there's such a thing as plant milk. That sure isn't something I've seen on the Goldenrod's menu.

"Cline?"

When Sylvie says my name, her voice is small.

"Yep, I'm here," I say.

"You . . . didn't need to hear all that," Sylvie mumbles. "Sorry."

Sylvie sounds embarrassed. About what, though?

"You don't need to say sorry," I tell her. "That *does* sound like a lot. I hope you can figure something out."

"Yeah." Sylvie still sounds uneasy. "So, how're you feeling about tonight?"

"Pretty good. I've been working on the lyrics and some chord ideas."

"Same. You know, I was thinking we could FaceTime. It'd be like workshop, only in our own homes."

"I like that idea." I find myself grinning, knowing that Sylvie's been thinking about us and our song.

"So, you want to now?" she asks.

"Want to what?"

"FaceTime?"

I whip around, facing myself in my dresser mirror like a possum caught dead in headlights. My hair's a frizzy mess, I'm wearing a sleep shirt with a big rip in the armpit, and I certainly don't have on my usual lip gloss. I really don't want Sylvie to see me like this.

"Uh . . ."

"Or not," Sylvie says quickly, like she's embarrassed again. "Just a suggestion."

"No, I like it!" I say, real quick. "But maybe we could do that another time?"

"Sure thing. I've got *your* number now, so you can count on it."

There's a sudden commotion on Sylvie's end, and when she speaks again it's to say, "Sorry. My sister's bugging me."

"Oh. Do you need to go?"

"Actually . . . I probably should," Sylvie says, sounding apologetic. "She's saying something about the toilet being clogged, and you never know with Maggie."

I'm sort of surprised to hear that Sylvie has a sister. It makes me want to know other things about her. Like what her house is like, and if she's always lived in Lexington, and if she thinks she'll be able to convince her parents to let her go to that rock camp in Nashville this year.

All the same, I think I've reached my limit of staying cool on the phone. So I keep my questions bottled up and tell Sylvie, "That's okay. We'll go over all this song stuff tonight. It was just . . . um, nice to say hi."

I make a face. Yep. It's high time I got off the phone.

"Well, hi," Sylvie says, sort of laughing. "And bye, too, I guess."

Sylvie hangs up, and I let out a giant breath. I don't *think* I came across all that weird. Even when I couldn't keep up with that stuff Sylvie was saying about school lunches, she didn't make me feel bad about it. And I didn't know someone like Sylvie could be embarrassed about . . . what? Talking too much? Like maybe she was worried about what *I* think. That possibility shoots a warm feeling through my chest—one that only gets warmer when I think about seeing Sylvie in person tonight.

20

"I KNOW WHAT the title should be."

It's the second half of workshop, and Sylvie and I are sitting alone in a music practice room. After break, Dr. Johnson took us up here, to the second floor of the Fine Arts Building, and assigned a room to each of us sixteen pairs.

"I've reserved these especially for you," she told us, "and I'll be checking in, room by room, for the next hour. Remember what we've learned today, and work with a spirit of *collaboration*."

For the first half of tonight's class, Dr. Johnson lectured on musical composition. She talked about some things I already knew, like tempo and chords and major and minor keys. There were plenty of things I hadn't heard of, though, like the "circle of fifths" and a bunch of Italian words: *forte, pianissimo, andante,* and *allegro*. When Dr. Johnson asked the class questions, folks around me raised their hands, ready with answers. Jamal explained what a coda is and Gia gave an example of syncopated time. Looking around the classroom, I got to feeling inferior again.

But then Dr. Johnson said something that put my mind at ease: "It's up to you how much technical theory you want to learn. Some musicians learn by the book, like me, and could ace a theory exam. But there have been successful musicians who couldn't read ledger lines to save their lives. You decide which approach works for you. If you can write songs, then *you can write songs*. Don't let anyone—myself included—intimidate that out of you."

So tonight, in our practice room, when Sylvie asked if I wanted to share what I'd been working on first, I found the courage to play our song to my chords, revised lyrics and all. And when I was through, Sylvie told me she knew what the title should be.

Now she says, "What do you think about 'Destination Unknown'?"

I try out the words in my head: *Destination Unknown.*

"It's perfect," I say.

Because it really is. It's a song title I'd definitely add to "Cline Kicks the World's Butt."

Sylvie has other suggestions, too. She wants to change some words in the verses—though still not the line about thinking of a girl—and she's got a way better idea for the bridge. It's only her last comment that sends me for a loop: "I'm not sure it sounds country enough."

"I made it so it *wouldn't* be," I say, laughing. "A little more Joan, a little less Emmylou."

Sylvie grins. "You listened to my list."

"You must've listened to mine, too."

Sylvie raises both hands, like I've caught her red-handed. "I *did* like some of the songs. Linda Ronstadt, especially. That woman can belt."

I tell Sylvie my own conclusions: I could do without so much screaming from Courtney Love, but I really liked Brittany Howard and the song she sings called "My Baby Is My Guitar." I tell her that Joan Jett's cover of "Crimson and Clover" got me dancing in my room and that I must've listened to Janis singing "Mercedes Benz" at least fifty times.

"That would explain the car metaphors," Sylvie says, winking. "A little subliminal Joplin never hurt anyone."

I laugh, even though I'm not exactly sure what "subliminal" means. I wonder if Sylvie knows bigger words than I do because her dad's a college professor. And maybe she has cooler clothes because her mom takes her shopping? Today, she's wearing a fringed velvet miniskirt and a button-up top, with a gold choker around her neck. I could *never* get away with a look like that, same as I wouldn't know what to do with lipstick or mascara.

That gets me to thinking of Hollie, and my stomach takes a dive. Maybe I can fake sick tomorrow, so I won't have to see her in school.

But no. That'd only be delaying the inevitable. I've got to face the music.

The music. *Ha.* I laugh aloud at my own bad joke.

"What?" Sylvie asks.

"Nothing," I say quickly. "You sure you don't want to play your own version for me?"

I learned today that Sylvie plays piano, not guitar. There's an upright piano in our practice room, but Sylvie hasn't touched the keys.

"Eh." She shrugs. "I messed around with some chords last week, but none of them sounded as good as yours. I'll just copy yours down, if you don't mind, and practice them at home."

If I don't mind. That's another joke. Here I was, nervous that Sylvie would hate my song. Turns out, we really are good collaborators.

"We could be the next Gram Parsons and Emmylou Harris," I tell her.

Sylvie arches a brow. "Or Lennon and McCartney."

"Who?"

Sylvie gapes at me. "I gotta make you another listening list, stat."

There's a knock on the door, and Dr. Johnson appears, stepping inside our room and asking to hear our song "in its current state."

Sylvie gestures at me. "Take it away, Cline."

I know she's only being nice, giving me the spotlight, but I freeze up, one hand stuck to the neck of my guitar. All that courage of mine from earlier? It's flown out the door. Playing for Sylvie was one thing, but Dr. Johnson is a *professor*—one who knows all the fancy Italian words. Not to mention, I'll be sharing my very personal lyrics. Sure, this time they're combined with Sylvie's words, but that doesn't make it any less of a big deal.

I swallow hard, not sure I'll be able to move, let alone play the right chords.

Sylvie must notice, 'cause she clears her throat and says, "It's called 'Destination Unknown.'"

She nods at me, like I've got this, and there's suddenly feeling back in my fingertips. I strum the first chord, then the next, and pretty soon I'm singing. When I reach the chorus, Sylvie surprises me by hopping in, singing harmony to my melody.

That's when it hits me that, up till now, I haven't heard Sylvie sing in her regular voice—no country or rock star impressions. And boy, can she *sing*. She doesn't try any fancy tricks, but her voice is rich and strong. There's not one off note, even though she's harmonizing on the spot. She sings the way she dresses: suave, with confidence.

Sylvie goes on to sing the second verse, as planned, and when we're through with the song, Dr. Johnson squints at the piano, like she's deep in thought.

"Well," she says, "you've got something really lovely here."

Relief rushes through me. Dr. Johnson liked our song. She thinks it's *lovely*, and she has plenty more to share, including a suggestion to help "tidy up" the bridge.

Dr. Johnson doesn't mention the line about thinking of a girl. I wonder if she even noticed. Or maybe she *did* and thinks it's just fine. Whatever the case, I feel like I'm on cloud nine. I've sung my own words, with my whole heart, for Dr. Johnson herself.

"I hope you'll consider auditioning," she tells us, before leaving the room.

"I wonder if she says that to *all* the pairs," Sylvie jokes.

I wonder, too. But I ask, "We really should do it, right?"

Sylvie nods, her face alight. "I'm still game if you are."

My insides whirl with excitement. Sylvie and I are making this happen. We're going to audition together next week with "Destination Unknown." I figure I can convince Delia to drive me one last time and come up with a story for my mama about hanging at Hollie's place. She doesn't know about our falling out. Actually, now that I think about it, Mama doesn't know much of anything about my life these days: Hollie, the workshop, my songwriting, my secret pact with Gram. . . . I can just add the audition to that list.

I'd be lying if I said I wasn't nervous about the audition. I want to show the world this side of me: Cline Alden, the *musician*. The Daylight Saving Bluegrass Festival could be my chance to do that. It could be, as Gram said, my big break. But now that I'm actually going to audition—not sometime in the future, but *next week*? Me playing onstage is less of a dream in my heart and more of a knot in my stomach.

All I can do is practice, though, which is what Sylvie and I do right up till the moment Dr. Johnson knocks on all the doors and dismisses us for the night. She reminds us that next Monday, our very last workshop, we'll be joined by *the* Marcia Hayes.

Around us, folks whisper excitedly, but I'm only watching Sylvie as we head downstairs. I guess I've been doing a lot of that tonight: noticing how the light catches on Sylvie's green-brown eyes, and how every so often she swoops her hand through her hair, sending it spilling over her shoulders and filling the room with the flowery scent of shampoo.

As she and I wait outside, dangling our legs off the stone wall, Sylvie looks up at the moon.

"Cline," she says, real soft—so soft I have to scoot closer to hear. "How'd you get brave enough to do this workshop on your own?"

My eyebrows shoot sky-high. Sylvie thinks I'm brave?

As I consider her question, I recall my performance of Emmylou in the Goldenrod kitchen on Labor Day. I remember listening to "Angel from Montgomery," wishing my dad could tell me what to do about the workshop. I think about the way the hymn "I'll Fly Away" flipped over in my head the Sunday I asked Mrs. Yune about the nursery job, and how "Cline Kicks the World's Butt" has been filling me with gumption these past few weeks.

"I guess it was the music," I say. "Does that make sense?"

"You mean, because you love music so much?"

"That," I agree, "but the music also inspired me, you know? I got to thinking about all those singers who came before me: Emmylou Harris and Bonnie Raitt and Wanda Jackson. They all found a way to make their own music, even when it wasn't easy."

"Yeah," says Sylvie. "I feel that way about Joan Jett. Did you know she was sixteen when she started her first band? And it was, like, a *big deal*."

Sylvie looks wistfully into the night sky and sighs. "I wish Nashville weren't so far away."

I scoot closer, even though I can hear Sylvie fine. "Because of that rock camp?" I ask.

Sylvie nods. "It's like my mom doesn't trust me. I know two weeks is a long time, and Nashville's three hours away, but I can handle it. Mom says maybe when I'm sixteen, but that's years from now. If I could convince her to let me go now, I'd work my butt off. I'd make the money. I'd give up, like, my phone and video games." Sylvie turns to me, eyes glistening like the moon's gotten caught inside them. "I'd do what you're doing, only . . . I can't sneak away to Nashville for two whole weeks. My parents would figure out pretty fast that something was up."

My chest squeezes tight, like a fist, as I figure something out: Sylvie and I? We're a lot alike. Sure, we've got different taste in music, but I know how Sylvie's feeling. We'd both give anything for our dreams. We don't care what the world says about being too young. Sylvie *gets* it. And I think I get her.

Just goes to show how rotten first impressions can be. I'm thinking about those awful three facts I came up with for Sylvie at our first class. Now, at last, I've got some good ones:

Sylvie's a top-notch singer *and* impressionist.

She's passionate about stuff like education and climate change.

And even though she seems like she'd be too cool for you, she'd never try to make you feel that way.

"I hope your parents change their mind," I tell Sylvie.

"Thanks," Sylvie says, shooting me a tiny smile.

As we go back to dangling our legs, I notice the little brown birthmark on her right knee, and I think to myself, *That's cute.* Because it just is.

"Did you figure out what you're going to do about your school project?" I ask.

Sylvie looks suddenly sly. "You mean, my '*Not* Milk' campaign?"

"Ooh, that's catchy."

"Thanks. So, at first I was taking a strictly scientific approach, you know? With the milk taste test. But now I'm thinking I can present my research in an *entertaining* way. So I called my friend Marie today to see if she'd do a skit with me, last minute, and she said she would, because she's big into theatre. In the skit, I'm going to play a queen, and she's going to play a king, and it's going to be all about how I want milk in my tea, but he wants oat creamer, and we have this whole royal falling out. Dad says it's a little out there but that it should still land. So, I'm thinking . . ."

Sylvie trails off, meeting my eyes.

"What're you smiling about?" she asks.

That's when I realize I *am* smiling. I hadn't noticed.

"I don't know," I say, but I make my best guess. "I just think it's cool when you get excited about stuff."

Sylvie's eyes flicker uncertainly. "You . . . don't think I talk too much? 'Cause, look, I *know* it's a problem."

I frown. "What's a problem?"

"Well, I get super passionate, or whatever, and talk a *lot*, and then people get bored."

I consider this. "Sometimes I don't know what you're talking about," I admit, "but I never get bored. You really care about things. That's not a problem. It's something I like about you."

Sylvie blinks at me.

"Not everyone feels that way. People made fun of me when I started middle school. This guy, Chase? He and friends used to call me Shrill Sylvie. Sometimes they still do."

I roll my eyes. "Well, they are clearly the worst."

"Yeah," Sylvie mutters, "they are."

"Anyway, I think the skit sounds great."

Sylvie nods. Then she raises one hand, as though she's holding an invisible teacup. She tips her chin dramatically before saying, in a regal British accent, "Thank you, my dear. It promises to be a smash."

"Well, cheerio to that, your highness," I say in a kind of *Mary Poppins* accent. It's bad—not at all like Sylvie's—but she doesn't seem to mind.

"I say, George," she tells me, after a fake sip of tea, "this oolong is most excellent. Whatever is your secret?"

I motion for Queen Sylvie to lean in closer. When she does, I whisper, "It's . . . *oat creamer.*"

Sylvie reels away from me, gasping in horror. In fact, she's

playing her part so well that she loses her balance and falls backward, right into the hedges.

I nearly bust my gut laughing as I help hoist her back on the
ledge.

"I wish you went to my school," says Sylvie, still huffing with
laughter. "You'd be great in the skit."

I give Sylvie a look. "I *wouldn't*. You're the one who does the
killer impressions."

That gets me thinking, though, that I wish I went to Sylvie's
school, too. Or that she went to mine. I feel a stab of sadness,
thinking about how our last class is next week. I've barely had
time to blink, and the workshop is almost over. When it is, will I
see Sylvie again?

I worry my lip, but Sylvie's still in the here and now.

"If my plan to become a rocker activist falls through," she tells
me, "I'll just audition for *Saturday Night Live*."

I've never seen an episode of *Saturday Night Live*, but if it's
anything like *The Porter Wagoner Show*, I'm sure Sylvie would be
a star. She and I go on talking, mostly about songwriting and
school, until her mom pulls up to the curb.

"Hang on!" Sylvie shouts to her, pulling a folded sheet of paper
from her pocket and handing it to me.

Then she runs to the SUV, waving goodbye.

Once she's gone, I open the paper to find that Sylvie's written
down a new list of music to listen to. This time, the list is made up
of songs. The first one is called "While My Guitar Gently Weeps,"

and I'm thinking how funny a title that is when my phone lights up with a text.

It's Sylvie.

I'm really glad we're partners, she writes.

Then, *Let's FaceTime practice soon, okay?*

I text right away, *Definitely.*

A few seconds later, Sylvie writes back, *AWESOME.*

I don't know how my heart got to beating so fast, but I think I like the feeling. A lot.

21

THE GOOD FEELING can't last forever, though. On Tuesday morning, school starts back up, and I'm nervous as all get-out waiting for my bus to arrive. Even with "Cline Kicks the World's Butt" playing in my ears, I feel like I might spew this morning's bagel.

Hollie will be on this bus. She still hasn't texted me, and I haven't texted her. It's been dead silence since Sunday, so I don't know what to expect. I've started worrying, though, about what she might say to our friends at DMS. If she would share my secret with a whole youth group, what would stop her from sharing it with Kenzie, Darlene, and Ava?

She wouldn't, though, I tell myself. She's not that kind of friend.

Of course, I didn't think Hollie was the kind of friend she turned out to be at the lock-in.

I'm about to hightail it on out of here, down the lane, and back to my house, when the school bus pulls up. My legs feel downright gelatinous, and my head's lighter than air, but somehow I manage to climb aboard, taking out my earbuds and scanning the seats for Hollie.

I'm thinking of what to say. Should I ask her about Sunday? Apologize for singing to her? Be angry and ask *her* to apologize instead?

Only, I find that Hollie's not in our usual seat. In fact, she's not on the bus, period. I stand there, dumbfounded, until Ms. Walker calls from the front, "Cline, pop a squat!"

I do as she says, sliding into the first open seat I find, next to a sixth-grade boy.

"Uh, hey," I tell him. "I'm Cline."

He stares at me like I'm Godzilla in the flesh, then looks out the window, scowling hard.

Welp. So much for that.

⌘

"When did Hollie tell you?" Kenzie asks breathlessly. She's run to catch up with me in the school hallway, tugging at my arm. "Have you had to keep it a secret for long?"

I stop my walking and stare at Kenzie. "Keep *what* a secret?"

Kenzie blinks at me. "That Hollie's not coming back to school."

On the bus ride here, I came up with lots of scenarios. Maybe Hollie got her mom to drive her to school. Or the Kendalls went on vacation, and Hollie forgot to tell me. Or Hollie's pulling the same stunt I considered—faking a stomach bug.

I didn't imagine *this*.

"What do you mean?" I ask Kenzie, as Ava joins us by my locker.

Kenzie gives me a funny look. "You didn't already know?"

Ava looks surprised, too. "Yeah, we figured she would've at least told *you*."

I shake my head, feeling unsteady, as Ava goes on to say, "She *transferred schools*. She's going to New Hope Christian now. Can you believe it?"

I can't.

Except, I can.

First period starts, forcing us to split up into our separate classrooms, and I'm left alone with my thoughts. As I watch Mr. Flores draw a parabola on the board, the awful suspicion I felt on Sunday gets stronger. Hollie *does* like her church friends more than me, so it only makes sense that she'd choose them over me, too—leaving DMS for New Hope Christian. But why would she leave so suddenly, with no warning?

At lunch, I learn from the girls that Hollie texted each of them yesterday with the news that her dad got a promotion at work, and he can afford New Hope's tuition now.

"It's plain weird," says Kenzie, picking at her canned pears. "I know she likes her church friends, or whatever, but you'd think she'd tell us she was thinking of switching."

"Maybe she was worried we'd get mad," suggests Ava.

"Too late for that," huffs Darlene. "We've been together since first grade. Now she's running off to her new friends? Like, bye forever, I guess."

"And she didn't tell you, Cline?" asks Ava. "Not even a hint?"

"Nothing," I say distantly.

I haven't spoken much through lunch, though I've felt the girls eyeing me. It's a known fact in our friend group that Hollie is closest with me. We were an unbreakable pair.

Or so I thought. But Hollie purposefully left me out of yesterday's text, which sure makes it seem like this whole thing is about *me*. Right after I tell her my secret, she up and decides to leave school. How could that be a coincidence?

I don't buy this stuff about her dad's promotion. Why wouldn't Hollie have mentioned it to me before? Then again, a voice inside me says, *I* didn't tell her about the Young Singer-Songwriter Workshop. I wasn't sure she'd understand. Did she think I wouldn't understand her wanting to change schools?

The rest of the day, my brain feels like a pan of scrambled eggs. Things were perfectly normal a week ago. How did they end up like this? Would Hollie really rather switch schools than ever face me again?

I ward off tears all afternoon, blotting the ones that come out with my turtleneck sleeve. On the bus ride home, I get off at Hollie's stop by accident. It's just habit. The bus drives off before I realize my mistake, and I'm left alone on the street. What should I do now? March up to the Kendalls' front door and knock?

Before today, I wasn't sure if I could forgive Hollie for what she did. All I knew was that I'd see her at school, and we'd *have* to talk it over. But now, Hollie's taken that chance away. She's decided, on her own, that we're simply not friends anymore.

That thought makes me want to cry again. Instead, I get out my phone and text Hollie: *Can we talk? Please?*

I shove the phone in my back pocket and walk on—not down Hollie's street but toward home. I haven't made it a full block when I get a text alert. I stop in my tracks, yanking the phone from my pocket; but I don't get a good grip and end up playing hot potato, nearly dropping it right there on the sidewalk.

All I can think is, *Hollie.* She's come to her senses. She realizes now how wrong she was. She's texting me back to let me know it's all better now, and she shouldn't have said those terrible things, and—

It's not Hollie.

I think I have a third verse to add to "Destination Unknown"?

I stare at the text from Sylvie as two more bubbles appear after it:

Or that might make it too long.

FaceTime me, and I'll play it for you!

My heart sinks way down low.

No, Sylvie, I think. *Not now.*

Because suddenly, it feels like everything's falling apart.

If things aren't right with Hollie, then they aren't right at New Hope. Maybe they haven't been, ever since Sunday. If folks at the church think I like girls, will they say I can't work there anymore? Mrs. Yune might feel differently, but, fact is, I don't *want* to work at New Hope if I'm going to be told by the likes of Tyler Evans that how I feel is the sign of a broken world.

Hollie's betrayal, New Hope, and all my secret keeping—it's just *too much*. A hard wind blows through my jacket, chilling my arms, and, like that, it becomes clear: I can't do this. Not any of it. Not anymore.

If I don't have that nursery job, how am I going to pay for the rest of the workshop? Even with the money I've earned, I'll still be over a hundred dollars short come Monday. I'd meant to do more haggling over that deadline. I was going to write a real persuasive letter to Jocelyn, send the money in my nightstand, and hope for the best. Now, though? The hope's cleaned out of me, and I'm too bone weary to come up with another three-box plan.

For all my planning, I didn't foresee *this*. Now, in the rust-colored afternoon light, my dream seems silly. Selfish, even. Gram could've spent her rainy-day money on actually useful things, like doctors' bills and her new medicine. Instead, I've spent it on this workshop, and for what? What's the point, if I can't pay for the rest? Keeping secrets from Mama is one thing, but Cline Alden's got a conscience about stealing, at least. It wouldn't be right to attend a workshop I can't pay for.

So I can't go. I can't show my face on UK's campus again. Not when there's an outstanding debt in my name.

No workshop, no audition, no *nothing* for me.

I remember last night, and how Dr. Johnson called Sylvie's and my song *lovely*, and how good Sylvie and I sounded when we harmonized. The Daylight Saving Bluegrass Festival preshow could've been the start of my musical career. Sylvie and I? We could have gone on making music together and becoming better friends.

But none of that's possible now.

This is the end of the line.

I trudge home, clutching my phone as tears fall fast down my cheeks. I'm thinking about a line Emmylou Harris sings in "Born to Run": "You don't get nothin' unless you take the breaks." All this time, I've been trying to beat the odds. Pushing ahead, running fast. Well, these right here are the breaks. The tough times. The unbeatable odds. I was born to run, like Emmylou. But now? I've fallen flat on my face.

∞

The ladies of country music have a load of sad stories to tell. I can near guarantee that if you pick up any old country album, half those songs will be tearjerkers—pretty melodies that fool you into thinking they're about something nice. If you listen close, though, you'll hear a real tale of woe. That sure is true of a song by Tanya Tucker called "Delta Dawn." It's got smooth harmonies and a chorus that sounds like a Sunday hymn, but the lyrics tell the sad story of an older woman named Delta Dawn, who roams the streets of Brownsville, Tennessee, grieving the no-good man who abandoned her in her youth.

It was Gram who told me that Tanya Tucker was only thirteen when she recorded her first album. Since then, I've considered her an inspiration. But now Tanya's story makes me feel as blue as the story of Delta Dawn. Fact is, I'm not Tanya. I'm Cline Louise Alden, and I'm stuck in Paris, Kentucky. Some big-shot Nashville songwriter could pen a real sad song about *me*.

I know it's not advisable to be feeling this morose, lying in bed on a Tuesday night. If Mama could see me now, she'd tell me to dry my eyes and start thinking practically. Crying never got a person anywhere. But I figure I'm allowed one single night to mourn a lifelong dream.

Tonight, I've come to terms with a hard truth. I've done the math, and if I split the workshop four ways, at seventy-five dollars apiece, that means I owe a whopping two-hundred and twenty-five dollars for the three classes I've already taken. That's ninety dollars more than I paid the first night, and *that's* sixty more than I currently possess.

Mama would be ashamed to know I've tarnished the Alden name like that. I can only imagine what she'd do if she found out my secret now, right as it's all going to pieces. I'd be grounded till next year, *and* I'd have nothing to show for it. So I guess it's a good thing Delia's not the kind to snitch. Mama will never know my secret. That's something to be grateful for, at least.

I call Mrs. Yune before it gets to be too late. On the second ring, she answers, "Yune residence! This is Edith Yune, Lily Rose beauty consultant."

Hearing Mrs. Yune's voice reminds me all over again that she gave me this job *and* rescued me from the lock-in *and* has been nothing but nice to me. And here I am, causing a heap of trouble. I can't bear to talk pleasantries, so I spit out the truth straightaway. I tell her that I've got to resign, and I'm unspeakably sorry for the inconvenience, and I can give back some of the money I've earned, so Mrs. Yune can offer more to a last minute worker tomorrow night.

Mrs. Yune won't hear it, though. "Take a breath," she tells me. "No one's angry, and there's no need to make a fuss."

"But you told me how shorthanded you were!" I just about wail. "Now I'm letting you down, and on one night's notice, too."

"Cline." Mrs. Yune sounds suddenly stern. "No more apologies out of you. Of course I'm saddened by the news. You've been a big help in that nursery, but I understand why you don't want to come back to the church. Matter of fact, I expected as much."

"You . . . did?"

I blink at a poster on my bedroom wall of Emmylou Harris playing guitar, illuminated by hazy orange stage lights.

Mrs. Yune says, "Do you remember what I told you on Sunday about standing up for yourself, or walking away—whichever felt right? I meant what I said. I hate that you had to go through what you did. And I think *you're* the best judge of what's right for you."

I feel like crying, but not for the reasons I thought I might when I first picked up the phone. Somehow, some way, Mrs. Yune truly understands my predicament. She's not blaming me at all.

After I've hung up, I stay sitting on my bed, studying my poster of Emmylou. I wish more people made me feel the way Mrs. Yune did: that I'm not in the wrong for being the way I am. Hollie, my own best friend, thinks my true self isn't normal.

And then there's Mama. She constantly makes me feel wrong for loving music as much as I do. It'd be so nice if I could walk down the hall and spill everything to her, knowing she'd listen without judging me. Only, the hallway feels more like a highway, Mama's room miles away from mine. I'm in so deep from lying to her, I don't know if I'll be able to have a real talk with Mama ever again.

I shut off my phone screen. Then I think better of it and turn off my phone altogether.

When I fall asleep, Tanya Tucker's still in my head, singing the sweet, sad chorus of "Delta Dawn."

22

Dear Jocelyn, or whoever else is in charge of money matters,

Here is thirty dollars toward what I owe for the Young Singer-Songwriter Workshop. I've decided not to attend the final class, since I can no longer afford it. I still owe you sixty dollars for the first three classes I took, and I intend to send that money as soon as I possibly can.

I hope you can understand the financial straits I've found myself in.

My sincerest apologies,
Cline Louise Alden

On the Wednesday afternoon bus ride home, I read over my letter, checking for spelling mistakes. I've been worthless at school, either thinking of how strange DMS feels without Hollie there *or* writing a million and one versions of my business letter. For this final draft, I added the thing about "financial straits." That's something Mama tells Hank Gilchrist at the pharmacy, and I think it helps my case.

The envelope is addressed. All I need now is a postage stamp from Mama's desk drawer at home. I figure since I'll be a few days early with the money, the workshop folks might forgive me for being tardy with the rest of what I owe. From here on out, I'm doing things the right way.

The right way sure doesn't feel good, though. I wanted to meet Marcia Hayes. I wanted to audition. I wanted the chance to be fully Cline for the world to see. All of that's gone. And the thought of letting down Sylvie? Of never seeing her again? It's got me torn up inside. So does the prospect of telling Gram the news. She's rooted for me from the beginning. She gave me her rainy-day fund. What's she going to say when I tell her that everything she's done for me has been pointless?

The bus drops me off at the end of my lane, and I walk home slow, crunching the fallen leaves in my path. I'm still a ways off from the house when I see something pink taped to our front door.

My heart takes wing like one of Stevie Nicks's white-winged doves.

Hollie, I think.

Maybe this is why she hasn't texted me back: she's been working on an old-fashioned letter instead. She's written out the reason for why she switched schools, and it *isn't* because she doesn't want to be around me.

When I reach the front porch, though, I can see it's not Hollie's handwriting on the envelope. My name's scrawled across the front, but the "i" in "Cline" is dotted normally—no star, the way Hollie dots hers. I'm not wholly disappointed, though. It is still a mysterious envelope with my name on it.

I open it right away, pulling out a pink and black zebra-striped card. As I do, something falls from the envelope, onto my bleached-white Keds.

I stare at the little green rectangles.

Money.

Twenty-dollar bills.

I pick them up and count: *nine* twenties, plus two tens still folded into the card.

Two hundred dollars.

My hands tremble as I open the card, and I look to the signature first, before any of the words.

Edith Yune.

Mrs. Yune was here. And she gave me two hundred bucks? Now I *have* to read what she's written.

Dear Cline,
Once upon a time, when I wasn't much older than

you, I was flat broke and trying to make my way in this town when a woman at my church gave me a stack of money to buy my very first Lily Rose selling kit. It meant the world to me, and I'm convinced it's what made me the woman I am today.

So that's what you've got on your hands. You can call it severance pay, or a token of gratitude for helping us out in a busy nursery season. Personally, I consider this something called paying it forward. I hope that one day, when you're successful at whatever you choose to do, you'll remember to pay it forward, too.

My best,
Edith Yune

I stare at the card and then the money. Card, money. Money, card.

Two hundred dollars. Money it'd take me over three months to make at the nursery. Money that could cover the rest of my workshop tuition, with sixty-five dollars to spare.

I've gone so long without breathing, I think my lungs might bust open. This money changes everything. Mrs. Yune paying it forward means more to me than she can ever know.

I open the front door, ready to holler to Gram that it's time for a dance party. But that's when I remember those big convictions I had, mere minutes ago, about doing the right thing.

I look again at the money in my hand.

Gram's rainy-day fund.

Two hundred dollars would *also* cover paying that back.

My buoyed hopes sink down again.

Haven't I learned my lesson? This money isn't for me and my dream. It'd be selfish to think that way. No. This is a chance for me to set things right.

I've been prepared to tell Gram the bad news. I need to stick to that plan, no matter how hard it hurts. I'll pay her back, and I'll send the rest of the money to the workshop, to pay my debt. I can spend the leftover money on guitar strings, if I'd like. Practical. Mama sure would be proud of that.

Not that she'll ever know.

With new resolve, I place one hundred dollars in my jeans pocket, fold the other bills in my hand, and head to the den, where Gram is listening to music on her old cassette player. I know who's singing. Of course I do. It's my namesake, Patsy Cline.

Gram pats the couch cushion beside her, and I join her, drawing my knees to my chest and listening along as Patsy sings "Walkin' After Midnight."

It's only when the song has ended, Patsy crooning the last "searching for me," that Gram pats my hand and says, "Land sakes, child. What's all that money?"

I have to act now, before I lose my nerve. I grab hold of Gram's hand and put the twenty-dollar bills in her creased palm.

"It's for you," I say. "I'm paying back your rainy-day fund." Then I breathe in deep, 'cause what I have to say next is the hardest part: "I'm quitting the workshop. It's complicated, but it's just not gonna work out."

The money rests in Gram's hand, but she doesn't grasp it. She's staring into the distance, eyes glazed over.

I get scared. Has she forgotten about the money she gave me? Is she going to cry about Papaw or call me by Mama's name?

But Gram doesn't do any of that. Quick as a whip, she grabs *my* hand, and she shoves the money back in my keeping.

"You listen here," she says, all business—sounding a lot like Mama, truth be told. "I said that money's for your music, and I stand by that."

I don't know when it started forming, but there's a giant lump in my throat.

"Gram," I plead. *"Take it."*

Gram shakes her head at me. "Do you mind explaining why you're quitting this workshop? Is the teaching no good?"

I shake my head.

"What about your music? The song you've been composing with that girl, Sylvie. Is *it* no good?"

"No," I mumble. "It's . . . actually great."

"So, what? You don't think driving to Lexington's worth your time? You're scared about that audition?"

"No," I say, miserably. "It's not any of that."

Gram arches a brow at me. "Then what, pray tell, is this big, complicated reason for quitting on your dream, Cline Louise?"

I sit in silence, picking at a hangnail. I can't give Gram a good answer without getting into a dozen topics I'd rather not talk about: the lock-in and Hollie switching schools and resigning from the nursery, and how I've had a revelation about my selfishness. How this whole plan of mine was harebrained and reckless, and how I've learned to take the breaks.

Gram doesn't know any of that, so she goes on, in her all-business tone: "It was real hard on me, Cline, to watch your mama give up the music that brought her joy as a girl. I don't want the same thing happening to you. Know why?"

"'Cause you're biased," I say flatly. "You think I'm a good musician because I'm your granddaughter."

Gram tuts, shaking her head at me. "I *do* think you're a great musician. And, yes, incidentally, we're related. But let me tell you something, Cline: I've worked with many musicians over the years. Roger and I saw them come and go in our shop. I watched them perform, listened to their records, broke bread with them. And I can tell you, without a doubt, that you've got as much grit as any of them. You haven't let anything stand in your way when it comes to this workshop, and I *know* it's been hard work. You've been sugarcoating things for me, so I won't worry, but I've seen the effort you've put in. You've got talent, Cline, there's no doubting that. But you've also got drive. *Gumption.* You have what it takes to live the life of an artist. Now, why on earth would you throw that away?"

I'm gaping at Gram. For all our *Porter Wagoner* nights, our shared suppers and dance parties and lazy Sundays, I've never heard her talk like this. It feels like an outright lecture. Only, I don't feel talked down to. I feel like I've been lifted up.

"You . . . don't think it's selfish, though?" I ask, finally saying what's been on my mind. "Spending all this money, just for my dream? You could spend your rainy-day fund on something practical. Like paying for your medicine, so Mama doesn't have to split your pills. Giving you back the money . . . it's the right thing to do."

"Says who?" says Gram. "It's not what's right in *my* books, and it's *my* money. Who're you to go telling me what I should do with it?"

I can't answer that. Gram's question hangs in the air, and the song on the cassette tape changes. The only sound left in the den is Patsy singing "The Wayward Wind."

Gram squeezes my hand—the one still holding the money. She nods toward the cassette player and says, "One day, Cline, that's gonna be you."

I feel strange inside, like I've never felt at once so sure and *unsure* of anything.

I only know that Gram believes in me.

She leans over and kisses me on the head.

"Now then," she says. "Bring my afternoon pills, would you?"

This time, I don't argue. Not about any of it. I go and fetch Gram's pillbox from the kitchen.

I'm staring at my phone and the three texts Sylvie sent me yesterday. I didn't respond to them then, because I didn't know what to say.

But it's funny the way life changes on you, switching feet faster than a two-step. The time that's passed between last night and right now feels more like a month than a day.

Now I have the money, and Gram's given me the pep talk I sorely needed.

She doesn't think I'm selfish for wanting to see this workshop through. She doesn't think it's foolish to audition for the festival. She hasn't once mentioned a million-to-one odds. Gram doesn't just think I *can* do this; she thinks I *should*.

I forgot, earlier, when I was moping about no one but Mrs. Yune believing in me, that Gram has believed in me from the beginning. And maybe all it takes is a couple of people to turn your bad breaks into big ones.

Things are still a mess with Hollie, and I still plan to never show my face at New Hope again. I'm still keeping secrets from Mama, and the odds remain stacked against me, but I'm two hundred dollars richer than I was this morning, thanks to Mrs. Yune, and I'm a whole lot more confident thanks to Gram.

My dream is back on.

First things first: I riffle through my backpack until I find the letter addressed to Jocelyn—the one still missing a stamp. I take out the money. Then I crumple up the letter. I'll be sending a different kind of letter, come tomorrow.

For now, though, I've got texts from Sylvie that require answering.

She asked me to FaceTime, so that requires me combing through my frizziest tangles and adding a fresh coat of Pretty in Peach lip gloss. Then I get to frowning at my shirt. I know it's perfectly clean and all, but it's just a plain green tee. So I head to my closet and pull out two other contenders: a baby blue sweater and a red turtleneck. I'm feeling brave, so I put on the turtleneck, and *then* I add my guitar charm necklace that Gram gave me two birthdays ago. It seems right for the occasion.

I check my reflection one final time, breathe in deep, and pull up Sylvie's number on my phone. I hit the FaceTime button.

The phone rings. Rings again.

Then, "Hello?"

Sylvie puffs after the word, like she's run to pick up the phone. Her image comes into focus, and even through the cracks on my screen, I see the pink in her cheeks. Her hair's done up in a braided ponytail, and she's wearing a black sequined shirt. Cool as always.

"Hey!" I say. "It's me."

Well, duh, Cline, I think, mortified. *She can see that.*

"Hey!" Sylvie smiles wide, her voice as bright as a major chord.

"Sorry it's taken me a while to call," I say.

I'm trying to think of how to explain, but Sylvie tells me, "No worries."

I let out a little sigh of relief. I don't know how I'd go about telling Sylvie that up until an hour ago, I was planning for the worst. Now, knowing how close I came to giving up everything? It's got me all the more fired up about "Destination Unknown."

"I've had time to think over that third verse," Sylvie tells me. "I've made some changes, and I thought . . . well, if it's not too weird, I could sing them to you and you tell me what you think?"

I press my lips together, trying not to look as excited as I feel. This is all so official, so *real*. We're collaborating together like true musicians.

"Singing what you've written isn't weird," I tell Sylvie. "We're singer-songwriters, aren't we?"

Sylvie laughs. "I guess we *are*."

She runs off camera to fetch her notebook. When she comes back, she sings through the lines she's been working on. We talk them over, and I make updates in my composition book. Then I grab my guitar, propping up my phone so I can play through chords as we talk.

Composing with Sylvie feels natural as anything. We pick out harmonies, fiddle with the bridge, and swap out a few words in the verses. Then we put everything back together, and soon our video call sounds as good as a studio recording: clear, strong, and pitch-perfect.

"I seriously can't wait to play this at the audition," Sylvie gushes when we're through.

I nod along, but I don't know what to say next. The audition isn't till next week, and it's clear that we've done all the work we can for tonight. Only, I don't want to say goodbye to Sylvie yet.

"Hey," I say, thinking back to the last time we talked. "Your presentation was today, right? How did it go?"

"Oh, 'Not Milk'?" Sylvie lifts her chin in a snooty fashion, and in her Queen Sylvie voice, she says, "Darling, it was marvelous."

I laugh as Sylvie drops her act and beams at the camera.

"My teacher loved it!" she says in her regular voice. "It sort of sucks, because it was only a class assignment, and it won't change our school's policies. I do think it's good that more folks know about the issue, but my classmates and I can't even vote, you know? Policymakers and adults need to hear this stuff. My dad suggested I write a letter to the editor of the Herald-Leader, but, like, do a lot of people read that anymore? Or I could start my own blog, but most people don't take thirteen-year-olds seriously. Then again, like I told you, the Greta Thunbergs of the world had to start somewhere."

"Y-yeah," I stammer. "I guess they did."

I wince at the way I sound: nervous and, honestly, boring. I love listening to Sylvie, but when it's my turn to talk, I can't think of anything smart to say. Sylvie's so cool and well-spoken and cute that I guess I get overwhelmed. All that confidence I feel when I'm singing turns shaky.

It's in this moment, as I notice just how shaky I am, that I figure out something. Something *big*. Something that's been right in front of me, obvious as the nose on my face. *Of course.*

I've got a crush on Sylvie Sharpe.

WHOA, says a loud voice in my head. *Slow down.*

Sylvie dresses like a rock star and sings like one, to boot. She makes me laugh, and she's real pretty and smart. I guess it only makes sense that I'd get a crush on her. I'm not sure I'd ever be able to *tell* her that, though. How could I even muster the courage to ask her if she likes girls? I guess I could do what I've done before and put it in a song. Maybe she'd get the hint. Or maybe . . .

My stomach drops to my feet. *Maybe* she'd react the same way Hollie did. I don't think I could stand it if that happened. The thought alone makes me want to sink into the floorboards of my room. Sure, Sylvie hasn't said anything about that line in our song, but maybe she's been meaning to. What if she wouldn't accept who I am? Or what if she accepts me, but she doesn't like me *that way*? Then I'll have stuck my foot in my mouth, and our musical partnership will be ruined.

Maybe, I think, falling for someone isn't all it's cracked up to be. Sure, there are nice love songs out there, but there are plenty of *sad* love songs, too—about the other person not loving you back or breaking your heart or leaving you all alone. Maybe I should try to ignore this crush. Maybe my time's best spent *writing* about love, not dabbling in it myself.

"Cline?" Sylvie says, and I realize we've both been quiet for way too long.

"Oh. Sorry." I force a smile. "Sort of spaced out." I realize how that sounds and add real quick, "I wasn't bored! I haven't had supper, is all. But I think it's great, what you're trying to do. Like . . . um, *really* great."

I want to bury my face in a pillow. Okay. So. Ignoring my crush is harder than I thought. I wonder if Sylvie can tell. Does she think I'm flirting? Is it written on my face, plain as day?

If so, Sylvie doesn't let on.

"I'm definitely not giving up on the cause," she tells me. "You don't get to be a rocker activist by sitting around."

I'm about to agree when I hear Mama pulling into the driveway. I glance to the window, downright shocked to find that the sun's gone down. Sylvie and I have been video chatting for over *two hours*.

My every nerve tenses as I hear Mama open and shut the car door. If she even caught a glimpse of Sylvie on my phone, I'd have to explain who Sylvie *is*, and all would be lost. I can't let that happen. Not now.

"Sorry, Sylvie," I say, hopping up from my bed to grab the phone. "My mama's back, I gotta go."

Sylvie nods solemnly; she understands my predicament. But thinking of my predicament reminds me of hers.

"Hey," I say, real low, as I hear Mama fitting her keys into the front door. "Maybe, if your parents see us play at the audition? Your mama might change her mind about rock camp. She'll get how much the music means to you."

Sylvie bites her lip, looking uncertain. "Yeah. Maybe."

"Music is medicine," I recite—Gram's treasured words. "I think it's strong enough to change minds, too."

Mama opens the door, calling out, "Cline! Help with the groceries, please!"

"Okay, *really* gotta go," I tell Sylvie.

She nods, her hazel eyes shining like sparkling suns. "See you at the workshop."

"You bet."

"And, Cline?"

"Yeah?" I say.

'Cause, truth is, I'd risk even Mama's temper for another second with Sylvie.

"Remember to bring your guitar."

"O-oh. Right," I say. "Um, see you then."

I hang up and run from my room, Sylvie's last words still ringing in my ears.

Bring my guitar. Sure.

The music, I remind myself. *Your song. The audition. Just keeping focusing on that.*

c∞೨

As I'm helping to unpack grocery bags in the kitchen, Mama asks why I'm smiling so big.

I shrug and say, "Just am."

Because these are my secrets to keep: the workshop and the audition; Sylvie and how I feel about her.

All the same, I feel a stab of guilt when I see that Mama's bought my favorite cereal—the expensive puffed chocolate kind. I see her eyeing me as I pull it from the bag.

"You like that one, right?" she asks, and it's funny the way Mama sounds. *Unsure.* Not like her usual all-business self.

"Yeah," I tell her. "I do."

Mama nods, looking pleased, and another guilty jab gets me right in the gut.

I try to ignore the pain. Sure, Mama bought me a cereal I like, but she won't help me out when it really counts. That's why, even now, she can't know the truth. I still have one more workshop and the big audition next week. I've got to keep my secrets safe till then.

As I finish unpacking, my thoughts wander back to my Face-Time with Sylvie, and a fluttery feeling springs up in my heart. That voice is back in my head, telling me to *calm down*. Sylvie and I are songwriting partners, that's all, and we've got a big audition number to work on.

If I focus on the music, I won't have time to think about that fluttery feeling. I won't have to stress over how Sylvie feels about *me*.

Back in my room, I pull out my guitar and start strumming every Emmylou cover I know.

One thing's for sure: it's less confusing to sing someone else's love songs than it is to think about your own crush.

23

BEFORE TONIGHT, I didn't think I was much of a Marcia Hayes fan.

Turns out, I am.

I'm at the very last class of the Young Singer-Songwriter Workshop. It's been my last day of picking up food early from the Goldenrod and skipping out on *Porter Wagoner* suppers with Gram. It'll be my last night of getting home after curfew. All I have left to worry about is the Daylight Saving Bluegrass Festival preshow audition this Saturday. Only five more days of keeping my secret from Mama. And if Sylvie and I are chosen to play at the preshow? Well, I'll cross that bridge when I come to it. I'd like to think Mama would see that as a sign I could cut it as a musician— one who plays actual shows, maybe one day for money. She'd see that . . . just as soon as she got over the fact that I've been sneaking off behind her back for a whole month.

By rights, I should be all nerves about the audition and

rehearsing with Sylvie tonight. Instead, I'm hanging on Marcia Hayes's every word. She began class by performing a couple of her songs, and then she told us what it's like living in Nashville and touring all over the world, how she got a record deal, and how it felt to attend the Grammys last February.

Marcia's decked out in white leather pants and a red jean jacket that stands out against her fair skin. There's a bandanna tied around her curly brown hair, and naturally, she's wearing yellow cowgirl boots—her signature look when she plays her hit song "Bootstraps."

I thought Marcia's songs were too "new country" for me. Like this, though—just her voice and an acoustic guitar? I get it. When Marcia sings, it's like the heating vents stop rattling and all thirty-something folks in this classroom simply stop *breathing*. Marcia's a darn good singer, that's plain as day. And "Bootstraps"? She wrote the lyrics and music on her own. I didn't know that before tonight.

Marcia finishes the song by repeating the first two lines of the first verse:

I'd like to be somebody's baby,
But not if that means they're making the rules.

Dr. Johnson's been a great teacher. She's taught me about Simon and Garfunkel, *abab* rhyme scheme, and what the word *crescendo* means. Hearing from Marcia is a whole other kind of learning, though. She talks about what a recording session is like and how folks in the industry have to "fight the man."

I'm disappointed when Dr. Johnson announces that Marcia has to leave at the break. Then again, Sylvie and I need the time to practice. After Marcia says goodbye, we decide not to waste our break on the bathroom or water fountain. We get straight to rehearsing in our practice room. I take out my guitar, fine-tuning each string, and I tell Sylvie my idea about singing the final chorus together, no harmony. She tells me that's a good plan, except we should still harmonize on the last line.

That's how it's gone between us since Wednesday night—throwing ideas back and forth by text. Turns out, Sylvie's suggestion for a third verse was genius. We've polished the bridge, too. Now we're playing it in a minor key to add what Sylvie calls a "haunting quality" to the song.

Sylvie's been practicing on her piano at home. Tonight, her hands glide over the keys, and when I tell her how good it sounds, she gives me a wink and says, in her Queen Sylvie voice, "Classically trained, darling."

It's only a wink and an accent, but my insides melt like cheese on a griddle. This whole trying to ignore my crush thing is *not* going well. Turns out, it's a lot harder to do when Sylvie's right in front of me. Today, she's wearing a bright green sweater dress, and when she leans close and asks me, confidentially, if she looks like a broccoli stalk, I laugh.

"You never look anything but cool."

I say it without thinking, 'cause it's true, but when Sylvie's eyes get big and her cheeks turn pink, I wonder if I've made a mistake.

I ask myself for what feels like the billionth time if Sylvie can tell how I feel. Or maybe this is like those times before, when she got embarrassed about talking too much, and she's only feeling self-conscious about her dress.

Whatever the case, Sylvie and I keep practicing, running through the final version of our song till we've memorized it inside and out. Dr. Johnson checks on us like she did last week, only this time she doesn't say a word when we're through. She just gives us two thumbs-up and leaves the room.

"Does that mean she thought it was extra great?" Sylvie whispers. "Or just extra *okay?*"

I don't have a clue. A memory comes to me, though. It's what Gram told me the night she insisted I keep her rainy-day money:

You've got as much grit as any of them.

Knowing that Gram believes in my determination? Well, that makes me *more* determined to play my heart out at the audition.

When it's twenty minutes till the end of class, Dr. Johnson calls us back down to the classroom. She tells us all what a privilege it's been to teach us this past month and how she hopes we'll carry these lessons with us into our future, whether that be as musicians or something else. Then she reminds us about the auditions this Saturday. As if we need reminding.

Once Dr. Johnson's dismissed class, I race up to her before anyone else and say, "Thanks for everything."

226

Dr. Johnson tells me, "Thank *you* for being here, Cline."

It's like she knows my coming to Lexington hasn't been a matter of simply showing up. It's been a choice, four weeks in a row, and this last week was the toughest choice yet.

I'm glad I chose right.

⚭

"There will be a keyboard, but they don't say if the keys are weighted."

"Does that make a big difference?" I ask Sylvie.

She gives me a look from beneath her choppy bangs. "Maybe not the same as between an acoustic and electric guitar, but *almost*."

"You're classically trained, though," I remind Sylvie. "You're gonna do fine on that keyboard, no matter what."

Sylvie and I are sitting in our usual spot, on the stone wall outside the Fine Arts Building. We're talking about the audition, 'cause how could we be discussing anything else? Auditions start at ten o'clock Saturday morning, and lucky for me, Mama's working the morning shift at the Goldenrod that day. Tonight, I asked Delia if she'd mind driving me into town one last time. I could tell she wasn't wild about the idea of giving up her Saturday morning, but in the end she said, "I got you into this. It's only fair."

Dr. Johnson has reserved practice rooms for those of us who want to run through our songs before the audition, so Sylvie and I have agreed to meet here at the Fine Arts Building an hour ahead of time. Once we've rehearsed, we'll head over to the Singletary Center, where the auditions are being held.

Thinking about Saturday sends shivers through my body, right down to my calloused fingertips. I'm still nervous about the audition—showing my whole self up onstage to judges and perfect strangers—but knowing I'll be with Sylvie eases my mind.

Sylvie and I have talked about names for our duo. I joked that we could be called "Country and Rock" and she suggested "Leris," as a tribute to both our hometowns. In the end, though, we decided it'd be best to stick to Sylvie and Cline.

"It's got a nice ring to it," Sylvie told me yesterday on the phone.

Tonight, when we're through talking auditions, I bring up the Beatles songs Sylvie asked me to listen to, and she tells me how the one called "A Day in the Life" is, in her opinion, the best song ever written.

"Other than 'Destination Unknown,'" I say, and we both laugh.

It's quiet for a moment before Sylvie says, "Cline?"

"Hmm?"

"That first song you wrote. 'Penny for Your Love'? Is it about someone in particular?"

I get a feeling like someone's vacuumed the innards out of me. My breathing turns shallow as I remember that night at New Hope. I played my song for Hollie, and then everything changed between us. The last time I talked to someone about this song, she straight up decided she never wanted to see me again. Even went

228

so far as changing schools.

Then again, I tell myself, Sylvie isn't Hollie. She's *Sylvie*. And she's not asking if I have a crush on *her*. All she's asking is if my song is about a real live someone.

So I tell her truthfully, "No. I've . . . never actually dated anyone. Or known someone who liked me that way."

I guess that's an embarrassing thing to admit, but somehow I don't feel weird telling Sylvie. Especially when she drops her gaze and says, "Same here."

I can't see how that's possible, though. Who wouldn't like Sylvie? There must be dozens of folks at her school who have a crush on her. She doesn't know about it, is all. Just like, hopefully, she doesn't know about *my* crush.

"It . . . *is* about a girl, though, right?" Sylvie asks, looking up.

Now I'm *really* breathing funny, staring at my bleach-white shoes.

"You don't have to say," she adds. "Sorry. If it's personal, that's fine."

"N-no," I say. "It's all right."

That's when I make my decision: I really am okay sharing this with Sylvie, even though it's scary. *Doubly* scary, because I like Sylvie so much. I'm downright terrified, but that won't keep me from answering.

If I've learned anything from the Young Singer-Songwriter Workshop, it's that bad things can happen when you take risks, but *good* things can happen, too.

Right now, I think telling Sylvie my secret is worth the risk. Maybe I'm not ready to say I like her, but I can share this much. I want to.

"It is about a girl," I say, meeting Sylvie's gaze. "Not anyone in particular. I just know it's about a girl."

Sylvie's lips stretch into a smile.

"Cool," she says. "I've written songs about girls, too. Guys and girls."

My lungs fill up with so much air, I think my ribs might break. "Really?"

"Yeah." Sylvie's got that look again, like she's unsure. "Mostly sad songs, though, about people not liking me back."

I shake my head, saying aloud what I only thought before: "I don't see how anyone could not like you."

Sylvie shakes her head back at me. "Don't see how they couldn't like *you*."

We're looking straight into each other's eyes, and I feel my heart beating hard in my ears. All those fears I had about telling my secret? They're gone now. I was brave, and this time, everything's turned out okay.

I just wish I were brave enough to say more. Because in this moment, it's clear: I can't keep ignoring my crush. Not with Sylvie this close.

Sylvie inches her fingers across the stone ledge, toward my hand. I inch my hand toward hers.

"Hey, Cline," she says, real soft. "Would you—?"

Bleeeeep.

I swear, we both jump a mile high. When we turn and look, Sylvie's mom is there in her SUV, Delia's truck parked behind her. I feel like someone's struck a match and lit up my whole body. How long have they been waiting there?

"Oh man," says Sylvie, laughing, as she hops off the wall.

I laugh, too, but it sounds wrong coming out. What just happened? What is *happening*?

"So, um, I'll see you Saturday at nine?" Sylvie asks, backing away.

"Saturday," I say, nodding till I feel my head's liable to fall off.

Then we run—me to Delia and Sylvie to her mom. I don't stop moving, don't look anywhere but straight ahead, until I'm in the truck and closing the passenger door with a loud slam.

"Whoa!" Delia shouts. "What were you running from, a bear?"

"N-nope." I laugh nervously. "No bears on campus today."

I don't feel like joking, though. My face feels flushed. My breathing is quick. I look in the rearview mirror, trying to catch a glimpse of Sylvie, but her mom is already driving off, passing us in a flash, the taillights of the SUV slipping into the night.

24

MY CHEEKS ARE hot as a furnace as I sit in Delia Jones's Chevy. I'm wondering what she saw of me and Sylvie. Could she see the way our hands were moving toward each other, like they might touch? Did it seem to her—like it sure seemed to me—that a second or two more, and Sylvie and I could've kissed?

My first kiss. What might *that* be like. My face explodes with more heat, and I can almost see the sparks showering down on the floorboard. Sylvie told me about the kind of love songs she writes. She was telling me that she likes girls, too. Wasn't she?

Could she also have been saying that she liked *me*?

My heart's beating fast with possibility but also with fear.

I keep glancing sidelong at Delia as she sings along to a pop song on the radio. I think I know how Delia feels about people being gay, thanks to the few times she's chewed out close-minded folks at the Goldenrod. After Hollie, though? I'm not sure. People can surprise you, and I don't know that I've got the guts for another surprise tonight.

But I have to say *something*.

"Hey, Delia?" I croak out.

She turns down the radio volume. "Yeah, Cline?"

"You're still okay with keeping this from my mama, aren't you? I mean . . . you don't think it's wrong?"

Delia squints ahead at Paris Pike.

"You deserve the chance to do what makes you happy," she finally says.

"And . . . if I had a secret to share, or . . . you found out something private about me, you wouldn't tell anyone about that either, right?"

Delia's quiet longer this time before she speaks.

"I think you should be able to choose who hears your story," she says. "What matters most to you. Your biggest dreams, and how you feel in your heart. If someone's not worthy of hearing that story, well . . . that's for you to decide. No one else."

I watch Delia closely—the way she grips the wheel and keeps her jaw tight. Gram says that, in this life, you'll get two kinds of advice: criticizing and empathizing. People will either talk down to you, acting like you should know better, *or* they'll tell it to you straight, coming alongside you as a friend. Well, it's clear that Delia's giving me the second kind of advice. I even get to wondering if she's talking from experience.

"When you were my age," I say, "did you ever feel you weren't like everyone else?"

Delia's jaw loosens at that. *"Every day,"* she says. "When I was in middle school? I didn't have friends. Not one."

"No way," I scoff.

Delia holds up one hand from the steering wheel. "Scout's honor. Old biddies at church would talk about how it was 'irresponsible parenting,' my stepmama allowing me to chop off and dye my hair, or how it wasn't 'appropriate' for me to not be wearing dresses to Sunday school. I didn't want to wear dresses, though."

Delia nods to the tattoo of a yellow rose on her arm. "I got this senior year of high school, and when I visited my mama over in Pikeville, she lost it. Going on about how it wasn't right, the way I presented myself. She said—now, I'm not lying—it was a sign of Satan's influence over me."

My eyes get big. *"Really?"*

"Some people are afraid of what's new to them," Delia replies. "They don't like being uncomfortable. Well, that's on them. I never hurt anyone, presenting myself the way I did. I did it because it felt like being fully, truly *me*. It took me a while to get there, though. I didn't find good friends until I started going to UK. Now I hang out with people who don't try to be what other folks say is 'normal' or 'right.' And you know what? It's great."

It sure sounds great.

I sigh. "I wish I could speed up time and be out of school already. Find friends like yours."

"Well, I don't know," says Delia. "Just because I didn't find them in high school doesn't mean you won't. Maybe you already have some of those friends, and you don't know it."

"Maybe," I say, thinking of Ava, Kenzie, and Darlene. I wonder what they'd say if I told them about my music, or even how I like girls. They're not Hollie, after all. They're Ava and Kenzie and Darlene, and they've got their own lives. Maybe it's not fair of me to assume they'd all react the way Hollie did.

Mostly, though, I'm thinking of Sylvie, wondering how she meant to finish that question of hers: *Would you . . .*

Want to change a lyric in verse two?

Want to hang out more?

Want to kiss?

I don't know what would've come next.

"Here's the last thing I'll say," Delia tells me, as we pass the Paris city limits sign. "It's tough, being uncomfortable, but it's part of life. You can run away from it, or you can embrace it—just acquaint yourself with that discomfort for a while. If you do, you might learn a thing or two. And you might find it's refreshing to be honest with yourself. Perfectly candid."

"Candid," I repeat. I smile as a new thought comes to me: "Candidly Cline."

"Some people want their world to be perfect," Delia says. "A pretty garden, with only the flowers they choose to plant. That's not real life, though. And personally? I find gardens boring compared to the great outdoors."

That gets me thinking about the lyrics to a song Gram and I both like: "I Beg Your Pardon (I Never Promised You a Rose Garden)" by Lynn Anderson. Lynn is sassy and confident as she tells her man that life's a mix of good and bad, and he'd better set his head straight if he thinks *she'll* be the exception.

"You're right," I tell Delia. "Gardens suck."

Delia doesn't reply. She's looking ahead with sudden worry on her face. That's when I spot three cars up the road, parked in front of my house. Mama's car is in the driveway, and by the looks of it, every single light in our house is on.

"Oh lord," Delia says under her breath, pulling up to the driveway. "Is that Luann?"

I don't say a thing. I can't. One second ago, there was a warm hope blooming in my chest. Now there's only cold, icy dread.

Mama is standing at the front door, pale as a ghost in the porch light, speaking to a handful of folks. Delia's right: Luann, owner of the Goldenrod, is standing on the porch with her husband, Vince. I've seen them plenty of times before. They tend to pop into the diner every so often for a chat, a staff meeting, or one of their family suppers. They're an older couple, both white with graying hair, and they're plenty nice, but I can't see why they're at my house.

They're not the only ones here from the Goldenrod, either. I see Bill, the head chef, and Martin, the busboy, and Polly, the new waitress Mama's been training. Mama is speaking with all of them, frantically waving her hands, when she sees me getting out of Brenda.

"CLINE. LOUISE. ALDEN," she bellows.

She walks right past Vince and Luann, stomping toward me across the lawn, and I swallow till I can't swallow anymore.

"Where is your grandmother?" she demands, looking me over. Then she and Delia lock eyes.

"I—I—I'm sorry, Judy," Delia sputters. "It's just me and Cline. We—"

Mama holds up a hand, meaning Delia should zip it right there.

"We'll talk later," she tells her, voice sharp as a razor.

I'm trying to look past Mama, at the house. I don't understand what's happening. Why is she home early? Why is everyone from the Goldenrod here?

As Delia zooms off in Brenda, Mama fixes her gaze back on me. I see now that there's fear in her eyes, and that's how I know that something is very wrong.

Mama tells me before I can bring myself to ask.

"It's Gram," she says. "She's gone missing."

25

I LEARN THE facts concerning Gram's disappearance soon enough. Mama got worried earlier tonight when she realized she'd left on her electric curlers. She called the house to ask me to unplug them, but of course I wasn't there. Gram didn't answer, either. No one did, all four times Mama called. That's why she left her shift at the Goldenrod, and that's how she discovered Gram was missing. She searched the house up and down, twice over, before finding the note Gram had left on the kitchen table, beneath the edge of her pillbox:

Going to find Roger. He isn't home yet.

After Mama found that note, she called up the diner to let them know what was going on. Luann was there for a supper with Vince, and she decided to close up shop and bring everyone out to help Mama.

Now she walks over to us with Vince and Bill.

"Listen, Judy," she says, placing a hand on Mama's shoulder. "We're going to head to Paris Cemetery and check it out."

Paris Cemetery is where Papaw is buried. I guess that's what Mama was telling the others when I showed up.

"There's no knowing where she's headed," Mama tells Luann, "but that's a start."

Meantime, Martin and Polly say they're going to drive around the Goldenrod, looking out for Gram in case she went searching for Mama there.

"I think I should stay near the house," Mama says. "I don't want to stray too far, in case she comes home. But there's no knowing how long she's been out. I just . . . I don't . . ."

That's when I realize that all this time, Mama's been trying not to cry. Luann squeezes her shoulder again and tells her, "We'll find her, hon."

Mama shakes her head. "You should be back at the diner, all of you. That's too much lost business. A whole three hours' worth."

Luann shakes her head right back. "This is what community's for," she says, real firm. "We take care of each other. Now how about you let us help you, huh?"

Mama doesn't say yes to that, but she doesn't say no, and Luann must figure that's good enough. She climbs into her Buick, along with Bill and Vince, and Martin and Polly get into their cars, too.

As everyone's driving off, I pick up Gram's note from where Mama set it on the porch table. A hundred arrows shoot through my heart, and I feel I might bleed forever.

Then Mama's gripping my hand. "You're coming with me, young lady," she orders, marching me to the Camry.

She takes my guitar case from me and lugs it into the back seat, while I buckle up in the front. I'm thinking frantically, running through all the places Gram could be, hoping so hard that she's all right and not hurt or in trouble. It's cold tonight, and dark—there's only the barest sliver of a moon.

Mama slams herself into the driver's seat and turns on the car, pulling out of the driveway.

"Keep your eyes peeled," she orders. "You look out that window, and you look hard."

It's quiet as Mama inches the car down the lane, and we peer into the darkness, looking between the oak trees along the old fence. There's no sign of Gram, so Mama turns right onto Cherry Lane, where the empty field around our house stops and a row of houses begins.

Mama's still looking out, past the Camry's high beams, when she tells me, "You have a world of explaining to do. Leaving your gram home alone at night. Running off to God knows where with that guitar of yours."

I'm glad I have an excuse to not be looking Mama in the face. I study every yard we pass, looking for Gram's familiar shape, telling my bleeding heart to keep it together.

"I can explain everything," I tell Mama meekly.

"Can you now? And can you explain *this*?"

Mama pulls something from the pocket of her waitressing uniform, holding it up for me to see: an empty envelope marked *Rainy-Day Fund*. She must have found it while searching the house for Gram. But Mama doesn't understand. She doesn't know anything about my big plan for the workshop, or how Gram and I were in cahoots.

I open my mouth, but Mama talks over me.

"I've never been so disappointed in all my life. What in God's name have you been doing while I've been at work? I've trusted you to care for your gram, and instead you're—what? Stealing? Sneaking off for some musical—"

Mama stops short, a stunned look on her face. She turns to me, real slow, bringing the car to a stop.

"This is about that workshop, isn't it? You've been . . . God help me, Cline. Is that what this is?"

Suddenly, it's too much to bear—my bleeding heart and my worry for Gram and all the half-truths I've been telling Mama for the past month.

"I'm s-s-sorry," I choke out. "I'm *sorry*."

Mama's eyes are like flint. "'Sorry' doesn't cut it, Cline. Stealing money, lying to me, running off to *Lexington*. You'd best believe there'll be consequences. You will pay back every cent of your gram's money, and—*no!*" Mama shouts over my attempt to protest. "I don't want to hear another word from you tonight, unless it's to tell me you see your gram on this road."

Mama's crying. The tears are inside her words, soaking them

to the bone. She throws the empty envelope onto the console and starts to drive again. Even though she's gripping the steering wheel tight as can be, her hands are shaking.

I want to explain everything, to get Mama to understand. That's the trouble, though: she's never understood me. If she had, I wouldn't have kept my secret from her. Mama gave up on music, and she as good as wanted me to do the same. She's never believed in my dream the way Gram has.

Gram.

This is all my fault. If I'd been home with Gram, watching our usual *Porter Wagoner*, this wouldn't be happening.

Gram left the house looking for Papaw, so that must mean she thinks he's alive again.

I thought Gram was doing better. I thought that breakfast when she cried about Papaw was the worst day she would have. I thought the new medicine was curing her. She hasn't been calling me Judy or forgetting where she's put things. Last Wednesday night, when she kissed my head and told me I'd be the next Patsy Cline, she was more like herself than ever.

So why would Gram go looking for Papaw now? Did she see something on television that made her think of him? It could be she heard the "Tennessee Waltz" and got to reminiscing on their very first date. Maybe she got sad, and I wasn't there to give her a hug and tell her everything would be okay.

I look out at the night. It's blustery outside, autumn wind bowing the branches of trees. Even with my parka on, I was chilly out there. I wonder if Gram thought to wear a coat.

The melody of the "Tennessee Waltz" dances through my head as I remember what Gram told me about that first date with Papaw: it was chilly that night, and he gave her his jacket to wear.

My breath hitches. Then I shout, "I know where she is!"

I expect Mama to tell me to quiet down. Instead, she looks me over and asks, "Where?"

So I tell her what I'm thinking, and I hope with all my heart that I'm right.

∽◦◦∼

I see Gram before Mama does. She's standing still as a statue in her faded pink pajamas. I unbuckle my seat belt and open my door as Mama stops the car.

"GRAM!" I call out, jumping onto the curb and running her way, across the park.

She stands on the bottom step of the gazebo in Magnolia Square. She only looks my way when I shout a second time, and when our eyes meet, hers are filled with confusion.

"Cline?" she asks.

That's good, I think. She at least knows who I am.

When I reach her, I throw my arms around her waist, only to find that Gram is freezing cold. Her arms are bare, and she's wearing house slippers for shoes. I hold her tight, wishing my body were a hot-water bottle—one that could warm her up till she's well again.

"I came here to find Roger." Gram pats my back as though

she's comforting *me*. "I thought . . . on our anniversary, we would always come here."

"Your anniversary's in May, Mother. It's October now."

I turn, and there's Mama, holding her coat out for Gram.

"Judy, why are you crying?"

Gram looks concerned, even as Mama wraps the coat around her shoulders. When Mama takes her hand and starts marching toward the car, Gram says, "Sweetie, it's all right. Everything's going to be fine."

Mama stops walking, and the streetlights wink off the damp edges of her face. Then she's turning around, and she's drawing me and Gram into a hug. She holds us close, and I can smell chicken-fried steak on Mama's apron and perfume on Gram's pajamas. I feel Mama's warm ribs and Gram's cold fingers, and for a moment it's simply the three of us, wrapped in each other's arms. Here we are, together. No secrets, no late-night shifts. No music to bring us close or pull us apart. It's just us Alden ladies—Cynthia, Judy, and Cline—holding each other in the dark.

"Come on, now," whispers Mama, after ages have passed. "Let's go home."

26

WHEN I WAKE, my toes are cold beneath my bedspread, and I have a sinking feeling that I've forgotten something big.

Remember, I tell myself.

Remember.

Then it comes back: Gram, Magnolia Square, and Mama's hug last night.

When we got back to the car, Mama called Luann and everyone else to let them know Gram was all right. Then she drove us home, and she sent me straight to bed. I stayed awake under the covers, listening as she helped Gram to a warm shower and tea. They spoke so low in Gram's room, I could only hear the talking, not the words.

I wonder if Gram is okay now. If she remembers Papaw's passing.

I hear someone rummaging in the kitchen, but when I check my clock I see it's early—six o'clock. I get out of bed and run down the hall.

"Gram?" I call. "You need help?"

Only, it's Mama in the kitchen, not Gram. She's at the counter, watching the coffee maker sputter fresh coffee into the pot.

I stop in my tracks, but it's too late to retreat. Mama knows I'm awake, and those consequences she mentioned last night? I know it's time to face them.

"Take a seat, Cline," Mama tells me, nodding to the kitchen table.

I take one, and she joins me.

"I had a talk with your gram last night," says Mama. "She told me she gave you the money in that envelope. Is that true?"

I fold my hands in my lap and nod.

Mama sighs so heavily, it sounds like an iron skillet's pressed down on her lungs.

"I'm sorry," she says, and I look up in surprise. "I shouldn't have accused you of stealing last night. I was upset. Though that's no excuse."

"I probably would've thought I'd stolen it, too, if I were you," I admit. "I mean, I *did* go to the workshop without telling you. You didn't know what to believe."

Mama touches a hand to her forehead, looking plain worn out. I wonder if she even slept last night.

"*Why*, Cline?" she asks me. "Why did you lie?"

Because you wouldn't believe in my dream, I want to say.

That won't help, though, so I say nothing at all.

"I suppose that *is* why you took on the job at New Hope?" she asks. "To pay for the rest of this workshop?"

I keep on keeping quiet, which I figure is as good as an answer.

"Understand," says Mama, "your silence isn't going to make my punishment less severe. I'll be discussing this matter with Delia, too."

That gets me talking. "It's not her fault!" I insist. "Don't be angry at Delia. She was only helping me out."

Mama lets out another sigh. "And I'm the villain in all this?"

I'm quiet again, trying to figure out what to say. Then I decide there's nothing left to do but be completely honest.

"I'm sorry I worried you last night," I say. "And I'm sorry I didn't tell you the truth. But . . . I'm not sorry I went to the workshop."

Mama parts her lips, looking stunned.

"I loved it there," I say with feeling. "It made me braver and a better musician, and—"

"*No.*" Mama raises her hands like she's had enough. "This is the problem. Being a better musician won't do anything for you. I've told you, music doesn't pay the bills. God knows they didn't for your grandmother. She can play you those old records and tell you to dream, but I'm the one taking care of *her.* Do you know why she moved in with us, after your papaw died?"

I frown at Mama. Of course I know why.

"To help out with me," I say. "Because you had to work more

hours at the Goldenrod."

Mama gives me a long, worn-out look. "No. It was because she and your papaw had no money. They didn't retire from running their shop in Asheville. It closed down because they were so deep in debt. When Papaw died, *I* had to pay those debts. I had to take in your gram and pay for her food and medicine. I know you idealize them, Cline. I did, too, growing up, and I still love your gram with all my heart. But *that* is why I have to work as much as I do. It's why Gram had to watch you so often when you were younger. She hasn't been taking care of me; it's the other way around. And I will be . . . I'll be *damned*, Cline, if I see you make the same mistakes my parents did. I'm telling you this because I love you: music will not pay your bills."

I didn't want to speak before, but now I can't. I never knew the things Mama's just told me. I guess because she kept them hidden. She didn't want me to think less of Gram and Papaw, maybe, and I don't. But I'm starting to understand a little better how Mama feels—and maybe why the music stopped moving her the way it did me and Gram.

I think about Mama's long shifts at the Goldenrod and all that time she spends haggling with folks on the phone, driving Gram to doctor appointments, and making sure Gram's taking the right medicine at the right time of day.

How could Mama be moved by music when she's barely got the time to listen to it?

Then it hits me, right smack in the face. My jaw drops, and my question comes out: "Is that why you sold the piano?"

Slowly, Mama nods. There are tears in her eyes, and I think back to the morning I saw her in here crying over Gram. I wonder how many times she's done that *without* me seeing.

All this time, I thought Mama had simply stopped caring. That she chose work over music, her piano, even my dream. Now I'm starting to see it wasn't like that at all. She never stopped caring about any of it. She just couldn't afford to anymore.

"Cline." Mama reaches across the table to take my hand. "I know I haven't been as involved in your life as a mother should, and I'm sorry for that. I'm going to make more of an effort, I promise you. I don't want you worrying about taking care of Gram, when that's my job. What happened last night wasn't your fault."

Mama must see the protest in my eyes, 'cause she squeezes my hand and shakes her head. "It *wasn't* your fault. Caring for Gram when I'm not home is a big responsibility. I shouldn't have put that on your shoulders."

"I want to help, though," I say.

I look at my hand—small in Mama's sinewy, calloused one. Then I say aloud what I'm seeing for the first time: "You already do so much for us."

Mama gives a tired smile, like her lips aren't strong enough to stretch too far upward. Then they falter and drop altogether.

"There *are* going to be consequences for your actions. Lying, leaving town . . . It'll be a while before we can rebuild the trust between us."

"I get it," I whisper. "I'm grounded, right?"

"You'll be going nowhere save school and home," Mama replies, in her all-business tone. "Not even the Goldenrod. I don't want you hanging around Delia until I've sorted things out with her. And no phone or internet for a month. At Thanksgiving, I'll reevaluate."

My heart's beating sharp, like a snare drum. I'll accept this punishment. I know it was wrong to lie to Mama, even though I felt I had to. So I'll do as she says. I'll stay grounded for a month. But there's one thing I *must* do before that.

"Mama," I say, "I have to go to Lexington this Saturday."

Mama's eyes narrow. "You don't 'have to' do anything."

I shake my head frantically. *No.* Mama doesn't see. The audition could be my big break, just like Gram said. I've worked so hard to get here. I nearly gave up on my dream already. I can't let it be taken away from me now.

"It's so, *so* important," I tell Mama. "It's an audition, and my friend Sylvie and I have been working on our song for weeks. If you—"

"Cline." Mama cuts me off. "Have you not listened to a word I've said?"

I grab the edge of the table, desperately trying to think of the magic words that will change Mama's mind. She can't do this to me. *I can't let down *Sylvie*.*

"I know you think it's impractical," I say fervently. "But this is . . . it's *everything*. Please, Mama. I'll stay grounded for two months, or three. You just have to let me go."

But even as I plead, I feel everything I've worked for slipping away. It's clear from the look on Mama's face: I can't argue her out of this. I can't fib my way around it, or sneak out without her knowing, like before.

Coffee gurgles out of the coffee maker, and my dream vanishes in the morning light.

⮔

Mama dismisses me from the kitchen table so I can get ready for school. She hasn't taken my phone away yet, but I have a feeling she will before I leave, so I've got to act fast.

I lock myself in the bathroom and text Sylvie:

Can't make the audition. Grounded. SO sorry.

I press send. I don't look over my words a second time, or let myself feel all the horrible feelings bubbling in my gut. I sit on the closed toilet lid, knees shaking as I wait for—no, *dread*—Sylvie's reply. The suspense is too much to take, so I get on Instagram.

The very first photo I see is of Hollie. She's wearing makeup and a flowy orange dress. She smiles into the camera, standing next to a boy I recognize: Scott. The location marker on the photo says *New Hope Church*, and Hollie's caption reads, *Love my new school & loved the autumn dance!*

Looks like Hollie's dreams are coming true, at least.

It hurts, seeing her on my screen. I can't believe it's only been a week since the lock-in, when it feels more like centuries. I've missed us hanging out after school, jumping on the trampoline, watching movies and quoting along. I even miss silly little things, like Hollie letting me borrow her scrunchies or yelling at Noah to leave us alone.

It seems like years have passed for Hollie, too. I didn't have a clue she'd be going to a dance at New Hope Christian, let alone with Scott. Normally, that'd be stuff she'd share with me. I'd tell her I was happy for her, and we'd eat ice cream to celebrate. But none of that's happening. Ever since she switched schools, Hollie might as well live on a different planet.

Not Sylvie, though. She's still my friend. Maybe she could be even *more* than that. Only, not if I've ruined everything.

I tap away from Hollie's photo and stare down my text thread with Sylvie.

Please, I beg silently. *Please text back. Tell me it's okay.*

There's a knock on the bathroom door. It's Mama, who's come to her senses and realized that I still have my phone. When she takes it from me, I realize she's taking away my music, too. No more "Cline Kicks the World's Butt."

Instead, as I head to school on this morning's bus, a new soundtrack plays in my head. I know the music and lyrics to this song by heart. It's Emmylou's "Beneath Still Waters"—the saddest song you ever did hear about a broken heart.

Today, that broken heart is mine.

I smile during lunch, while the girls talk about the Harvest Dance. I even pay attention in class, answering a question in social studies. I act like everything's normal, and I'm not worried sick about Gram or wondering how upset I've made Sylvie or thinking how I'll never get to play "Destination Unknown" for an audience.

I keep my eyes dry, and I playact that everything's fine.

But beneath still waters, I feel I could cry for years.

27

THIS NEW SOUNDTRACK of mine—the one in my head? It plays nonstop. When I wake up Friday morning, Patsy Cline's version of "Crazy" is on my mind, spinning a tale of broken hopes and shattered dreams. As I head to school, I hum Dolly Parton's "I Will Always Love You." As I eat lunch with the girls, eyeing the place where Hollie used to sit, I think of Kitty Wells's "You Don't Hear," and reflect on how, like Kitty, there's no one listening to what's on my mind.

I've been agonizing over Sylvie. I forgot to warn her that Mama was going to take away my phone, and no matter how hard I've begged, Mama won't give it back, even for one text. Sylvie's got to feel like I've abandoned her. I should've taken more time on that text. I could've worded it differently, or apologized more. No matter what I could've written, though, it wouldn't change the fact that I'm going back on my word.

I hope Sylvie will play a solo version of "Destination Unknown" for the audition. She's got a voice that sounds like a million bucks, and even if the audition keyboard doesn't have weighted keys, I know she'll impress the judges all on her own. I just wish I could be there to play alongside her. I wish I'd had the chance to show the world who Cline Alden is: a girl who loves music with her whole heart and who sings fearlessly.

On Monday, the future looked so bright. I was almost sure that Sylvie was going to hold my hand. I wish I knew how she planned to finish her question: *Hey, Cline. Would you—?*

Now Sylvie's question is a mystery that might never get solved. She was part of my life in Lexington, but I'm grounded in Paris. I would be Cinderella, mopping floors and washing windows till kingdom come. I'd give up my phone and the internet for a *year*. I'd do all that if it meant I could go to tomorrow's audition. But Mama has put her foot down, and there's no budging it. I can't outhaggle the woman who taught me haggling, and neither can Gram.

"I told you before, Judy," Gram said over supper on Tuesday, "I gave that money to Cline. She shouldn't be in trouble on my account."

Mama replied that lying to your mother is worth *plenty* of trouble.

That didn't stop Gram from making her case again the next morning or the next. Yesterday, I could tell, Mama was worn down thin. She snapped at Gram, "Now that's *enough*. Cline is my daughter, and I make the rules in this house."

Gram has been doing all right the past few days. The morning after we found her in Magnolia Square, she was back to her old self, as though nothing bad had happened. But here's something I've started to understand: Alzheimer's isn't like an ordinary disease, where you get sick for a while, and then you get better. Sometimes Gram seems sick, and other times she seems well. And though the pills she takes are supposed to help slow down her disease, there's no guarantee they will, or that Gram won't eventually lose her memories for good.

See, I can say it now: Gram really does have Alzheimer's. I've been stopping up my ears and shutting my eyes for so long, telling myself the doctors were wrong, or maybe they were right, but nothing would change. I didn't *want* things to change.

Monday night taught me a lesson, though. Things are gonna change, whether I want them to or not. I can't stop whatever's going to happen down the road. All I can do is hold on to the here and now, watching *Porter Wagoner* with Gram in the den and hoping she keeps laughing and singing along.

When I get home from school, Mama's car is in the driveway. That's unusual, seeing as how she works Fridays till six o'clock. My first thought is a bad one: Has Gram gone missing again? I fling open the front door, shouting, "Mama, what's wrong?"

She pokes her head out the kitchen doorway and shushes me. "Cline. Indoor voice."

Like that, I calm down. If Mama's scolding me, then all is right in the world.

Gram is in the den, snoring through a black-and-white rerun on TV. Mama's bustling about the kitchen, which is filled with the savory smell of biscuits and gravy.

"Why're you home early?" I ask Mama, pulling up a stool to the counter. "And why're you making *breakfast*?"

Mama looks up from stirring the gravy in a frying pan. "This is something your gram used to do when I was little," she tells me. "Every Friday, we'd have breakfast for supper—her, Papaw, and me."

I blink at Mama. She rarely talks about what it was like growing up or being my age. I think I've learned more about her in this past week than I have in the rest of my thirteen years.

"Anyway," Mama goes on, "I took off early today. I wanted the three of us to have a nice evening together."

I chew my bottom lip. Mama did tell me that she meant to be more present in my life. I guess that's what this is, and I'm not complaining: I'd take breakfast over leftovers any day. I just don't know how much of supper I can enjoy, knowing that tomorrow morning I'll miss out on the audition. No amount of buttery, ten-layer biscuits can make that better. No gravy can serve as a balm to the ache I feel over leaving Sylvie high and dry.

When Mama orders me to bring Gram to supper, I do as I'm told, nudging Gram awake in the La-Z-Boy and holding her hand as she gets to her feet. We take our seats at the kitchen table, which

Mama's piled high with food: a plate of piping hot biscuits, a big dish of gravy, and a bowl of chopped fruit. Mama serves Gram first, scooping apple and melon slices onto her plate.

Just then, there's a knock at the front door.

I wonder who'd come by the house at suppertime. Could be one of those kids from Cherry Lane, selling holiday wrapping paper for school. Mama glances up from the table, squints at the door, and goes back to dishing out fruit.

But whoever's at the door knocks again.

Mama sets down the serving spoon, muttering about people being "terribly inconsiderate" as she heads down the hall. I watch her, peering over the back of my chair as she opens the door.

There's a woman on the front porch, and it's a woman I *know*: Dr. Mireille Johnson.

I stare from my seat as Mama asks, "Can I help you?"

Dr. Johnson introduces herself, saying how she's my teacher at the Young Singer-Songwriter Workshop. Then she catches my eye from down the hall.

"Hello, Cline!" she calls.

I don't know what to do, so I sort of wave.

"Who's that?" Gram whispers across the table.

I turn to tell her, "My workshop teacher."

Gram's eyes get big and she shoos me from the table, saying, "Don't be rude, missy."

So I join Mama at the front door, where Dr. Johnson is telling her that she's found out I don't intend to audition tomorrow morning.

I just about fall over at that. Dr. Johnson knows. Did Sylvie tell her? Does that mean Sylvie's mad at me? Mad enough to tell on me to our teacher?

With her arms crossed tight, Mama tells Dr. Johnson, "Cline is grounded. She needs to learn there are consequences to her actions, and missing this audition tomorrow is one of those."

There's a stitch in Dr. Johnson's brow as she says, "I respect that. But the reason I drove out all this way is because I think your daughter has real talent. I don't give preferential treatment in my workshop. I try not to, anyway. However, in confidence, I can share that I thought your daughter and Miss Sharpe were two of the most promising musicians in my class. And that includes a good many high school seniors."

I'm not sure how much longer I can stand on my own two feet. Dr. Johnson is here, at my house, saying I'm *promising*? Somebody pinch me.

"I don't know the circumstances surrounding Cline's grounding," Dr. Johnson goes on. "Of course, as her parent, you must do as you see fit. I'm only asking that you reconsider. Opportunities like this don't come around often, and I think what your daughter and Miss Sharpe have is very special. They're not only good musicians in their own right; they make an excellent team."

Mama's arms stay crossed, but when she speaks again, she sounds less severe. "Who's this . . . *Miss Sharpe* you keep mentioning?"

Dr. Johnson looks surprised. "Cline hasn't told you about Sylvie?"

Mama's face hardens. "There's a lot Cline hasn't told me apparently."

"I see." Dr. Johnson glances at me, which makes me wish I were invisible. Now that she knows I'm a lying sneak, maybe *she's* going to reconsider.

Dr. Johnson keeps on, though. "Miss Sharpe—Sylvie—is Cline's age. They've been collaborating on a song the last three weeks and were planning to perform tomorrow for the audition."

I told Mama all this on Tuesday, but Dr. Johnson saying so seems to have a different effect. Mama's arms loosen and drop to her sides. She studies Dr. Johnson and then looks at me, shaking her head like she's disappointed. But something else, too . . .

"I suppose I see your point," Mama tells Dr. Johnson. "It doesn't seem fair that this other girl should suffer on account of Cline's poor decisions. She shouldn't lose her partner last minute—especially if she needs one to audition."

Dr. Johnson nods encouragingly. "I do think Sylvie's performance would suffer. She's a talented musician and could certainly carry the piece on her own, but it's the girls' harmonies that give their number that extra oomph. I really do think that, together, they stand a chance of getting a spot in the preshow."

"And this is for some festival?" asks Mama, looking suspicious.

"A bluegrass festival, yes. It'll be held in Lexington this March."

Mama seems to be thinking hard, and I wonder if she's deciding whether or not I'll still be grounded in five months' time. I don't make a peep. I stand there, watching Mama, hoping against hope.

At last, she says, "Fine. I'll allow Cline to go. For this Sylvie girl."

I think I've died and gone to heaven. I'm feeling woozy when Mama adds, "But I've got work tomorrow. There's no way I can—"

"Delia will drive me!" I cut in. "She already agreed."

Mama's face darkens, and I'm sure I've made a huge mistake. Delia must've been in a heap of trouble with Mama at the diner this week. I hope, after all that, she'll still consider driving me into the city. I think she will if she knows she's got Mama's permission this time.

Mama's quiet for a while, and I'm pretty sure she's trying not to lose her temper in front of a perfect stranger. It takes her a moment, but she ends up smiling politely at Dr. Johnson and saying, "That settles it, then."

She asks Dr. Johnson, "Would you care for tea or some food? You did drive all this way."

Even now, Mama hasn't forgotten her manners. Dr. Johnson waves her off, though, saying she needs to get going but thanking Mama again for her time. We watch from the doorway as Dr. Johnson gets in her sedan, and once she's driven off, Mama turns to face me.

"Mama—" I say, but she holds up a hand.

"I'm doing this for that girl," she says, real firm. "I'll be the one to call Delia and be sure your ride is arranged."

I nod. I'll go along with anything Mama says. *Anything*, so long as I don't break this spell. I do have to ask a question, though. When we're back in the kitchen, I say, "Can I call Sylvie? She needs to know."

Mama's eyes burn like forest fires, and at first, I think she's gonna say no. But then she walks to the kitchen cabinet over the fridge and, standing on her toes, pulls something out: my phone.

"*One* call," she says. "And you make it right here, in front of me."

So that's what I do. I don't stop to read any of the thirteen missed texts on my phone. I'm too afraid of which ones are from Sylvie and what they might say. Instead, I open my contacts, punch Sylvie's name, and hold my breath.

The phone rings. And rings. And *rings*.

I get scared, thinking that Sylvie won't answer, and my one chance will be over.

But then . . .

"Hello?"

I exhale.

"Sylvie?" I say. "It's me, Cline."

I glance nervously at Gram, who's chewing a biscuit at the kitchen table. She gives me a big thumbs-up.

"Yeah. What do you want?"

Sylvie's voice is thin. *Angry*, I think. She sounds a lot like the

Sylvie I met at the first workshop.

"Do you . . . have a migraine right now?" I ask.

"Nope."

Oh. Then she's just mad at me. The thought stings, and I get this funny feeling in my wrists, like I'm liable to drop the phone.

"I'm so sorry about bailing," I say, hoping Sylvie can hear my sincerity. "My mama grounded me, like I said, and I couldn't use my phone."

"How'd you get it back, then?"

"Well, that's the thing. I'm using it now with special permission, 'cause Dr. Johnson came by, and she . . . uh, well, Mama's agreed to let me audition with you, after all."

Sylvie's quiet. Too quiet for too long.

"I mean, if you'd still want to do that," I mutter.

Sylvie says, "That hurt a lot, you know. Getting that text? I've been miserable all week."

"I'm *real* sorry," I say, gripping the phone close to my ear. "It's my fault, what happened. I never meant to hurt your feelings or mess with your chances for the audition."

Sylvie's quiet some more before she says, "You really can make it?"

"Nine o'clock," I tell her. "Like we agreed before. I'll be there."

"Promise?"

"I do."

"Then it's a plan." Sylvie's voice is fuller now. I think I can almost hear a smile in it.

"It's a plan," I repeat.

I look over to see Mama scowling at me, over the counter. "Uh. Sylvie? My time's up. I gotta go."

"All right. But . . . *hey*."

"Hey?" I say—or squeak, more like.

"I think we've got a shot at this."

I know then that Sylvie did call Dr. Johnson. Not because she was angry, but because she's a good friend. And maybe?

Maybe something more.

"Thank you for believing in us," I say.

This time I *know* I hear a smile when Sylvie says, "That's what collaborators are for."

28

MAMA WEARS A faraway look the rest of supper. She only eats half the biscuits on her plate before excusing herself to her bedroom. It's almost like she's . . . *embarrassed*. Maybe because, in the end, she got outhaggled by Dr. Mireille Johnson.

Dr. Johnson saved the day. Sylvie, too. And now? I've got an audition to attend.

I barely get a wink of sleep. "Destination Unknown" plays in my head all night. I hum the melody, whisper the lyrics, and tap the chords into my pillow. It's early when I rise, but with my nerves tingling and brain whirring, I know I won't be able to fall asleep again. Instead, I do something useful and run through "Destination Unknown" on my guitar. I sing and strum softly, so as not to wake up anyone, and I only stop when I hear Mama's door open.

I listen as she heads down the hall and out the front door. Then I scurry to my window, watching as she pulls the Camry out of the driveway. She's gone off to work at the Goldenrod without so much as a "Good luck, Cline!"

Maybe she thought I was sleeping and didn't want to wake me. Or maybe she still doesn't want me to audition today.

For this Sylvie girl.

That's why Mama gave in to Dr. Johnson: not for my sake, but for Sylvie's—a girl she's never met. Thinking that way sends my stomach on a loop the loop. I can't focus on Mama. Delia will be here to pick me up in less than an hour.

It takes me time to choose what to wear. I put on and pull off three dresses—the only ones I own—before I decide on my purple skirt and a denim button-up shirt. And of course, I lace up my Keds. I put on lip gloss, wishing I could wear *real* makeup. Standing on that stage, pale as I am, I'll be washed out in the stage lights. But I'm not pressing my luck by sneaking makeup from Mama's room. I'll play by the rules as best I can.

Once I'm dressed, I put my guitar in its case and head down the hall. I rap gently on Gram's door and poke in my head to say goodbye. Gram's not there, though. Her bed is made up, nice and neat.

"Gram?" I whirl around, looking down the hallway. The bathroom door is open. No sign of Gram there.

"Gram?" I say again, heading for the kitchen.

That's when I hear music coming from the den. I step inside, and there's Gram, looking like the belle of the ball. She's dressed to the nines, her lips painted cherry red. Her hair's done in a smart updo, and she's wearing a velvet dress that goes past her knees and is colored—well, *goldenrod*.

"Gram," I say, breathless.

She smiles big and turns up the volume on the cassette player. Music blasts through the speakers. I know the song. It's Wanda Jackson belting "I've Gotta Sing."

"I didn't know you were coming with me," I say, awed.

"Well naturally, sweetie pie." Gram places her hands on her hips. "And you'd best believe I'll be asking for your autograph afterward. Now come on. An audition dance!"

I'm grinning like a loon as Gram shimmies my way and takes my hand.

We start singing along with Wanda, belting out the chorus of "la, la, las." Gram spins me in a circle, and we dance to and fro. I spin so many times that I get dizzy, and I'm clutching the sofa when I hear an engine rumbling outside. Delia's here.

"Come on!" I say to Gram.

Together, we head outside. Delia has pulled Brenda into the driveway, and she's giving me a look I can't quite read. I run up to her open window and ask, "Is it all right if Gram comes along?"

"Can she manage the step up?" Delia asks, eyeing the floorboard doubtfully.

That's something I hadn't thought of, but Gram surprises us both. All she needs is my hand to steady her, and she's up in the cab in one go. I follow her, hauling my guitar onto the floorboard.

During my tossing and turning last night, I thought through this moment—what I'd say to Delia, and how. But when I open my mouth, she shakes her head and says, "Don't even, Cline."

"But I'm sorry," I tell her. "I'm real sorry I got you in trouble with Mama, and in front of Luann and everything."

Delia tsks at me, backing the truck out of the driveway. "I don't want to hear it. Things are fine at work, and, anyway, I'm the one who gave you that flyer and agreed to drive."

"Well, you did that stuff for *me*. And I bet Mama hasn't been so pleasant at the diner."

Delia snorts. "You know how your mama gets. Not gonna lie, I was shocked to get that call from her last night."

"You and me both."

Delia snorts again, slowing at a four-way stop. As she does, an awful, shrieking sound emits from Brenda.

"What's that?" I shout over the noise.

"Oh God," says Delia, gripping the wheel. "Not *now*."

"Not now, *what*?"

That's when the steam starts hissing out from under the hood.

"Brenda's a piece of crap, that's what," Delia moans. "This hasn't happened in weeks, I swear."

"W-what's happening?" I ask, getting scared.

"The engine's overheated." Delia turns off the truck as more steam billows out, clouding the windshield.

"But we can still drive, can't we?"

I already know the answer to that one, though: Brenda's broken down.

Right away, I start flipping through the names of anyone who might help us out of this bind. Normally, I'd call Hollie, but that's not an option anymore. Or Delia, but she's here in the truck with me. I even think of Mrs. Yune, because of how nice she's been. But that's the thing: she's been *so* nice. She gave me a whole two hundred bucks that I haven't even thanked her for yet. No way I can ask another favor.

Anyway, the point is moot, 'cause I can't call a soul. I don't have my phone.

Delia does, though. She's got it held up high, on speaker, waiting through a series of rings. Someone picks up and says, "Goldenrod, how may I help you?"

Oh *no.*

Mama is the last person I want to call. She'll tell me this serves me right. She'll say music doesn't pay for car repair bills. She'll say it's too bad, there's nothing she can do.

There's got to be something *I* can do, though. Determination's flowing through my veins. I check the clock. It's five past eight, and I've still got time to think up a plan and get to Lexington on time. I can—

"Y'all sit tight. I'll be there."

I jolt at Mama's words. I didn't pay any mind to what Delia was telling Mama about our predicament. I already knew what Mama's answer would be.

Or so I thought.

"*Mama*?" I call out, panicked that she's already hung up.

"Yes, Cline?"

"But . . . you're working."

"Well, the Goldenrod will have to survive on its own two feet for one Saturday morning."

Mama hangs up for real then, and I'm left staring ahead.

"That went better than expected," Delia says.

"Yeah," I say vaguely, not sure what to think.

"It's a *miracle*," Gram says.

Delia guffaws at that, but, thing is, "miracle" sounds about right. Mama up and leaving work to come get me, her wayward daughter, bound for an impractical audition? I'm so flummoxed, I can't properly breathe.

Delia calls a guy named Sean, some mechanic she knows in town. Afterward, she rolls down her window and waves the few cars who come our way around poor, broken-down Brenda. The minutes tick by, and I must get on Delia's nerves, asking every so often what time it is. Ten past eight, then fifteen, then *twenty-five*. If we don't leave town soon, I'm going to be late to my practice with Sylvie. After I bailed on her before, she might not forgive me for this.

Then I see a wink of silver in the rearview mirror. It's another car, cresting the foggy hill behind us. The headlights grow closer, and then there's no mistaking Mama's Camry. I don't stop staring, even when Mama rolls down her window and calls out, "Get in the car!"

Delia tells me and Gram to go on. She'll be fine waiting for Sean, she says; he's a friend. So I help Gram out of Brenda, and we get into the Camry—Gram up front, and me in the back, with my guitar. Once I've shut my door, I get an awful suspicion: Mama said she'd pick us up, *not* that she'd drive us to Lexington. What if she's only come out this way to drive me home and say, "too bad, so sad"?

But then Mama holds out her phone to me and says, "Plug in the address."

I do what I'm told, and when I'm through, Mama props the phone on the dash.

"We're behind schedule if you need to be there at nine," she says, "but I'll do the best I can."

When I look at Mama's eyes in the rearview mirror, I could swear up and down they're filled with tears. That makes me worry that there was a big to-do at the Goldenrod about her taking off work for *another* emergency. Is she in hot water? Or is she just stressed about missing her shift? I don't know.

I can see Gram's face in the mirror, too. She's not crying. She puckers her red lips into a kiss.

I've gotta sing, I remind myself.

That's my focus. Not broken-down trucks, Goldenrod shifts, or running late. So I whisper the lyrics of "Destination Unknown" for the umpteenth time, dreaming of how it will feel to sing them under shining stage lights.

29

SYLVIE'S WAITING FOR me where we agreed, in practice room number sixteen. I'm running ten minutes behind, but it could've been worse. Mama *sped* down Paris Pike, and when we reached the Fine Arts Building, she didn't bother with parking. She told me to run ahead, and she and Gram would meet me at the Singletary Center.

I can add both those things to my list of Stuff I Didn't Expect from Judy Alden. I've never seen Mama break the speed limit, and on account of my being grounded, I didn't think she'd let me out of her sight. But I'll have time to mull over that later. Right now? I've got some explaining to do.

"I'm sorry," I tell Sylvie, breathless from running all the way to our practice room.

She's sitting on the piano bench, hands folded in her lap. She doesn't look mad, exactly. More relieved. Her hair's done up in a crown braid, and she's wearing a flowy, hippie-style dress, colored lavender. Our outfits couldn't be more complementary if we'd planned them.

"I was worried you wouldn't come after all," Sylvie tells me. "I tried texting."

I pat my empty skirt pockets. "Still grounded."

Sylvie looks thoughtful. "Does that have anything to do with your mom not knowing about the workshop?"

"Everything to do with it," I mumble.

"That sucks," says Sylvie. "But I'm glad she changed her mind."

"That was *your* doing," I say. "How'd you convince Dr. Johnson to talk to her?"

Sylvie shakes her head. "I was hoping she might *call* your mom, not show up at your front door."

"It was dramatic," I admit. "And . . . really nice of her, too."

Even in the fluorescent lighting, Sylvie looks like a dream. She's not wearing any makeup either, but her face glows without it, and her green-brown eyes shine. My stomach turns over like a steamboat wheel. As much as I've told myself to ignore my feelings, there's simply no denying it: I have a full-blown, honest-to-goodness crush on Sylvie Sharpe.

And truth is? I'm *really* glad we're here together. I wouldn't want to be playing music alongside anyone else. If you'd told me a month ago that I'd be auditioning with and *crushing* on Rude Girl in Sunglasses? I wouldn't have believed you. No way.

Life sure is full of surprises.

⌀

It feels like, over the past few weeks, Sylvie and I have practiced our song a hundred thousand times. But that saying about practice making perfect? It's especially true when it comes to music. That's why we run through "Destination Unknown" a half dozen more times this morning. When Sylvie and I finally feel ready, we leave the practice room and follow the signs marked *AUDITIONS* to the Singletary Center auditorium. I know Mama and Gram must be somewhere in the audience and, according to Sylvie, both her parents are, too. We can't sit with them, though. A volunteer directs us to the front three rows, where the other auditionees are gathered.

Most of the folks here are way older than me and Sylvie. I knew we'd be auditioning with adults, but seeing them all around us gets my heart pounding. I thought it was scary enough, taking a workshop with high schoolers. How much more expertise do *these* people have? Some of them look like they've been playing music for ten, twenty, *thirty* years.

The festival directors—our judges—sit three across at a table onstage, with papers before them and pencils in their hands. They call up the first act: a guitar and vocal solo by a woman who looks to be in her twenties. She sings an Alison Krauss song, and though I think she's good, she hits some notes flat. I sure can't blame her. The auditorium's huge and dark, and dozens of random folks are watching. It's a lot of pressure.

I'm relieved when I see other students from the Young Singer-Songwriter Workshop get onstage. Like me and Sylvie, they're younger than most of this crowd, and it's nice to see familiar faces—even Veronica, the girl who called me "precious." Chris and Jamal give a knockout performance, playing the fiddle and banjo and harmonizing to a foot-tapping chorus. Everyone has a song to sing, and each musician is unique. I don't know how the judges mean to pick only five acts from us hundred-something auditionees. What are the chances that Sylvie and I can win them over?

I breathe in deep and shut my eyes, forming fists with my shaking hands.

The singing voice of Emmylou Harris reaches my ears: *You don't get nothin' unless you take the breaks.* Dr. Johnson's voice follows, saying, *Your daughter has real talent.*

I open my eyes to find Sylvie watching me.

"I'm fine," I mouth to her, but even so, she reaches across the seat and takes my hand.

Just like that, I feel I could sing a whole *album's* worth of songs. I could play dueling guitars with Johnny Cash himself. I could perform before a roaring audience at the Grand Ole Opry. Though, if I think about it, this audience right here is more intimidating than the Opry's. A few weeks ago, I didn't expect that I'd be auditioning for anyone, and up until a few *hours* ago, I had no idea Mama or Gram would be in this room. My two worlds—one in Paris and one in Lexington—are smashing together.

Or maybe, I consider, those two worlds were never all that separate. Because even when the people who believed in me weren't

275

by my side, they were supporting me from afar. This was never just me, Cline, out on her own. Folks have been there for me every step of the way. Delia gave me a flyer and a ride. Gram gave me a guitar and her rainy-day fund. Ms. Khatri in fourth grade gave me online guitar lessons. Mrs. Yune gave me support when I needed it most. Dr. Johnson gave me her knowledge and a second chance. Even Mama gave me her Saturday shift at the Goldenrod.

And now? Sylvie's giving me her hand.

When one of the judges calls out, "Sylvie Sharpe and Cline Alden," Sylvie and I exchange a final glance. She gives my hand a squeeze that sends my heart flipping all over again, and then lets go. The audience applauds as we walk onstage, and I grin, knowing that one of those people clapping is Gram. She's rooting for me. So this is for her. It's for Mrs. Yune and Ms. Khatri, for Delia and Dr. Johnson, and even for Mama. For all the women who got me here.

But also? It's for me. Cline Louise Alden.

After Sylvie and I ensure that my guitar's in tune with the keyboard, I count us off, and we begin. We're in perfect synchronization, just like we rehearsed, only now the notes of our song are bouncing off the walls of a big auditorium.

I sing the first verse, and though I'm quaking inside, my voice comes out steady, hitting every note right. I don't even think twice when I sing "you're the girl I'm thinking of." It feels as natural as can be. Sylvie joins me at the chorus, harmonizing, and I can practically see vibrations in the air—our voices dancing together, creating a new sound. Sylvie sings the second verse in her strong, rich tone, and then our voices dance again for the chorus, harmonizing right into the bridge and the third verse.

I miss one chord close to the end, my fingers pressing into the wrong frets. I correct myself, though, and we're back in sync for a strong finish, the two of us harmonizing on the final line:

If we're together when we drive.

The last notes ring out, drifting across the lit stage into the darkened auditorium. It's like Sylvie and I have cast a magic spell, and for a moment, the world's hushed, perfectly still. Then the audience applauds, and Sylvie and I take our bows, and it's over.

༼༽

When the final auditionee has left the stage, one of the judges—a tall Black woman in a checkered dress—takes a microphone and announces that she and her fellow judges will be posting their decision online by next Sunday. Then the houselights come on, and everyone starts bustling about.

I'm scanning the faces around me for Mama and Gram when a man and woman come scurrying up to our row. I recognize the woman from the nights she's picked up Sylvie: it's Sylvie's mom, Mrs. Sharpe. Beside her, a white man with glasses and a beard greets Sylvie by lifting her clear off the ground and saying, *"Magnificent."*

Sylvie laughs as he lowers her to ground. "*Dad.* You're embarrassing me."

"That's my job," he replies.

Mrs. Sharpe smiles. "It *was* impressive."

I nod eagerly. "Sylvie's got real stage presence. Folk music's good and all, but she's even better at rock. Have you heard her do a Joan Jett cover?"

Sylvie gives me a sidelong glance, a twinkle in her eye. She can see what I'm trying to do. Sylvie is the queen of impressions, and I figure it won't hurt for her parents to know that, too.

"So," says Mr. Sharpe, "you're the famous Cline. We've heard a lot about you."

I blush, wondering what all Sylvie's said about me to make me *famous.*

That's when a brown-skinned girl in pigtails who looks around five or six pushes past Mrs. Sharpe, yelling, *"Way to go, Sylvie!"*

Then the girl turns on me, beaming, and shouts, *"I'm Maggie!* I'm Sylvie's sister, and I've got a soccer game!"

"Too true," Mrs. Sharpe says, checking her watch. "Sorry, Cline, but we've got to get going."

"O-oh," I say, as Mrs. Sharpe starts shooing Maggie and Sylvie down the aisle.

I didn't know exactly what to expect, after the audition. I guess I figured Sylvie and I would have time to talk, like we've always had after Monday night workshops. But now Sylvie's leaving, and I've got no way of talking to her again—not with my phone privileges revoked.

"U-u-uh . . ." I stammer, not knowing how to tell Sylvie goodbye. "Maybe my mama will let me call you next week, when they post the results?"

Sylvie nods with big eyes. She looks flustered, like she wasn't expecting to be whisked away, either.

"Sylvie girl!" Mr. Sharpe calls from down the aisle.

"Coming!" Sylvie shouts, her eyes still locked on mine.

I'm trying to make out what she's silently telling me:

We played great, maybe.

Or, *I hope we see each other again.*

Or, while I'm dabbling in possibility, *I've got a crush on you.*

But then Sylvie turns away, and those possibilities evaporate. I watch her leave, dress fluttering behind her like a lavender wave.

A hand rests on my shoulder. It's Gram. Gently, she turns me around and pulls me into her arms, filling my nose with the scent of her floral perfume.

"Sweetie pie, that playing did your namesake proud."

"Thanks, Gram," I whisper. "I could hear you clapping for me."

I look up to find Mama standing beside us. Her eyes are glistening, like they were before in the car, and there are winding wet tracks down her cheeks.

"Mama," I start to say, but there's another familiar voice calling my name.

Dr. Johnson is running down the aisle, her thick braids bouncing. Mama wipes away her tears real quick, just as Dr. Johnson reaches us and says in her booming, classroom voice, "A job well done."

"Thanks, Dr. Johnson," I say. "I couldn't have done it without you."

She waves her hand, as though to say, *No big deal.* Or, *You could've done fine on your own.* But it is a big deal, and I couldn't have done any of this alone.

"I meant to catch Sylvie, too," Dr. Johnson says, looking around. "Is she already gone?"

I nod, and Dr. Johnson puckers her lips. "Well. Something tells me this isn't the last I'll see of you two. I'll be doing plenty of work at the festival come March. Whether or not you get a spot, I hope you'll attend."

"Yeah." I give Mama a furtive glance. "I guess we'll see."

Dr. Johnson turns to Mama. "As I said, Ms. Alden, you have one talented daughter. I imagine she gets some of that from you."

"Oh, nothing of the sort." Mama lets out a papery laugh, looking uncomfortable. "I'm a waitress, not a singer."

"Well!" says Dr. Johnson. "That's the noblest profession in the musical world."

"I suppose," Mama says, with a humorless smile.

"It's true. You talk to anyone in Nashville hospitality, I

guarantee they'll have more talent in their pinkie finger than last year's Grammy winners. Just biding their time, making a living so they can sing. Waitressing's the profession that's sustained us through and through."

Mama clears her throat. "Well, it *is* practical."

"Indeed." Dr. Johnson looks like she's fixing to introduce herself to Gram when one of the other workshop students calls out from a few rows over.

Dr. Johnson waves to him and tells us, "Nice to see you again."

She excuses herself, and we three Alden ladies are left alone.

It's a quiet ride home, and neither Gram nor Mama say a word about "you're the girl I'm thinking of." I wonder if they heard the lyric. Even if they did, I don't think they can know how important those words are to me, or even that I'm the one who wrote them. Maybe they assumed that Sylvie did, or that they weren't meant to be romantic.

After a few minutes on the road, Gram is snoring in the passenger seat. I can't sleep, though. After today, I'm not sure I'll get any shut-eye for a week. It happened. I performed. It wasn't how I ever expected: a duet with another girl and Mama of all people driving me to the audition. But it *happened*. I think about Sylvie holding my hand before we went onstage and our voices in harmony as we sang "If we're together when we drive." I look out the window at passing black fences and autumn trees—leaves colored bloodred, golden, and orange. I feel a stirring in my chest. The audition is over, but I've got a feeling that something new—something *amazing*—is starting.

Mama pulls into our driveway, wakes Gram, and heads into the house. It's not till Gram is settled in the den with *The Mary Tyler Moore Show* that Mama catches me in the kitchen.

"Cline," she says. "Did you make up that song on your own?"

"Well, with Sylvie," I say.

"But you wrote those lyrics and music together? *You* did that?"

"Yeah."

Mama shakes her head. "It was . . . Seeing you up there, I couldn't believe that was my daughter."

I'm not sure what to say. I wonder for a second if Mama's going to mention the line about thinking of a girl, after all. But she goes on.

"Cline, I don't know you the way a mother should. I haven't been here."

"You've been busy supporting the family," I say, real soft.

"There are different ways to support a family. I've been doing an okay job at one of those. The others, not so much. Your performance reminded me—" Mama's voice stoppers up. She shakes her head, and after a moment, she starts again. "It reminded me of many things. Most of all, it reminded me of how proud I am to be your mother. We may not always see eye to eye, Cline, but I'll never not be proud."

"Th-thanks," I say, the word quivering like jelly.

"Have you written other songs?" Mama asks, like she wants to know where I've hidden buried treasure.

"Some," I reply. "Lots of love songs. Not that they're based on real life."

I pause, thinking about Sylvie.

For the first time in I don't know how long, I feel comfortable telling Mama about my music. I think now, if I wanted to, I could even tell her about my crush on Sylvie. I finally have the words to express the way I feel. Only, I decide, that's a conversation for another day. For now, I'm content talking about the music.

But *that* gets me thinking about how I've tried to ignore my crush on Sylvie and focus on the music instead. I wonder if Mama would understand that, at least.

"I've been thinking," I say, "that musicians write better songs when they're *not* in love. When they don't get happy endings. For one thing, they can focus better on the job. And for another, there's more heartbreak that way. Better song material."

As I speak, deep ridges form across Mama's forehead.

"Cline," she says solemnly. "That's poppycock."

I slump my shoulders. Mama doesn't understand, after all.

Only, she's not finished. "You be a musician if you must," she tells me, "but I won't have you moping about, expecting heartbreak. That's where I draw the line."

"I'm just telling it like it is."

"No," Mama replies. "You can have music *and* love. Your gram taught me that."

"But . . . you said Gram—"

Mama holds up a finger, cutting me off. "She and your papaw

weren't successful in business. Heaven knows their finances were a mess. But one thing I can tell you: they were plenty successful in love."

I think about Gram, freezing cold in Magnolia Square, where she and Papaw once met. Even with her memory under attack, she hasn't forgotten about the love she shared with him.

Mama says, "Your father was more like those two than I am."

I stare. "Like . . . Papaw and Gram?"

Dad's own parents both passed a while back. I figured he shared stuff in common with them, but not *Mama's* folks.

"Do you know, he insisted we dance at our wedding to 'Angel from Montgomery'?" Mama smiles like she's reminiscing. "I told him it was a sad song, better suited to a funeral. But he said it made him feel things deep in his bones. You got that from Gram, Cline, but you also got it from him. Your father felt music as much as he felt love. You can have both. So don't let me hear you say otherwise again."

Mama fixes her eyes on me, and I realize something: she's given me permission. She said I could be musician, if I must.

And naturally, I *must.*

"You, too, Mama," I tell her.

She raises a brow. "Me, too, what?"

"I got it from you, too," I say. "The music. I remember when you used to play the Yamaha. And Gram always says you named me Cline for a reason."

Mama's eyes turn soft. She opens her arms, and without saying another word, I fold myself into them. It's here, in this hug, that I can at last picture what Gram told me about Mama holding me as a baby, singing me to sleep with "Blue Moon of Kentucky." Before, that didn't seem like the Mama I knew. Now I know better. The music's still in her, beating inside her heart. I feel it—a steady rhythm against my ear.

30

IT'S WEIRD, NOT having the internet or a phone. Awful in some ways. Like how I can't FaceTime Sylvie so we can fret together over audition results. Or how I can't talk to Sylvie in general. But in other ways, it's nice. For instance, I can't waste time checking the Daylight Saving Bluegrass Festival's website, hoping they posted the audition results early. Mama's given me *one* chance to do that, this Sunday evening.

I'm not able to see any photos, either, of Hollie and her friends at New Hope Christian. I guess that's a good thing, too. I sometimes wonder if Hollie ever texted me back, but I've got a gut feeling she didn't. If she was going to do that, it would've been back when I had my phone. From what I can tell? Hollie's moved on, plain and simple.

I'd be lying if I said my heart didn't get sore when I think about that. I don't see how friends like us could be close for so long and then split apart. I have so many memories of Hollie, both in my head and in my room: a bottle of hyacinth perfume we made together at her place, a papier-mâché koala bear in my closet, and the *Princess Bride* cross-stitch over my dresser that reads *As You Wish,* embroidered with hearts and rodents of unusual size. Hollie always gave the best birthday gifts.

We shared more with each other than crafts and gifts, though. We swapped stories and secrets and dreams. A year ago, I could write down a list of Hollie's favorite foods, movies, songs, and her entire school schedule.

Now? There's so much she doesn't know about me: the workshop, the audition, my crush on Sylvie, Gram's disappearance. There's so much I don't know about *Hollie,* like how just yesterday she announced that she and Scott are officially boyfriend and girlfriend. That's something I don't hear about till I'm at school, sitting at lunch with Kenzie, Darlene, and Ava.

"Can you believe it?" Darlene stage-whispers. "My mama won't let me date boys till I'm fifteen."

What about girls? I think to myself, prodding at the fruit cup on my tray.

"What's that look for, Cline?" asks Ava.

"Nothing," I say real fast, but when I look up from my tray, the girls are staring at me.

That's when I remember the promise I've made to myself. I've decided that, from here on out, I'm going to be more honest with my friends. They're still sticking around, long after Hollie's left. They've proven that they're dependable. So this past Monday, I told them about the workshop. They were going to find out about my being grounded anyway, and I figured I might as well tell them the reason why.

They weren't even mad. Darlene called me a badass. Ava looked me up and down and then gave me a slow clap that lasted for what felt like a whole minute. Kenzie said she was sad I hadn't felt like sharing before, but she understood what it's like to want to keep your art to yourself.

"It felt weird when I first started selling my portraits," she told me. "It's, like, the art is *so* personal, but suddenly it's not fully yours anymore."

That's when I realized that Kenzie *got* it. Ava and Darlene, too, in different ways. Darlene talked about how her mom is Shania Twain's number one fan, and how even though Darlene herself isn't big on music, she really likes Shania's new album.

"It's about her getting cheated on by her husband with her *best friend* and then being, like, 'Forget *you*, I'm going to be happy anyway,'" she said. "Like, get it, girl."

Ava told me she knew what it was like to scrimp and save for something you love.

"Color guard costumes are *way* too expensive," she explained. "Sixth grade, Mom had to really stretch the budget. I almost had to quit the team, just because of those gross silver leggings that made us look like robots."

It feels good—*real* good—to be honest with my friends. Before,

I was too worried about Hollie and what she'd say. Turns out, I had three other great friends right here all along. Now I don't have to keep School Cline apart from Singer Cline. I can be both. I can be *me*.

Sure, there are some things I still don't feel ready to share. I didn't tell the girls about the New Hope lock-in or how I've got a massive crush on Sylvie Sharpe. Maybe I won't want to share that part of me till I'm older. Or maybe I'll feel ready in a few months. Whatever I decide, I've figured out it's *my* decision to own. I can't control how anyone will react. Maybe they'll accept me, like Delia and Sylvie have, or maybe they won't, like Hollie didn't. It's not my job to make anyone happy, though. It's just my job to be me.

And I know I'm fully me when I'm sharing my music. It's been in my veins ever since I can recall, burning inside me well before I realized I liked girls. I guess that's why it feels fitting I open up about the musical part of me first. I know the rest will follow in time.

Meantime, I plan to work on being a good friend, paying more attention to Ava and Darlene and Kenzie and what's important to *them*. So when I find everyone's eyes on me at the lunch table today, I break into a smile and say, "Who's ready for the Harvest Dance?"

Darlene squeals and starts gushing immediately about her date.

"Hey," says Kenzie, glancing at me. "Cline's not going. Don't rub it in her face."

"It's okay," I say. "I wouldn't have brought it up if I minded."

"We'll take pictures, for sure," Darlene tells me. "You will flip when you see my costume."

"Are you still going to dress up for Halloween?" Ava asks me. "Like, to give out candy?"

Honestly, I hadn't thought about dressing up. I was just figuring on cuddling with Gram in my pajamas tomorrow, watching our favorite old scary movie, *The Ghost and Mr. Chicken*. I hadn't considered handing out candy to kids. Maybe I could throw something together.

"*What*, Cline?" Darlene demands. "What're you smirking for?"

This time, I can give a truthful answer: "I'm going to be Emmylou Harris."

Kenzie squints at me. "Is that, like . . . Michael Myers? But a girl?"

I laugh and say, "Know what? Once I'm not grounded, we'll have a listening party. The four of us."

"Like a slumber party, but with music?" asks Ava. "I'm down."

"Yeah," Kenzie agrees.

"And," says Darlene, "you'll play a song for us?"

I consider that. I do want to play for my friends, but not "Destination Unknown." I want to keep that one to myself. I do know there are more songs inside me, though—other Cline originals waiting to come out.

So I nod and say, "I sure will."

⌒◠⌒

What with all the treasures in Gram's cedar chest, it's not hard to come up with the perfect costume on Halloween night. I use Mama's flat iron on my hair till it's stick straight, and I part it right down the middle. I wear a button-up shirt, simple and white, and pair it with blue jeans. Then there's the finishing touch: a paisley scarf from Gram's collection, which I knot atop my head. I even place my guitar by the front door, so if kids ask who I am, I can strum a few notes and say, "Emmylou. The legend."

It'll be downright educational.

Mama's working late tonight, helping Laila at the Goldenrod. Luann makes a big deal about Halloween, decking out the diner with decorations and offering a free slice of pumpkin pie with every entrée, which causes a real Halloween rush. So it's just me and Gram at home. I've whipped us up a tub of caramel, heated in the microwave, along with apple slices and a bag of kettle corn. Gram asked Mama specially to get apple cider from the grocery, and we drink it cold in mugs.

We watch *The Ghost and Mr. Chicken* in the den, and every time the doorbell rings, I run down the hall to give the kids a handful of Hershey's kisses. We're at the part in the movie where Luther, the main character, is showing folks around a haunted house, when the doorbell rings again.

I scurry out of the room and open the front door, armed with a fistful of candy.

Only, there aren't little kids on the other side.

I'm so startled, I don't understand at first.

There's a girl standing on the porch with short, choppy black hair. She wears red pants, a leather jacket, and oversized shades.

I recognize those sunglasses. I've seen them before, on the first day of the Young Singer-Songwriter Workshop.

"Sylvie?" I whisper, 'cause I'm still not sure how it can be true.

The girl takes off her sunglasses, grinning at me, and then it's clear as day: Sylvie Sharpe is at my front door. She's wearing a wig and a costume, and I recognize the look well enough from the music videos I've seen on YouTube.

"Joan Jett, at your service," she says in a raspy voice that's a killer impression of the rocker queen herself.

I feel suddenly loopy. Sticking my hand out for a shake, I say, "How d'you do, Ms. Jett. I'm Emmylou Harris."

Sylvie laughs, breaking out of her Joan imitation. "You *would* be."

I shake my head in awe. "How the heck are you here?"

"You mean, *why* the heck am I here. The how was easy: you're the only Aldens listed in Paris, Kentucky. Anyway, Dr. Johnson made it seem like such a fun thing to do, showing up unannounced." Sylvie scrunches her nose. "It was the only thing to do, actually, since you wouldn't answer your phone. Still grounded?"

I nod.

"Thought so. I convinced my mom it was worth the drive, since it *is* a matter of professional importance."

Sylvie waves toward the street, and that's when I see a familiar SUV parked in front of the house.

"Hi there, Cline!" Mrs. Sharpe calls from the driver's seat.

I give her a limp sort of wave, 'cause I'm still focused on Sylvie.

"What's a matter of professional importance?" I ask.

Sylvie breaks into the biggest grin I've ever seen. "We got it," she says, so low I think I didn't hear right.

"Got . . . what?"

"What do you think? *It*. One of the slots for the preshow! They posted the results early."

My knees feel as shaky as Jell-O salad. I stumble forward, but Sylvie grabs both my hands, and she doesn't let go.

"You . . . mean it?" I wheeze. "This isn't a Halloween prank?"

"Why would I prank you?" Sylvie demands. "We got it, Cline. We're going to be playing at the festival."

That's when it really hits me. I squeeze Sylvie's hands, and we jump up and down till Gram calls from the den, "Sweetie? Everything all right?"

"It's fine!" I call back, but Sylvie's eyes have grown big.

"Am I getting you in trouble?" she asks. "I know you're still grounded, so I don't mean to stay and make a scene. It's just, when I saw the news, I *had* to come tell you. I told Mom, 'I don't care about Irene's party, I've got to see Cline.'"

Sylvie and I are still holding hands, and I never want to let go. I'm not even embarrassed that she's here at my house, where the paint's peeling and our driveway is made of gravel. She doesn't seem to care, and I don't either.

"Thanks for coming out all this way for me," I say.

"Not just for you. For me, too." Sylvie's smile turns confidential. When she speaks next, it's to whisper, "Guess what? Mom's changed her mind."

"About rock camp?" I ask, lighting up.

Sylvie nods, her eyes crackling with excitement. "After the audition, I heard her and Dad talking downstairs. You were right: the music changed her mind. Well, that *and* everything I've been doing at school. I'm looking into starting a petition about the school lunch thing and getting a teacher to sponsor a climate change club. Dad said I'd really proved how mature and responsible I was this semester, and how it'd be a disservice if I didn't go to Nashville this summer, and Mom *agreed*. I think she actually gets it now. If I'm old enough to get a preshow performance . . . well, I'm old enough for rock camp."

"That's *awesome*," I nearly shriek. "I'm so happy for you!"

But now Sylvie's got a serious look on her face. She glances back at her mom and then to me.

"So, um . . . I know you're in trouble right now, but I've been wanting to ask: Would you want to keep practicing with me on Monday nights? I was thinking we could alternate, back and forth—my house and yours. You know, spend the time we usually did at the workshop, only just the two of us, making music."

Butterflies burst from my stomach, fluttering into my chest, filling my heart, soaring all the way up to my head.

I've finally heard what Sylvie meant to say. The end to her *Would you—?*

She wants to keep seeing me every week. She wants to make music together. And she still hasn't let go of my hands.

"I'll need to ask permission," I admit.

Sylvie's face drops, which I can hardly stand, so I add, quick as I can, "I'd *love* that, though."

"Really?" Sylvie still looks uncertain.

"Believe me, Joan," I say. "It'd be an honor."

Finally, a smile returns to her face, and she puts on that same raspy accent from before. "Well then, Emmylou, we've got ourselves a deal."

She steps closer to me—so close I can smell the chocolate candy on her breath.

She asks, "Would it . . . be all right if I kissed you?" Then her eyes get big, and she adds, "I mean, just on the cheek!"

I don't rightly know how to breathe. I think, for a split second, about all that time I spent trying to ignore my crush. What was the point? How could I ever deny how I feel about Sylvie? Mama's words from audition day come back to me: *You can have music and love.*

In this moment, I know for sure that's true.

Sylvie's waiting on an answer, her hazel eyes still wide. A million butterflies are crowding my head, but I manage to nod.

Then Sylvie's lips press against my skin, soft and warm, and it's like I'm listening to the greatest song of all time. When she steps away, her face is more radiant than the moon, and I feel like I could float past the stars.

"Later days, Emmylou," she says, raising her hand in a peace sign.

"See you around, Joan," I say back.

Then Sylvie's running off to her mom's SUV.

I don't care that Mrs. Sharpe may have seen the kiss. I don't mind how many more weeks of grounding I have to endure to see Sylvie again. Right at this moment, I'm near exploding with happiness.

31

MAIN STREET LIGHTS up in December with flickering candles in storefronts and twinkle lights wrapped around balconies. Wreaths hang from the lampposts, and a banner strung over the street says *Holidays on Main 74th Anniversary*. That's when the whole town gathers for free cocoa and carols and the lighting of the Main Street Christmas tree. The festivities take place this weekend, and for the first time in I don't know how long, Mama will be attending along with me and Gram.

Mama always had an excuse for why she didn't join us before: bills to sort out, an unexpected shift, kitchen cabinets to clean. But there have been a lot fewer of those this past month. Not bills or cabinets in need of cleaning. *Excuses.*

As for me, you could say I've been watching Mama with a new set of eyes. I've noticed how hard she works at the Goldenrod and home to make things comfortable for me and Gram. I guess you don't pay attention to that stuff when you're younger.

You don't see why your mama would do a thing like sell her piano out of the blue.

Now, I see that diner tips and extra shifts add up, but so do the chores at home. So I'm cleaning the kitchen cabinets every so often, rather than watching TV with Gram. I'm taking out the trash on my way to school, so Mama doesn't have to after a long day at the diner. Mama showed me on audition day that there was still music inside of her. It's about time I showed her that there's practicality in me.

Mama and I understand each other better these days, and I think my dad would be pleased to know that. I think he'd be happy, too, to see me playing guitar or listening to Brandi Carlile sing "Hard Way Home"—my own style of worship, good as Mrs. Yune going to church or Bill from the Goldenrod planting azaleas.

I've been officially un-grounded since Thanksgiving Day, which means I've had my phone back for a week. I've been texting up a storm with Darlene, Ava, and Kenzie, who are coming over for a listening party this weekend, after the Christmas tree lighting. And I've been texting Sylvie. Of course I have. Just thinking of her puts a grin on my face so wide, you'd think it'd split my jaw in two.

Starting tonight, Mama's agreed to let me and Sylvie practice together. She says it'll have to be on Sundays, rather than Mondays, and only every other Sunday night, *and* only if Sylvie comes out to our house for the first couple of weeks, so Mama can keep an eye on me. She did mean what she said about rebuilding trust.

But Sylvie and her parents were all right with that. And me? I've been over the moon.

I'm in an extra good mood this afternoon as I walk down Main, listening to "Cline Kicks the World's Butt." It's queued up to a song from the *Trio* album—a dream collaboration of Dolly Parton, Linda Ronstadt, and Emmylou Harris. This is one of their most famous numbers, "Wildflowers." It's a song about how, no matter where they're planted, wildflowers—resilient women, that is—grow strong.

I'm crossing the street, heading toward the Goldenrod, when I hear a muffled voice behind me. I yank out my earbuds and look around, and there is Mrs. Edith Yune waving me down.

It's cold out, but my heart feels warm. I haven't seen Mrs. Yune since the weekend of the lock-in at New Hope. I've *thought* about her a whole lot since then, though.

"Cline!" she says, clapping her mittened hands. "I thought it was you."

Mrs. Yune is fashionable as always, wearing leopard-printed pants, black boots, and a purple peacoat.

"Mrs. Yune. *Hey.*" I stand there, staring at her like she's a movie star.

She's better than that, though. Mrs. Yune gave me a chance to go after my dream. And now I'm thinking how wrong I've been to not call or write a letter. Life was so hectic at first, with the audition and being grounded, and then I got to feeling awkward about the situation. How do you thank someone for giving you a whole *two hundred dollars*? For telling you that you're perfect the way you are?

I didn't say anything, in the end, but seeing Mrs. Yune now, I really wish I had. So instead of saying "thank you," I blurt out, "I'm sorry."

Mrs. Yune looks baffled. "Sorry for what?"

I shuffle my Keds, which are a lot more brownish-gray these days than white. "I should've said thank you before," I tell her. "For your gift."

Mrs. Yune raises a brow and asks, "Did it help, in the end?"

"It did," I tell her earnestly. "A *lot*."

"Well," she says, "that's all I need to know. I just wanted to say hello, and I hope you're doing well, and I'm here if you ever need an adult to talk to."

"Thanks, Mrs. Yune. I mean it, really. *Thanks*."

"Did you know," she says, "I happen to be a bluegrass fan myself?"

I recall the Loretta Lynn playing in Mrs. Yune's car, and I figure that makes sense. But I'm wondering why she's brought up bluegrass right up until she tells me, "I saw a certain someone's name in a festival lineup."

That's when I understand. The Daylight Saving Bluegrass Festival released an online poster last week, advertising the folks who will be performing in March. There are *big-time* singers coming, and their names are, naturally, printed in giant bold font. But way down at the bottom of the poster, in tiny print, are the names *Sylvie Sharpe and Cline Alden.*

I have been *real* excited about that.

"You must've had to use glasses to read my name," I tell Mrs. Yune.

"Everyone starts in small print at first," she replies, winking. "Just remember, once that print gets bigger, what I wrote about paying it forward."

"I won't forget," I say, as Mrs. Yune's phone starts ringing.

She reaches into her purse and checks the screen.

"I've got to take this," she says, "but I'll see you onstage in March!"

See me onstage. I beam at the idea.

Then I wave goodbye and watch as Mrs. Yune walks away, talking cheerily into her phone.

⸎

When I pass by the Goldenrod's storefront, I stop in my tracks and do a double take. My eyes have not deceived me. Sure enough, there's Hollie, eating at a booth with her family. Mr. and Mrs. Kendall and Noah sit with her, but it's only Hollie who spies me through the glass. Our eyes lock for one instant, and then, like a spooked horse, I run. I skid around the building, heading to the back entrance. When I reach the kitchen, I turn a corner without looking and nearly run headlong into Delia.

"Whoa!" she yelps. "Jeez, Cline. Always a kitchen hazard."

"Sorry!" I say, backing away.

Delia swishes past me to dump a load of dirty plates in the

sink. "Brenda gives her regards, by the way."

I was happy to hear that Brenda got the lifesaving repairs she needed, even though Delia's mechanic friend says she's living on borrowed time.

"As long as her engine's beating, she's the only girl for me," Delia told him.

On a normal day, I'd laugh and tell Delia I give my regards right back. Only, I've just seen Hollie for the first time since the New Hope lock-in. So today is most definitely not normal.

Delia notices my silence. "Hey," she says, from the sink. "You know I'm just giving you a hard time, right?"

I nod through the lump in my throat. I feel like I might hurl.

"I need to . . ." I don't finish. I scurry out of the kitchen and down the narrow hall toward the restrooms.

At first, I pay no mind to the girl standing by the door. It's only when I turn the handle that she says, "Cline?"

I look up, and there she is: Hollie Kendall, former best friend, standing a foot away from me.

The queasiness lifts from my stomach, leaving behind nothing but a hollowed-out feeling.

"Hi," Hollie says.

I stare at her like she's a two-headed chicken. I don't say hi back.

"I thought maybe I'd find you back here," Hollie goes on. "I'm glad, 'cause I wanted to say . . . I should've texted you back, in October. I didn't want to at first, and then so much time passed, I thought you wouldn't *want* to hear from me. But it's weird, right? Going from hanging out so much to not talking at all."

I feel like saying, *You're the one who left school.* And, *You're the one who didn't text back.* And also, *You betrayed me in the worst possible way.*

But I keep quiet.

It's shocking how much older Hollie looks. She's got makeup on—the same mascara and pink lipstick I first saw her wearing the night of the lock-in. I guess that's a usual thing for her now. She purses those pink lips, like she's expecting something from me that I'm not delivering. Then she folds her arms and says, "Look. My parents were planning on sending me to New Hope Christian, anyway. That was before . . . you know, what happened. Dad got a raise at work, and he and Mom decided they could afford tuition, and I'd known that for a while before I left. I just couldn't think of a good way to tell you."

"So you didn't," I say.

Hollie shrugs, looking askance at the photographs on the wall: pretty landscapes of horse country.

Like that, I've got my answer to the question that's been burning in me for weeks: Did Hollie switch schools because of me? As it turns out, she'd been thinking about it for a while, but she didn't want to tell me. Maybe she thought I wouldn't understand any more than I thought she'd understand about my workshop. Maybe we were both right.

A part of my heart is aching all the same. It's clear to me now that Hollie's becoming a brand-new person. In some ways, she's the same girl I met in kindergarten, who can quote *The Princess Bride* straight through. In other ways, she's changed.

I've changed, too. I'm sure not the same Cline I was before my first workshop in Lexington. For one thing, I've learned how to say what's on my mind. I've learned how to take big risks and express myself honestly.

Well, I'd say a little expressing myself is in order now. See, Hollie's apologized for not texting me back, but not for leaving me and our friends without a proper goodbye, and certainly not for what she did at the lock-in.

I'm remembering something Mrs. Yune told me that Sunday. Seeing her on the street has brought her words back to mind, when I need them most. She told me that maybe Hollie has some mind changing to do, but that doesn't mean I need to let her treat me bad in the meantime.

You can stand up for yourself, or walk away, she told me. *Whatever feels right.*

So I take her advice.

"I forgive you for not texting back," I tell Hollie.

We were real good friends, after all. *Best* friends. That doesn't go away in two months' time. Friends forgive each other, so I do that for the memory of the friends we used to be.

Then, I do something for me.

I tell Hollie, "It wasn't right, what you did at the lock-in. But even if you're not sorry, I forgive you for that, too. And I hope life goes real well for you."

I don't wait around for Hollie's answer. I've stood up for myself, and now I'm walking away—down the hall, back to the kitchen, where Delia's hooting about some joke and Bill's sizzling meat on the grill.

It hurts so bad, knowing for sure that I've lost Hollie as a friend. I think it's going to hurt for a while, like a scabbed-over wound that keeps getting knocked around and bleeding fresh.

But somehow, even though I'm hurting . . . I feel better.

I'm looking forward to what's ahead. Like the Daylight Saving Bluegrass Festival. A party this weekend with my DMS friends. The Sunday night right in front of me. And beyond that? An exciting, mysterious future.

I'm traveling to a destination unknown.

32

"FIFTEEN MINUTES, CLINE, and then we're off."

Mama's in her element as she bustles into the Goldenrod kitchen, whisking away a tray of piping hot food. She shouts an order to Bill, who acknowledges her with a spatula salute. Moments later, she's back to recite a new table's order.

The fifteen minutes pass, ticking away on the kitchen clock. Then, true to her word, Mama takes off her apron and joins me where I stand, holding two plastic bags filled with takeout for four—food for a nice Sunday sit-down supper with me, Sylvie, and Gram.

See, after the night Gram went missing, Luann sat Mama down and told her she was working her heart out. Right then and there, she gave Mama a raise and told her we Aldens deserved a good takeout twice a week. That means Mama can spend less time in the diner on Sundays and more time with us. *This* Sunday, Sylvie will be joining us to eat and, afterward, to practice music with me in the den.

Tonight's the first time I'll be seeing Sylvie since Halloween, when she gave me that better-than-music kiss. I've replayed that moment so many times, you'd think I'd be sick of it, but no. I'll never be sick of Sylvie or imaging what it would be like to kiss *her*—this time, maybe, on the lips.

One day soon, I might want to tell Mama and Gram that I think of Sylvie as my crush, not just my friend. I might even explain to them what that line in our audition song means to me. For now, though? I'm happy with the parts of me I've let them see.

Mama and I leave the Goldenrod for the Paris Community Center, where Gram is finishing up an afternoon with her new senior group. Mama found out about the group by way of a neighbor on Cherry Lane, who'd heard about Gram's disappearance that Monday night.

Turns out, Gram's got a couple of old childhood friends in the group, and now she spends three hours a day playing cards or gabbing over pimiento cheese sandwiches—whatever's on the daily agenda. Once she's home, we watch *The Mary Tyler Moore Show* or throw dance parties or reminisce on her old life in Asheville. Every day, I try to make a memory with her. 'Cause even if one day those memories might slip from Gram's mind, I figure I can treasure them for the both of us.

Once we've picked up Gram, we Alden ladies head home,

where Gram talks a mile a minute about how Joan Merriman won bingo today, and how the group will be putting together holiday presents for the homeless shelter next week.

Meanwhile, I'm looking at my composition book. It's the same one I used for the Young Singer-Songwriter Workshop, but now it's a book for my nights with Sylvie. There's a song in the back that I'd like to share with her soon. I'm not through with the lyrics yet, but I've given it a title. It's called "Candidly Cline."

I've got Delia Jones to thank for that.

This song isn't about loving a person. It's not about heartbreak, either. It's about being honest—with friends and family, yes, but most of all with yourself.

I look over the chorus:

I'll always love my roots,
But I like how I've branched out.
I hear whispers in my heart
That I have to shout about.

I might not do it pretty,
And I'll mess up every day.
Rest assured of one thing:
I'll be candid all the way.

It needs work, I know, but I like the gist of what's on the page. What's more? I don't think I could've written these words back in

September. Not before the Young Singer-Songwriter Workshop or before I fell out with Hollie or met Sylvie. Not before I went looking for Gram on a chilly October night or before I auditioned in front of my mama and three judges.

But now? I'm being candid.

Candidly *me*.

The doorbell rings, jolting me out of my thoughts. I close up the notebook and run for the door. When I open it, Sylvie's there with a smile that could light up all of Paris. I take her hand in mine, bringing her in from the cold.

I can't wait to hear about the new online climate change petition Sylvie's created for the Fayette County school district. I can't wait to watch the dead-on impression she's been practicing of Joan Jett singing "Bad Reputation." I can't wait to compose together and to see all that's in store for the both of us.

"Ready to make some music?" Sylvie asks me with shimmering eyes.

I think right then of Emmylou Harris and how she was born to run.

I tell Sylvie, "Been ready all my life."

Acknowledgments

My earliest memories of my grandaddy involve me sitting in his old pickup truck, listening to his favorite singer, Patsy Cline, croon tunes like "Blue Moon of Kentucky" and "Walkin' After Midnight." Since those days, my love of music has been inextricably tied to a love of place. I grew up jamming to the greats of old country, bluegrass, and folk, whether I was singing along to Patsy with Grandaddy on his Kentucky farm or listening to Alison Krauss belt "Oh, Atlanta" in my Aunt Laura's Nashville home. I am forever grateful to songstresses Emmylou Harris, Dolly Parton, Linda Ronstadt, Patsy Cline, and so many others for igniting my enduring passion for storytelling.

Little did young Kathryn know that one day she'd be writing a story about a redheaded girl who, like her, adored music and liked girls. I would not have had the strength, resources, or ability to tell Cline Alden's story without the help of dozens of individuals, and I'd like to thank each of them here.

First, gigantic thanks to Beth Phelan, agent extraordinaire, for rooting for Cline and finding her a home. You helped fine-tune this novel to the perfect pitch, and I'm eternally grateful. My thanks, too, to the tremendously warm and talented folks at Gallt & Zacker and to Addison Duffy (Go Ducks!).

Thank you a hundred times over to my editor Stephanie Stein for believing in and championing Cline every step of this publishing journey. Your incisive notes, thoughtful care, and brimming enthusiasm made Cline's story shine. Many thanks to assistant editor Louisa Currigan for your help, so much of which I know was tirelessly given behind the scenes. Thank you to the inimitable Jessica Berg, Gwen Morton, and Allison Brown, and to rock star copy editor Martha Schwartz.

Peijin Yang, you brought Cline to life with vibrant color and palpable optimism. Thank you! I'm so grateful, too, to Chris Kwon and Alison Donalty for the phenomenal design work. I could not be more in love with this cover and book design.

Aubrey Churchward! Fellow fan of many a pop culture masterpiece and the brilliant publicity force behind past YA titles, we meet again. Just as before, I'm so grateful for all your brilliant work. Oodles of thanks to the marvelous Delaney Heisterkamp and Audrey Diestelkamp for their work in marketing, and to everyone else at HarperCollins Children's Books who helped bring Cline's story to the bookshelf.

Thank you, thank you to the brilliant Ashley Herring Blake, Lisa Jenn Bigelow, and Nicole Melleby for providing blurbs so kind they knocked the wind right out of me. I'm a huge fan of each of you and so grateful for your support of Cline.

My warmest thanks to the usual suspects of dear friends and family who have supported me and my work, including Annie and Matt Snow, Shelly Reed, Destiny Soria, Mai Shaffner, Vicki Rymill, and an extended list so long that, if I wrote it down, it'd roll right off this book and into the farthest reaches of the galaxy.

Your love and advice have carried me through a pandemic, forest fires, and, you know, 2020 in general.

Thank you, Grandaddy, for the memories and music you gave me. I miss you more than lyrics could ever convey. Thank you, Laura Ashby, for taking Younger Me to see Alison Krauss at the Grand Ole Opry and Older Me to see Brandi Carlile at the Nashville Symphony. Those two concerts left indelible impressions on me, and their songs played on a loop as I drafted this manuscript.

Alli Ormsbee, music has always been deep at the heart of our story together. I treasure the memories of that Ronnie Spector Christmas concert where we stared awestruck at Wanda Jackson's yodeling; the magical night we spent watching First Aid Kit perform my longtime favorite, "Emmylou"; and the moment we told each other that love songs hadn't made much sense till we met each other. You have unfailingly supported me through some of the most devastating valleys and triumphant peaks of my life. You've been Cline's biggest fan, and you're the reason I made it through weeks of hermit mode. I love you beyond belief, and I'm gobsmacked that I get to call you my wife. This one's for you.

Finally, to my young readers, thank you for reading this story. If you, like Cline, are trying to find your voice, I hope you know how unique that voice is and how important your songs and stories are. As a queer gal who grew up in the South, I know that sometimes it can be tough to feel fully accepted. My dearest hope is that you meet folks who love you as you are (I did!) and that you are buoyed by the stories of others who have walked in your shoes (or boots, or bleached Keds, as the case may be). Just like Cline, you can find your voice and sing your truth, all in a way and time that's right for you.